R
e
D

ReD

alison cherry

Quercus

First published in the USA in 2013 by Delacorte Press,
an imprint of Random House Children's books,
a division of Random House Inc., New York

This edition published in Great Britain in 2014 by

Quercus Editions Ltd
55 Baker Street
7th Floor, South Block
London
W1U 8EW

A CIP catalogue reference for this book is available
from the British Library

ISBN 978 1 78087 890 4

10 9 8 7 6 5 4 3 2

Printed and bound in Great Britain by Clays Ltd, St Ives plc.

For Mom and Erica,
My all-time favorite redheads

Part One

Redheaded women! Those blood oranges! Those cherry bombs! Those celestial shrews and queens of copper! May they never cease to stain our white-bread lives with super-natural catsup.

—Tom Robbins, "Ode to Redheads"

1

The banner fluttering in the breeze outside City Hall read SCARLETVILLE, IOWA: NATIONAL REDHEAD SANCTUARY.

Felicity St. John, who had lived in Scarletville all her life, couldn't even begin to guess how many times she had encountered the phrase "national redhead sanctuary." It blasted from her clock radio every morning, repeated over and over by the DJs at Scarletville's classic rock station, KRED. It was printed under the masthead on the town's newspaper, the *Scarletville Gazette*. It was etched onto a plaque on the front of Scarletville High School. And Felicity was probably going to hear the clichéd phrase a hundred times more today.

It was Scarlet Sunday, the anniversary of the founding of Scarletville, and the yearly carnival was in full swing. The lampposts in the center of town were festooned with red flowers, and the breeze carried the popcorn-and-fried-dough smell of celebration. The town was turning seventy-five this year, and the mayor's carnival committee had really outdone itself. Main Street was lined with food vendors, game booths, and displays of local crafts, as it was every May. But this year, the number of rides in the town square had tripled, and they were significantly more terrifying than usual. Felicity couldn't even look at the paralyzing vortex of doom called Zero Gravity without feeling slightly ill. Her twin half brothers, on the other hand, had no such qualms. From all the way across the plaza, she could hear Andy's and Tyler's seven-year-old voices shrieking with joy as the flying swings whipped them around in dizzying circles. Felicity hoped they would keep their cotton candy securely in their stomachs, but judging from past carnivals, it was highly unlikely.

The mayor must have publicized Scarletville's anniversary quite aggressively this time around—the dinky local press was there, of course, but there were also representatives from neighboring towns, including a reporter from the *Des Moines Register*. Right now, all the reporters and a sizable portion of the town's population were gathered in front of the grandstand, where the mayor was holding a press conference. He was just finishing his opening remarks, using the same speech he always gave on Scarlet Sunday. Felicity and her best friends, Haylie and Ivy, had heard it so many times they could recite it along with him.

"Less than *four percent* of the world's population is blessed with red hair, and in my grandfather's day, those redheads were scattered far and wide across the globe!" boomed the mayor. "And to add insult to injury, these poor scattered redheads were often much maligned in their communities, where they were considered oddballs and curiosities. Our priceless recessive genes would have been bred out of existence within fifty years had no one stepped up to prevent it! But my forward-thinking grandfather saw that we should bond together in solidarity, making precious redheaded children and raising them in a safe, supportive environment. Let's hear it for Scarletville, our nation's one and only redhead sanctuary!" The crowd applauded wildly, as it always did.

When the mayor finished the Gospel of Scarletville, reporters peppered him with questions about the town's history and redheadedness in general. A small blond journalist raised her hand high. "Mayor Redding!" she called. "How would you respond to the accusation that Scarletville discriminates against people with other hair colors, particularly among the younger generations? According to my sources, the student council, the Scholastic Bowl, the cheerleading squad, and several of the athletic teams at the high school are composed exclusively of redheads."

The mayor's undersized orange mustache twitched like an agitated chipmunk, and Felicity had to work hard not to snicker. "Of *course* we don't discriminate against people with other hair colors," Mayor Redding said. "We love *all* our children here in Scarletville. But are we really to blame if we've created an environment where redheads can blossom and live up to their full potential?" There were shouts of approval. "Besides, nearly seventy-five percent of the students at Scarletville High are redheads. Statistically, it makes *sense* that most of our highest achievers would have red hair. Redheads are Scarletville's finest natural resource!" This was another of the mayor's pet phrases.

"Do you think Redding can possibly be his original family name?" Ivy whispered. "His grandfather must have changed it back in the day, right? Don't you think it's just a little too convenient?"

Felicity shook her head, and her long, sideswept bangs fell into her eyes. "There's just something about that mustache. I can't get over it."

Haylie smacked her on the shoulder. "Don't bash Mayor Redding. I think he's adorable." One of the news vans on the corner crept a little closer, and Haylie eyed it with excitement. "Hey, do you think we'll be on the news?"

"*You* won't, shorty," Ivy snorted. "All the cameras will be able to see are two little red buns with butterfly barrettes."

Haylie looked outraged. "Look who's talking! You're half an inch taller than me, if that!"

Felicity always felt like a giant next to her best friends. She was only five seven, but she had a good five inches on both of them.

"The difference is that I don't want to be on the news," Ivy said.

"Want me to carry you on my shoulders, Hays?" Felicity offered. "You weigh about forty-five pounds. Hop on."

"I'm such a shrimp. I'm never going to win the Miss Scarlet Pageant with stumpy legs like these."

Haylie was a ballerina and had an appropriately tiny frame, but she was anything but stumpy. "Haylie, short people win pageants all the time," Ivy said. "Don't you ever think about anything besides the stupid Miss Scarlet Pageant? Why do you care so much?"

"It's not stupid! And how could you *not* care? They're announcing the competitors as soon as the press conference is over!"

"I don't care because I *didn't enter*. Which part of me says 'pageant girl' to you? Is it my flowing tresses? Or perhaps my bodacious bosoms?" Ivy gestured to her rust-colored hair, which was cropped in a messy pixie cut, and her virtually nonexistent boobs. Today she was dressed in her swim team T-shirt, a fleece vest, cargo pants, and flip-flops. Ivy in a ball gown made about as much sense as Mayor Redding in pink footie pajamas.

To be honest, Felicity didn't see herself as a beauty queen, either. Haylie was the one who had always loved the town's pageants. But Felicity had done them both with her: Little Miss Scarlet when she was eight, Miss Ruby Red at twelve. And now here she was, a junior in high school, waiting to see if she had been chosen to compete for the all-important title of Miss Scarlet. Countless times, she had considered backing out and saying she just wasn't interested in pageants.

But there was no chance of that. Not when her mom was the one who ran them.

Ginger St. John had been crowned Miss Scarlet the year the town turned fifty, and from the moment that crown landed on her head, the pageant was the love of her heart. She had been grooming her daughter to follow in her footsteps since Felicity had been two years old. Felicity suspected her mom had gotten pregnant at twenty-five on purpose, just so her daughter would be the right age to compete in Scarletville's seventy-fifth-anniversary pageant.

And so far, Felicity had done everything right. She had been born a girl. She had dutifully played with the other little girls Ginger considered potential stars. At her mother's urging, she had learned to pose, answer interview questions, and strut down catwalks. To be a better pageant contestant, she had taken tap, jazz, and ballet with Haylie instead of the art classes she'd really wanted. And although she didn't enjoy competing, she had grown quite good at it—her fear of disappointing her mom had always motivated her to work hard. She hadn't won anything so far, but she had been first runner-up in the Miss Ruby Red Pageant, to Ginger's unending delight.

Miss Scarlet was Felicity's final pageant, but it was also the most important one. It was her last chance to become the winner her mom expected her to be. And the prize money that came with the title would be a huge help to her family. As Ginger constantly reminded Felicity, fifteen years of costumes and dance classes didn't come cheap.

The mayor concluded his remarks, and Felicity's mom approached the podium. The whole town grew quiet as Ginger adjusted the microphone. Haylie forgot about her argument with Ivy and grabbed both her friends' hands for moral support. Her grip was so tight that her nails carved little crescents into Felicity's skin.

"Hi, everyone!" Felicity's mom beamed at the crowd. "My name is Ginger St. John, and I'm the director of the Scarletville Pageant Committee! I'm here to announce the competitors for this year's Miss Scarlet Pageant!" The crowd roared its approval. "There are seventy-eight eleventh-grade girls this year, all of whom are eligible for the competition, and sixty-four of those young ladies chose to enter. Our competitors were selected based on their photos, their accomplishments, and their essays about how holding the title of Miss Scarlet would help them achieve their personal goals. I just want everyone to know what a tough decision we had this year. All you girls are spectacular, and I wish we could have taken everyone. But as always, there are only twelve slots in the competition." She made an exaggerated sad face, and Felicity sighed. She hated it when her mom slipped into beauty queen mode and mugged for the crowd.

"But enough suspense! Let's get to it! Georgia, may I have the envelope, please?"

Georgia Kellerman, the reigning Miss Scarlet, left her seat near the podium and strutted across the stage. There was a storm of screams and whistles from the candy apple booth, where the cheerleaders were assembled—Georgia was their captain and queen. Today she was wearing her Miss Scarlet sash and crown over her cheerleading uniform, which should have looked ridiculous but somehow came off as chic. Her curled red hair hung loose to the center of her back and bounced as she walked. Had she been auditioning for a shampoo commercial, she would have booked the job for sure. When she reached the podium, she did a little spin, then presented Felicity's mom with a large red envelope.

"Thanks, Georgia! Before I read the names, I just want to assure everyone that I did not help choose the contestants this year. That wouldn't have been fair, since my Felicity's in the running." Ginger blew a kiss to Felicity, who blushed and wished she had something larger than her garden-gnome-sized best friends to hide behind.

"And now, ladies and gentlemen, the moment you've all been waiting for. This year's Miss Scarlet contestants are . . ."

Felicity's heart started hammering, and she squeezed Haylie's hand tightly. If she wasn't chosen, her mom might never recover. She was Ginger's only daughter, her one and only chance to relive the most glorious experience of her life. If Felicity failed her now, seventeen years of careful planning would crumble to nothing.

The weight of responsibility pressed down on Felicity until she felt like someone had piled several boulders on her lungs.

Ginger pulled a piece of paper out of the envelope and unfolded it. Felicity searched for a telltale facial twitch indicating whether her name was on the list, but her mom's expression didn't change at all. "Madison Banks!" she called with a smile.

Madison was next in line to be cheerleading captain, and there was another round of screaming from the candy apple booth. She had won the Miss Ruby Red Pageant in seventh grade, so it was no surprise that she would be competing again. Her perky red ponytail bounced wildly as she jumped up and down and hugged her teammates. Felicity and Ivy made gagging gestures at each other, but Haylie seemed too nervous to notice anything except that the first name hadn't been hers.

"Lorelei Griffin!"

Again, this was no surprise. Lorelei had been the star of last fall's production of *Little Shop of Horrors* and had played the lead in *Annie* the year before. It was a good day for the Griffin family. Earlier that morning, Lorelei's mother had won the Magnificent Mommy award for having produced seven redheaded children, the highest number in the community. It was a good thing the award came with a hefty check, as she was rumored to be pregnant again.

"Haylie Adams!"

Felicity barely had time to brace herself before Haylie came flying into her arms. "I made it I made it

11

I made it!" her friend shrieked at the top of her lungs, drowning out the crowd's applause. Ivy squeezed both of them, forming a Haylie sandwich, and Felicity struggled to stay on her feet. She was happy for Haylie, but that was three names down already—there were only nine slots left. What if she didn't make the cut?

Haylie clambered back down to the ground as Ginger called Cassie Brynne's name. "Don't worry," she said, reading Felicity's mind. "You're definitely going to make it."

"You don't know that for sure."

Haylie rolled her eyes. "Um, hel-*lo*, you have the reddest hair in the whole school. I wish I had your color." Her hair was lighter than Felicity's, closer to carrot than copper. "And you're the best artist, and you're smart, and you're *so* pretty. And everyone loves you. And, um, *your mom runs the freaking pageant*."

"That doesn't help. My mom didn't get to vote," Felicity said, but she felt buoyed by her friend's compliments. There were still eight names to go. Maybe everything would be fine.

"Ariel Scott!" called her mom, and a small group of strawberry-blond girls near the edge of the grandstand shrieked with joy. Ariel was so overwhelmed that she started to cry.

"Ariel? Seriously?" scoffed Haylie. "Her hair's hardly even red!"

"They always put one strawbie in the pageant," Ivy said. "It looks bad if they don't. Especially after the mayor's whole speech about 'loving all our children regardless of their hair color.'" She twitched her upper lip in an imitation of Mayor Redding, and Felicity giggled despite her nerves.

"But, I mean, it's called the Miss *Scarlet* Pageant for a reason," Haylie said. "It should really be for redheads only, don't you think?"

Felicity had just opened her mouth to respond when her mom called, "Ivy Locklear!"

Ivy's eyes widened until they were dangerously close to popping out of their sockets. *"What?"* she gasped as Haylie jumped up and down, squealing and clapping. "But I— How did this— I didn't—"

"I did your application for you, doofus. I wrote your essay about how you wanted to assert your feminine side because people see you as such a jock."

"Are you *kidding* me? How could the committee possibly have believed that?"

"It's exactly what they want to hear! There's nothing they like better than a reformed girl who's seen the light and realized how important pageants are." Haylie beamed. "Don't be mad, Ives. I just wanted the three of us to do this together, like we always used to dream about when we were little! Don't you remember how we played Miss Scarlet every day at recess?"

Ivy was turning redder by the second. "Haylie, we were in *first grade*! I stopped caring about beauty pageants when I stopped playing with My Little Ponies!" She whacked Haylie with her plastic bag of cotton candy, and Haylie squealed and ducked as sugary wisps flew everywhere.

13

Ivy turned to Felicity, holding up the half-empty bag threateningly. "You were in on this, weren't you?"

Felicity shook her head and took a quick step out of Ivy's sticky reach. "I didn't know anything about it. But it won't be that bad, will it?"

"C'mon, Ives, don't go all Grouchy McSourpuss on us. It'll be great. I'll help you." Haylie tried to pat Ivy's shoulder, which gained her another whack with the cotton candy.

"I don't want you to *help* me! I want you to tell the committee what you did and get me out of this! Felicity, you can have my spot."

"Shut up, Felicity's going to have her own spot!"

Felicity wasn't so sure that was true. She barely caught the next two names over her friends' commotion, but neither of them was hers. There were only four slots left now.

Ivy stuffed a wad of the abused cotton candy into her mouth. "What am I supposed to do for my talent? I can't very well swim the butterfly or do advanced math in a pageant."

"You're really good at walking on your hands," Haylie suggested.

"You're a virtuoso on the kazoo," added Felicity. She tried to read her mom's face again so she could tell if her name was among the last four. She wished they had worked out some sort of secret hand signal in advance. *Raise your right eyebrow and tug your ear twice if I'm in. Mime slitting your throat if I'm out.*

"Great," said Ivy. "That's exactly what I'm going to

14

do, just to spite you guys. I'm going to walk on my hands while playing the kazoo. In my freaking ball gown. I'm going to make a complete spectacle of myself, and you'll be sorry you ever filled out that application."

"You don't wear your gown for the talent portion," Haylie pointed out.

"Amber Neilson!" called Felicity's mom.

Three names left. Felicity's heart was beating so fast it felt as if there were a hummingbird trapped inside her rib cage.

And then her mom looked straight at her and winked. "Felicity St. John!"

Felicity's knees almost buckled as a wave of relief swept through her. She was in. She had lived up to everyone's expectations, including her mom's. Haylie danced around, screaming, "I knew it! I told you!" then smashed Felicity into another group hug.

Ginger called the last two names—Jessie Parish and Savannah King—and then invited the twelve contestants up to the grandstand to take a bow. Ivy tried to escape into the crowd, but Haylie clamped a hand around her wrist and dragged her toward the stage. For such a tiny girl, Haylie was surprisingly strong, and Ivy seemed to realize that resistance was futile.

Felicity brought up the rear, accepting kisses, high fives, and shoulder squeezes from her friends and acquaintances as she snaked through the crowd. Everyone seemed to want to touch her and congratulate her. Though her mom had always kept her in the limelight, hoping to ensure her popularity, being so visible had

15

always made Felicity uncomfortable. It seemed strange that anyone cared about her personal business. Sometimes she longed to hide in the shadows for a change.

"Felicity!" Her boyfriend, Brent, was fighting his way out of the tiny ring toss booth he was manning to raise money for the football team. She paused as he jogged toward her, his crimson jersey billowing in the breeze. When he reached her, he swept her up in a hug and spun her around, knocking her into several other people. "Congrats, sexy. Knew you could do it." Brent was economical with his words, as if he were always texting instead of talking. He rarely said anything longer than 140 characters.

"Thanks," said Felicity. Brent twined his hands through her wavy hair and gave her a kiss, and her stomach fluttered, just as it always did when he touched her. He was very attractive, with floppy auburn hair, dimples, and football-toned muscles. Felicity just wished she *liked* him a little more. He wasn't exactly the brightest crayon in the box, and it was impossible to pretend otherwise. But he adored her, and there wasn't any other boy in Scarletville she liked better. Every time she considered ending the relationship, it seemed like more drama than it was worth.

Brent held her tightly around the waist and clearly had no intention of releasing her any time soon. "Um, I've gotta go up onstage now," Felicity reminded him.

"Oh. Right. Come by my booth later? I'll give you a couple free tosses."

16

"Sure." She kissed him one more time, then gently pulled free and headed toward the grandstand.

As she walked by the sunblock vendor, Felicity passed a group of her brunette classmates, all of whom were staring at her coldly. She smiled at them—she tried to be friendly to everyone, regardless of their hair color—but their stony expressions didn't change at all. "This pageant is so lame," Gabrielle Vaughn said to Marina Rios, loudly enough to ensure that Felicity heard her. "I can't believe I have to write about this crap for the *Crimson Courier*."

"Why are you so pissed? It's just another newspaper assignment. It's not like any of us entered." Marina flicked her dark ponytail over her shoulder.

"The point isn't that we *want* to be in it," Amanda Westin said. "The point is that even if we *did*, this stupid town would never let us."

"Exactly. It's not like that herd of redheads up there is any smarter or prettier or more talented than we are. Trust me, we deserve the recognition and the prize money a lot more than *some* people." Gabby met Felicity's eyes with a look so hostile it was like being doused with a bucket of ice water.

"Come *on*, Felicity!" Haylie called.

Felicity followed her friends, but she wasn't paying attention to the crowd around her anymore. A pit had opened deep in her stomach, and all her relief about being named a contestant was spiraling into it like bathwater down a drain. As she made her way to the grandstand, she could feel a dozen brown eyes on her back.

She was the last one to reach the stage, and Ginger waited until she had mounted the grandstand steps to shout, "Let's hear it for all our Miss Scarlet contestants!"

The crowd cheered and whistled and catcalled, and the wave of sound washed over Felicity. Despite feeling completely overwhelmed, she tried to keep a smile plastered on her face. Pageants were all about smiling through your feelings. She might as well start now.

Parents began pushing through the crowd to hug their daughters, and Ginger St. John was no exception. The moment she was done announcing the whens and wheres of the pageant, she fled the podium and pulled Felicity into a bone-crushing embrace. "Baby, I'm so proud of you!" she gushed.

"Thanks, Mom." As uncomfortable as Felicity felt, she was relieved to see her mom so pleased with her.

"I could barely keep from jumping up and down when I saw your name on that list, but I think my poker face was pretty good, wasn't it?"

"A little too good, actually. You totally freaked me out. I thought for sure I wasn't in."

"Oh, I'm so sorry, baby, I didn't mean to scare you. But this is *so exciting*! We're finally on our way to becoming the very first mother-daughter pair of Miss Scarlets!" Ginger held Felicity at arm's length and beamed at her, then pulled her close again and did a little happy dance, jiggling her awkwardly up and down. "Everything is going exactly like we always dreamed it would.

This win is right there for the taking, baby. All you have to do now is reach out and grab it."

Over her mom's shoulder, Felicity spotted the little brunette island in the sea of red and saw that her disgruntled classmates still hadn't stopped glaring at her. She quickly looked away. Though everything did seem to be going according to plan, all those cold dark eyes reminded Felicity that she didn't deserve any of the praise she was getting. She didn't deserve to be competing in the pageant at all.

Because unbeknownst to the adoring crowd, Felicity's hair color—that bright coppery red that made her so enviable in Scarletville—was completely artificial.

There were only two other people in the entire world who knew her secret. One was her mom. The other was her stylist, Rose Vaughn.

Gabby's mother.

2

MONDAY, MAY 3

MONDAY, MAY 3

Every town has a dirty little secret. Some have underground drug rings. Others look away while prostitution flourishes. A select few shelter branches of the Mob.

Scarletville's secret was Rouge-o-Rama.

There was rampant speculation among the town's residents over where the underground hair salon was located and what it looked like inside. Some thought it was sleek and white and sterile, like the flight deck of a science-fiction spaceship. Others whispered that it was more like an early-twentieth-century abortion clinic, with bare lightbulbs and rusty sinks. There were even rumors that it moved around to avoid detection, like a heroin stash house. Of course, there wasn't anything illegal about hair dye, but it certainly felt that way in

Scarletville. Being an artificial redhead—an "artie"—carried such a strong social stigma that everyone who colored their hair went to great lengths to keep it a secret.

Of course, the biggest mystery of all was the identity of the salon's owner. The mayor had been trying for years to sniff out the culprit who was diluting his redheaded gene pool with arties, but much to his frustration, he'd had no success. The only ones who knew about Rose were her clients, and they would never reveal her secret. If they exposed her, they exposed themselves.

Felicity had been visiting Rouge-o-Rama every few weeks since she was a toddler. Ginger, who had the reddest hair in town, had been shocked and appalled when her daughter was born a strawbie. It was bad enough that her high-school-sweetheart husband had left her six months pregnant and run off to California with a blonde. But the fact that Ginger didn't even get a redheaded baby to show for her failed relationship felt like a slap in the face. When she brought Felicity home from the hospital, her friends stroked the infant's tiny head and said, "Don't worry, Ginger, her hair will get darker." But they couldn't hide the pity in their voices. *Their* babies' hair had been flaming red right from the start.

As soon as it became clear that Felicity's strawberry locks weren't going to get any darker, Ginger took matters into her own hands. Her daughter was the only thing she had left, and none of her plans for Felicity could come to fruition with that washed-out hair in the way.

It took months of research to locate Rouge-o-Rama, but Ginger was wily and more motivated than the mayor, whose reputation wasn't at stake. She presented her squirming toddler to Rose and instructed her to dye Felicity's hair one tiny increment redder every visit. That way, it would look to the world as if her daughter's hair were darkening naturally as she grew.

By the time Felicity started preschool, the vibrant color of her hair was the envy of every parent in Scarletville. Ginger felt as if she had done her job.

Her daughter's social standing was safe.

The night after Scarlet Sunday, Felicity had The Dream.

It was always the same. She woke to the blaring of her alarm, took a shower, and got dressed. She perfumed her hair with her customary sandalwood oil and brushed it until it shone. She ate breakfast—in The Dream, it was usually Life cereal and a banana. Then she drove to Scarletville High.

Nothing was out of the ordinary until she entered the school and noticed that everyone was staring at her and whispering. It got worse as she walked down the hall; some people gasped in horror, and others laughed at her outright. Even the littlest freshmen, the ones who would never dare to speak to her in real life, were giggling. Had she remembered to put on her clothes? Yes, she seemed to be fully dressed. Was there something on her face? Was the back of her skirt tucked into her underwear?

With mounting panic, Felicity raced to the bathroom. And there in the mirror, she saw . . . *roots*. A whole inch of shining, platinum-blond roots, lacking even the slightest hint of strawberry. There was no way to hide them. Everyone had already seen her. Everyone in the whole school knew she was a big artie *fake*.

She usually woke herself up when she screamed.

Felicity switched on her bedside lamp and rushed to her mirror with a pounding heart. Her fingers scrabbled through her hair, parting it over and over. But there were no roots. She had gotten a touch-up at the salon only eight days ago. She breathed slowly in and out, willing the adrenaline to stop pumping through her body. It was only a dream. Her secret was safe.

Felicity climbed back into bed. It was four in the morning, but she couldn't relax enough to fall back asleep. The feeling was distressingly familiar — sleep had often eluded her in the weeks leading up to Scarlet Sunday. Sometimes she had tossed and turned all night, worrying about how her mom would react if she was rejected from the pageant. But everything was okay now. She was officially a Miss Scarlet contestant, a status symbol that could only lend credibility to her red hair.

But every time Felicity closed her eyes, all she could see were the icy stares of her brunette classmates. Had one of them discovered her secret? It seemed impossible. Sure, Gabby's mom owned Rouge-o-Rama, but Rose kept security tight. She had once told Felicity that her own family didn't even know where the salon was. And even if Gabby and her friends had stumbled on Rose's appointment book, all the listings were under code names. There was no way for anyone but the stylist herself to know who Raspberry Ripple was.

Felicity decided she was being paranoid. The brunettes were probably just jealous of her. And who wouldn't be? She was in an enviable position, one coveted by every girl in town.

When her alarm went off a few hours later—for real this time—Felicity felt as if she had been up all night. Her mom took one look as Felicity slumped into her chair at the breakfast table and asked, "Baby, do you feel okay? You look awful."

"Thanks, Mom. You know how much I love hearing that."

"You're not sick, are you?" Ginger felt her forehead, then combed her fingers through her daughter's hair. It felt like an affectionate gesture, but Felicity knew her mom was probably just checking her dye job.

"I'm not sick. I didn't sleep well." Felicity squirmed out of her mom's reach. "Could you hand me the phone? I want to make an appointment at the salon for later today."

"But you're already scheduled for Thursday."

"I had The Dream again last night, Mom. It would really make me feel better to go today instead. Please?"

"Okay, baby. You just eat your breakfast and I'll call for you." Ginger kissed Felicity on the top of the head, then yelled, "Boys! Breakfast!"

Andy and Tyler barreled in from the den, carrying action figures they had mummified in tinfoil. They both had pumpkin-orange hair — the hair Felicity *should* have had. The twins were the result of the short fling her mother had had with a redheaded pageant judge from out of town when Felicity was in fourth grade.

"Hey, Lissy, which is awesomer, Captain Spacepants or Captain Rocketpants?" Andy scrambled into his chair and placed his spaceman neatly in the center of his eggs.

"I like Captain Rocketpants." Felicity winked at Tyler, who beamed. His adult front teeth were much larger than his baby teeth, which gave him a rabbity look.

Andy pouted. "Nooooo, Captain Spacepants is *way* awesomer!"

"Andy, eat your toast-pants," said Ginger, sending both boys into gales of laughter. These days, they both thought adding "pants" to the ends of words was the funniest thing in the world.

Felicity tried to keep her brothers quiet while her mom phoned Rouge-o-Rama. For maximum discretion, the salon had an 800 number that showed up on the caller ID as a tech support hotline. "Hi, Rose. Do you have any appointments open this afternoon?" Felicity crossed her fingers. "Oh, that's perfect. She'll take the four o'clock. Raspberry Ripple." Ginger wrote down a four-digit code on a Post-it note. "Four-seven-two-three. Got it. Thanks so much."

Ginger hung up and stuck the Post-it to Felicity's arm. "That's the code for the door today. Four o'clock.

Will you pick up the boys from day care on your way home?"

"Sure. Thanks, Mom." Felicity gulped down the last of her orange juice, kissed Ginger's cheek, and grabbed her backpack. "I've gotta go. I'll see you later."

"Okay. Chin up, baby. Even if you're not feeling your best, you've got to make everyone else believe that you are. It's the face you present to the world that matters, not how you feel inside."

Felicity nodded. She'd heard that advice from her mom countless times.

"That's my winner. Have a good day. Boys, say bye to your sister."

"Bye, Lissy," they chorused.

Felicity walked out into the breezy spring air and headed for their car. The unwieldy Chevy was a hand-me-down from their neighbor Victor, who lived in the other half of their duplex. When he had upgraded to a hybrid last year, he had given his old car to Felicity. It was lime green, and it had multicolored peace signs stenciled on the trunk, the hood, and the driver's-side door. Victor called the car Yoko, a tradition Felicity faithfully maintained. Although Ginger was always on her case about getting Yoko a new paint job, Felicity liked the absurdity of the peace signs. She had worried at first that she would be ridiculed for driving such a flamboyant car, but it had only made people consider her delightfully quirky. A non-redhead never could have gotten away with it.

Felicity stopped for her daily double-mocha latte,

then pulled into the student parking lot at Scarletville High. She parked in the row closest to the doors—the best spots were unofficially reserved for the students with the reddest hair. When she entered the school, everyone looked up at her and started murmuring amongst themselves, and for a horrible moment Felicity thought she was back in The Dream. But there was no jeering, only broad, warm smiles. School was always like this the day after the Miss Scarlet competitors were announced—Felicity had just never been on this side of the equation before. The pageant would be everyone's main topic of conversation for the next month, which meant she'd be in the spotlight even more than usual. She tried to follow her mom's advice and hold her head high as people cleared a path for her, but she had no control over the squirmy feeling in her stomach.

Haylie and Ivy were waiting by her locker. As she got closer, Felicity noticed the homemade sign taped to the door that read CONGRATULATIONS, FELICITY! GO MISS SCARLET! in glitter. It was signed from SASH, the Spirit Association of Scarletville High. When she glanced down the hall, she saw that there were signs taped to the other contestants' lockers as well. Ivy carried the remains of her sign, folded into quarters and leaking a steady stream of glitter onto the floor.

"So, we need to go dress shopping," Haylie said in lieu of a greeting. "Which weekend are you free? Can we take Yoko? All the good dresses in Scarletville are going to get snapped up right away, so we'll probably have to drive down to Iowa City or Cedar Rapids. My mom's college roommate owns this boutique in Iowa City called Lulu Levine, so we can probably get discounts there. And she's a redhead, so I trust her to show us good stuff."

"Good morning to you, too," Felicity said. "I have to ask my mom. And I have a bunch of stuff to do for the art show and the prom committee."

"Seriously? Dress shopping?" Ivy gave her sign another twist. "I didn't realize I'd have to spend *money* on this stupid pageant. Can't I just wear one of your old gowns, Hays?"

Haylie looked at Ivy as if she had just suggested wearing a dress made of dead weasels. "Are you kidding? You can't wear a *hand-me-down* for Miss Scarlet! And stop mutilating your sign. You're getting glitter all over your shoes."

A pair of strong freckled arms locked around Felicity's waist from behind, followed by a nose nuzzling her neck. "Hey, Lissy," Brent's voice said close to her ear. "You smell awesome."

Felicity had repeatedly asked Brent not to call her "Lissy," a nickname that was reserved for her brothers. She thought about reminding him again, but really, what was the point? He'd be genuinely sorry, and his wide-eyed, penitent look would make her forgive him. But he'd do the exact same thing tomorrow. It was less work to just swallow her annoyance. Besides, the nuzzling was sending a rather pleasant shiver down her spine. So she just smiled and said, "Thanks. How're you?"

"Better now." He kissed her neck. "We had a solid practice this morning. Coach says I have great hustle."

Felicity didn't have the slightest idea what that meant. "That's great, babe." He nuzzled her again in response.

"Get a room, people." Haylie wrinkled her tiny nose. Felicity knew her friend was jealous that she had such a cute redheaded jock for a boyfriend. She wished she could explain that dating Brent was usually more like caring for a puppy than having a relationship, but Haylie would just think she was playing things down to be nice. Plus, her friends could never know she felt ambivalent toward Brent, or they would wonder why she stayed with him. The truth was that in addition to having some genuinely good qualities, Brent was insurance for Felicity—he added to her redhead credibility, or her "red cred," as she secretly thought of it. People were less likely to suspect her hair color wasn't natural when she was dating one of the most popular guys on the football team.

"Hey, do you guys want to come over after school and look at pageant dresses online?" Haylie asked.

"Oooh, I'd *hate* to miss that, but I have swim practice," said Ivy. "Thanks anyway."

"Sorry, Hays, I've got to pick up the twins," Felicity said. Her supposed babysitting duties were very convenient excuses whenever she had appointments at the salon. "We'll do it soon, though."

The first bell rang, and Haylie and Ivy took off down the hall. Felicity's first class, History of Redheadedness, was just around the corner, and she gently unlatched Brent's arms so she could dig through her locker for her textbook. "Can I come over and see you tonight?" Brent asked. "We could watch a movie. Or not watch one." He wiggled his eyebrows.

"Maybe," Felicity said. "Call me, okay?"

"I'm going to the gym after school. Coach says I should be able to bench about fifteen more pounds. Gotta work on my arms. Call you after."

"Great." Felicity gave him a quick kiss, then watched as he walked away. He already had really great arms.

The day passed in a blur of admiring looks, praise, and congratulations from her fellow students and teachers. Three giggling freshmen approached Felicity in the cafeteria and made her and Haylie promise to sign their yearbooks, which wouldn't even arrive for another four weeks. Unlike Felicity, Haylie soaked up the attention. "Everyone needs celebrities to adore," she announced. "We're providing a valuable service to the school. We have to do our civic duty and let everyone gossip to their heart's content." Ivy responded with a sound that closely resembled that of a cat expelling a hairball.

Felicity tried hard to remember Haylie's comment when she caught Sayuri Kwan and Marina lurking near her locker after school, stealing quick glances at her as they laughed and whispered. *They're just talking about how much they wish they could switch places with me,* she told herself as she headed to the salon. *There's no reason to worry.*

Rouge-o-Rama was located in the Jefferson Building, where many of Scarletville's dentists, lawyers, and real estate agents had their offices. The building's main elevators stopped only on the first six floors. The salon was on the seventh, which looked like part of the roof from the outside. Felicity went to the third floor and waited until the hall was empty, then ducked into the women's bathroom, marked CLOSED FOR RENOVATIONS. Once inside the room, which reeked of cheap floral air freshener, she approached a plain metal door near the back and pressed on a wall tile next to the doorknob. It flipped up to reveal a keypad, which always made Felicity feel like a secret agent. She pulled out her mom's Post-it note, punched in that day's salon code, and flipped the tile back down. The door unlocked with a click, and she pulled it open.

Behind the door was one of Rouge-o-Rama's two private elevators. This one carried clients up, and the other, at the opposite side of the building, took them back down after their appointments. The other elevator let out on the second floor, which ensured that clients never accidentally met coming to and from the salon.

Felicity boarded the elevator and punched the only available button, and the car ascended to the top floor with its usual clanking and grinding noises. Rose opened the door almost immediately when Felicity rang the bell. "Hey, honey!" the stylist said, pulling her into an enthusiastic hug. "Congratulations on Miss Scarlet!"

"Thanks," Felicity said. "I couldn't have done it without you."

"Of course you could've. You got in 'cause you

deserved it, not just because of your hair. If it was *all* about red hair, they wouldn't have chosen Ariel, right?"

"Yeah, but Ariel doesn't have a chance. Is it even worth competing if you can't possibly win? That's so much work for nothing."

"I think Ariel might disagree." Rose shrugged. "Come inside. Let's make you even more beautiful."

Rose led Felicity into one of the salon's two main rooms, handed her a smock, and went into the back to mix the dye. Contrary to all rumors, Rouge-o-Rama just looked like a regular hair salon. The walls of the main room were papered in a crimson and white pattern intended to hide errant flecks of red dye. The mirrors had decorative, low-wattage lightbulbs around the edges — Felicity had spent a lot of time posing in front of them as a kid, pretending she was a Hollywood starlet. It was a comfortable, warm space that made people feel optimistic about their hair, even if it wasn't naturally red.

Felicity sat down in the chair and snapped on her smock, which had a big red rose printed on the front. After a few minutes, Rose came out shaking a plastic squeeze bottle, her gloved finger over the hole in the top. "So, are you excited about the competition?" she asked.

"Yeah, definitely. It's going to be great." Felicity tipped her chin up so Rose could smear Vaseline along her hairline to prevent accidental drips from dyeing her skin. It was slimy and cold, and she had to force herself not to pull away.

"What are you doing for your talent?" Rose started

squeezing the dye onto the roots of Felicity's hair, using a small paintbrush to spread it around evenly. The harsh chemical scent of it scratched at the inside of Felicity's nose, the olfactory equivalent of fingernails on a chalkboard.

"I'll tap-dance. That was Mom's talent, too. I already learned a routine, just in case."

"I can't wait to see you strut your stuff. You're all so talented. Katie, my youngest, is totally obsessed with the pageant this year. You should see her practicing her runway walk in the living room every night. It's adorable how she idolizes you girls." Rose grinned at Felicity in the mirror. "Is everyone treating you like a celebrity at school?"

"Yeah, most people." But her brunette classmates' cold stares were still fresh in her mind. She tried to figure out how to ask Rose if anyone could possibly know who frequented the salon, but she couldn't think of a way to phrase the question that didn't sound paranoid.

Rose brushed on one final squeeze of dye and stretched a plastic cap over Felicity's hair. "Come on, it's time for the dryer."

Felicity tried to concentrate on reading *Macbeth* for her English assignment while the dye set, but it was hard to focus with so much on her mind. There was also something very disconcerting about reading the "Out, damned spot!" scene while her hair was drenched in blood-colored liquid. Eventually she just closed her eyes and listened to Rose's radio, which informed her that Ruby Johansen, Scarletville's fiftieth redheaded baby of the year, had just been delivered. Rose did little chores around the studio until the timer on the dryer went off, then led Felicity to the sink and started scrubbing out the dye.

"Rose?" Felicity asked timidly. Now that she couldn't see her stylist's face, it was easier to say things that might sound accusatory.

"Yes, honey?"

"I don't want you to think I don't trust you or anything, so please don't take this the wrong way. But you would never tell anyone whose hair you dye, right?"

Rose's fingers stopped moving against her head. "Of course not, Felicity. You know that. I signed a contract with your mom when you were just a little kid. I would never violate client confidentiality."

"I mean, I didn't think you would. I know you're a professional and everything. But there's no way that someone could accidentally find out who comes here, is there?"

Rose sighed. "I know you're nervous because of the pageant, but you don't need to worry, okay? Your hair looks so natural. If I didn't color it myself, I'd think it was real."

"Okay. You're probably right." Felicity started to relax a little as Rose resumed scrubbing at her scalp with strong, competent fingers. They were both careful. Nobody was going to unearth her secret.

When Felicity's hair was clean and conditioned, Rose spritzed it with sandalwood oil to hide the smell of the chemicals and blew it dry. She carefully inspected

Felicity's hairline for runaway flecks of dye, then removed her smock and gave her shoulder an affectionate squeeze to show there were no hard feelings. "Good to see you," she said. "I'll email your mom the bill for today. Congratulations, and don't stress, okay? You look beautiful. I'll see you in two weeks, and we'll recolor all the way to the ends."

"Okay." Felicity gave her roots a quick check in the mirror. They looked bright and coppery and natural. She smiled at Rose. "Thanks a lot. I'll see you soon."

She boarded the down elevator and rode it to the second floor, where it opened onto a small room made up with mops and brooms and a large corroded sink. The only way it differed from a normal supply closet was that under a sliding section of dirty wall tiles, there was a concealed screen showing video feed from two security cameras in the hall. Felicity saw three men in suits passing by, and she waited in the closet until they were out of sight.

Just as she pushed the door open to leave, her sunglasses slipped off the top of her head and clattered to the floor. She ducked back into the closet to retrieve them, and that was when she noticed something on the monitor that she hadn't seen before.

There was someone else lurking in the shadows near the stairwell.

Felicity frantically pulled the door closed again, swearing under her breath as it made a louder click than she'd expected. How could she have been so careless? Even as a preschooler, she had known the rule

35

about the video monitor: check twice, sneak once. *The door was only open for a second*, she told herself. *They probably didn't see you. Just wait here for a minute, and whoever it is will go away.*

But the person didn't leave. Felicity stared hard at the grainy footage, trying to figure out who it was, but all she could tell for sure was that it was a dark-haired girl. For ten agonizing minutes, as she paced around the tiny closet and tried to calm her racing heart, the mystery lurker stayed right where she was. It almost looked like she was watching the closet door, waiting patiently for Felicity to emerge.

Finally, just when Felicity thought she couldn't take one more minute, the girl pushed open the door to the stairwell and disappeared.

Sweaty and shaking, Felicity slipped out of the closet and hurried out of the Jefferson Building as fast as her legs could carry her. She was still trembling all over by the time she reached her car. She tried to believe there was no reason to be afraid; someone could have been lurking in the hallway for any number of reasons. Maybe she was waiting for a friend. Maybe she was looking something up on her phone. Why assume the worst?

Still, Felicity couldn't help feeling as if the mystery girl had been trying to catch her in the act of emerging from the closet. And if someone knew she would be in the supply closet of the Jefferson Building after school today, that person probably knew why.

3

When Felicity arrived at Scarletville High the next day, she ducked her head and hurried inside as if she were fleeing from the paparazzi. Her experience at the salon yesterday had spooked her. She told herself it was just a coincidence and that nobody was following her, but she couldn't shake the feeling that something wasn't right.

She slowed when she saw a brown-haired boy leaning against her locker. Though she couldn't tell who it was from the back, he couldn't be a friend of hers — Felicity didn't have any brown-haired friends. Perhaps he just wanted to congratulate her on the pageant. She wasn't in the mood for gushing this morning, but she remembered Haylie's comment about doing her civic duty. So she put on her best magnanimous smile and approached.

But when the boy turned around, Felicity saw that it was only Jonathan Lyons, the senior who was curating the student art show with her. He was tall and wiry, and he wore glasses with thick dark frames, walking the fine line between nerdy and trendy. Jonathan was an impressive painter, and the smear of green acrylic on the shoulder of his T-shirt indicated that he had already spent time in the school's art studio that morning. He was probably trying to finish his piece for the show by the submissions deadline. When Ms. Kellogg, the art teacher, had appointed Jonathan and Felicity as curators, she had also guaranteed them spots in the show. Felicity wondered what Jonathan was working on; he was in the other art class this year, so she hadn't seen any of his recent paintings. Whatever it was, it was sure to be spectacular.

Her forced smile turned into a genuine one. "Hey, how's it going?" she called.

Jonathan nodded, his glasses slipping down his nose a little. "Pretty good. I just checked the art show cubby in the main office, and we have a ton of submissions. Like, a *ton* of them. They wouldn't even all fit in the cubby, and there were CDs piled up in this whole separate box on the floor." He talked rapidly, as if he were worried Felicity might find something better to do before he finished. "So we have a lot to choose from, which is really great. Do you want to go through all the stuff after school on Wednesday? I mean, if you're free." His hands fluttered around like nervous birds, straightening his glasses, slipping into his pockets and out again. They seemed unwilling to settle anywhere.

"Yeah, sure. I can do Wednesday." Felicity set her coffee cup on the floor and opened her locker door, the inside of which was plastered with postcards of paintings and sculptures by Cézanne, Rodin, and Picasso. A small red envelope fell out and landed at her feet, and she picked it up. It looked like some sort of invitation.

"Okay, great," said Jonathan. "So, do you want to meet at a coffee shop, maybe? We could go through the submissions on my laptop."

A coffee shop was a bad idea. Felicity liked Jonathan, but being seen with a non-redhead outside of school would be a crushing blow to her red cred. "Maybe we should just use the computer in the art room," she said, trying to sound casual. "That way, we won't have to lug all the CDs out of the building."

"Yeah, sure, okay. That makes sense. I'll probably finish my piece in class today. Are you almost done with yours?"

While Jonathan was talking, Felicity tore open the red envelope and pulled out a small card. Handwritten in the middle of the creamy stationery were the words

I know your secret, artie.

For a few seconds, Felicity's heart completely stopped beating. She clutched the card to her chest so Jonathan wouldn't see what it said. Maybe this was just another version of The Dream and she was actually safe in her bed. *Wake up,* she urged herself. *Everything's fine. You're just asleep.* She pinched her arm, hard. But nothing changed, and Felicity could only conclude that this time, her nightmare was very, very real.

Images rushed through her mind like a slide show gone haywire, showing her everything she would lose if her secret got out: her boyfriend, her popularity, the respect of all her peers. Even her closest friends probably wouldn't stand by her if they found out she'd been lying to them about something so important. She might be kicked out of the pageant for having "questionable morals." Ginger would be crushed, and she might even lose her job in the mayor's office.

"Felicity?" Jonathan reached out to touch her shoulder, but his hand stopped a few inches short of her and then retreated. "Are you okay?"

"What? Yeah. Yeah, I'm fine." Felicity shoved the note into her back pocket. Jonathan was still looking at her expectantly, but she couldn't remember what they'd been talking about.

Oh, right—the art show. The whole thing suddenly seemed totally unimportant. If someone at school knew she was an artie, she could be a social outcast by the end of the day. The art show would be the least of her worries.

But she couldn't very well lose it in the middle of the hallway, so she smiled and tried to look normal. "I'll be done by then. I'll see you Wednesday, okay?"

"Great, okay. See you later."

As soon as he was gone, Felicity scanned the hall. Whoever had left her this little gift might be lurking nearby, waiting to see her reaction. Gabby was most likely the one who had discovered her secret, considering her mom's connections with the artie population. But she could have told her friends, and any one of them could have decided to use the information to her advantage. Felicity's eyes flitted from brunette to brunette, searching her classmates' faces for signs of guilt or hostility.

Unfortunately, that was no help—Felicity found hostility on the face of *every* brunette. Marina and Sayuri were chatting happily at their lockers, but they looked up and glared when they caught her staring. Amanda Westin and Sarah Lowes rolled their eyes at her and turned their backs. Gabby shot her a "What are *you* gaping at?" look. Did the entire brunette population of Scarletville High know her secret? Or had these girls always given her dirty looks, and she'd just never noticed before? Was this note the only step the culprit had taken, or was a widespread announcement on the way? Gossip at Scarletville High spread faster than head lice at a day camp, so if even a few people knew her secret now, everyone would know by lunchtime.

Everyone.

Felicity stumbled through the morning in a fog of panic. She didn't hear a thing her teachers said about radians, Hemingway, or light refraction, and she completely botched her pop quiz about Vikings in History of Redheadedness. Every time she walked into a room, she expected to be greeted with wide eyes and horrified whispers. But class after class, nothing happened. Felicity felt as if she were in the dentist's chair, listening to the high-pitched whine of the drill as it approached a cavity. She almost wished the actual drilling would begin, just so she would know how much pain she was up against. Right now, she could only imagine the worst.

The drill touched down just before fifth-period lunch. When Felicity opened her locker to retrieve her books for the afternoon, a second red envelope landed at her feet, and her heart leapt into her throat. She snatched up the incriminating message before anyone could see it, then locked herself in a bathroom stall so she could read the contents unobserved.

> Starting right now, you will act like you
> want every brunette in this school to be
> your best friend. Fail to impress us, and
> everyone finds out what you really are.

Felicity swallowed hard. It would be difficult to make that look natural, but she would have to find a way to make it work. The good news was that nobody had spread her secret around yet. Sure, she was being blackmailed, but at least she had the opportunity to protect herself. The situation could be infinitely worse.

The first thing Felicity saw when she entered the cafeteria was Lorelei Griffin and a crowd of her theater friends standing menacingly around the table where Gabby, Marina, and Sayuri were sitting. That particular table was prime real estate: close to the windows and the vending machines, far from the chaos of the lunch line. "What are *you* doing here?" Lorelei was saying to the girls. "This is our spot. Get out."

Gabby made a big show of inspecting the surface of the table. "I'm sorry, but I don't see a reserved sign with your name on it."

Lorelei's eyes widened — nobody ever talked back to her. "Do you seriously want to mess with me? You've had your little joke, and now it's time to go back where you belong before I get really pissed."

"No thanks, we're good here," Marina said. "But I see a free table for you over there." She pointed at a table near the trash cans, right under a banner proclaiming RED IS RAD! Gabby and Sayuri snorted with laughter.

A dark cloud passed over Lorelei's face. Then she very deliberately removed the plastic lid from her soda and tipped it off her tray, directly onto Marina's white shirt. "Oops," she said sweetly as Marina jumped up with a shout. "*So* sorry about that. But look, your shirt matches your hair now!" Lorelei's friends laughed as ice cubes cascaded from Marina's lap and skittered across the floor. From the far corner of the room, a copper-haired lunch monitor glanced up disinterestedly, then returned to her gossip magazine.

Felicity took a deep breath. Then, praying her black-mailer was watching, she grabbed a handful of napkins and headed straight into the fray. "Hey," she said, dabbing at Marina's shoulder. "Let me help you."

Marina jerked away. "I don't need your help."

"Well, here. At least take these." She put the napkins on the table, and Marina grudgingly grabbed several. As she blotted at her shirt, Felicity turned her attention to Lorelei. "What is your problem?" she hissed, making sure all three brunettes heard her. "They didn't do anything to you."

"They were sitting at *my table*. I asked them to move very politely. It's not my fault if they're too dumb to follow directions. Why do *you* care, anyway?"

Felicity bit back the "I don't" that was forming on her lips. "You don't have to be such a bitch about it," she said instead.

Everyone was looking at her now, probably wondering why someone with hair as red as hers would stick up for a brunette in a fight. This could be a serious blow to her red cred, and it was time to get out while she was still ahead. She turned away quickly, face flaming, and hurried toward the table she always shared with Haylie and Ivy. Hopefully her blackmailer had seen her selfless act, and everyone else would forget about her strange behavior by the end of lunch.

But then Gabby, Marina, and Sayuri fell into step beside her, carrying their lunch trays.

"That was surprisingly decent of you," Gabby said.

"Yeah, well, I— You're welcome," Felicity muttered.

They reached Felicity's table, and Haylie looked up. "Hey, don't you think Ivy should—" She broke off as she registered that the three brunettes weren't just walking *near* Felicity, but *with* her. A tiny crinkle of confusion appeared between her eyebrows. "Why are you—"

"We can sit here, right?" Marina said. She looked straight at Felicity, her eyes steely. It was clearly a test, and Felicity's stomach turned over. It was one thing to stick up for someone when she'd just had a Coke dumped on her and quite another to spend the entire lunch period with a table full of brunettes. But Marina might be her blackmailer, which meant that turning her down could have unspeakable consequences. Felicity knew what she had to do.

"There's not really room—" Haylie started, but Felicity cut her off.

"It's okay. We can squish."

Haylie and Ivy both shot her perplexed looks, but she pretended not to notice. She grabbed another chair from a neighboring table and tried to get everyone seated as inconspicuously as possible.

Felicity hoped the brunettes would talk amongst themselves and leave her to talk to her own friends, and Marina and Sayuri did exactly that. But Gabby dug into her mini pizza, then looked at Felicity expectantly, clearly waiting for her to say something. "I like your sandals," Felicity finally said, at a loss for any other common ground between them.

"Thanks," Gabby said. "They were on sale at Flame Footwear. Pretty much everything in there right now is covered in glitter and rhinestones, what with prom and the pageant coming up. It's absolutely vomit-inducing." She wrinkled her nose as if she'd just found an unexpected anchovy on her pizza. "But I guess that's all you guys are thinking about right now, huh?"

"Not really," Felicity snapped, before she remembered the note.

> Act like you want every brunette in this school to be your best friend.

She softened her tone. "I mean, there's still a lot coming up before that, like the art show."

"Right, you're curating that. Must be nice to be in charge of something, huh?"

Felicity nodded, letting the irony of the statement sink in. She had never felt less in control than she felt right now.

Sometimes Felicity had dreams in which she was performing in a play but had forgotten all her lines, and that's exactly what the rest of lunch felt like. Her stomach clenched into a tight knot that left no room for her sandwich, which she threw out after only two bites. When Amanda Westin passed their table on her way to the vending machines, Felicity complimented her new haircut, and Amanda stared at her as if she'd sprouted several additional heads. Gabby continued to make disparaging comments about the pageant, and Felicity couldn't refute them, just in case her blackmailer was listening. She prayed she was getting credit for her self-sacrifice. It was possible her rival didn't even have fifth-period lunch, in which case she was doing all this for nothing.

When the bell finally rang, it sounded sweet as a chorus of angels. Felicity finally allowed herself a sigh of relief after the three brunettes had gone.

"What was *that* about?" Haylie asked as soon as they were alone. "Since when are you all buddy-buddy with Gabby Vaughn and her weird friends?"

"I'm not," Felicity said. "I just felt bad 'cause Lorelei was being so awful. She dumped her entire drink on Marina."

"That stuff happens all the time," Haylie said. "Since when is it our problem?"

"I guess it's not. But they were standing right here being like, 'Can we sit with you?' What was I supposed to do, say, 'No, please leave so I can talk to my friends?'"

"Well, yeah. That's what anyone would have done. That's what I was trying to do, before you were all, 'Please sit down and be my BFF.'"

"Sorry," Felicity said, a little desperate. "I didn't know you would care that much. I was just trying to be a decent person."

"It's fine," Ivy said. "It's not a big deal. I think it's nice that you stood up for them."

Haylie tossed her bag over her shoulder. "Whatever. But if you want to be friends with brunette freaks, could you maybe do it on your own time?"

Ivy started laughing. "God, Hays, you're such a jerk."

"I am *so* not! I don't see what's so terrible about wanting to eat lunch alone with my own friends!"

Felicity followed Haylie and Ivy out of the cafeteria,

only half listening to their bickering. Her head was starting to throb, and she closed her eyes and massaged her temples. She couldn't let a simple conversation with a bunch of brunettes rattle her like this. After all, this was probably just the beginning of what was in store for her.

She was going to have to toughen up.

Felicity was exhausted by the end of the day, and she had to force herself not to skip the prom committee meeting after school. She had only joined the committee because they'd needed an artist to design the decorations, and it had seemed like the perfect compromise. Felicity could spend hours painting after school, and her mom never complained that she was wasting her time making art when she was surrounded by popular people, working for a "worthy cause." She was always bored to tears by the meetings, but at least there were no brunettes on the committee, so she didn't have to worry about being ambushed.

When she arrived, everyone except Madison Banks was grouped around Cassie, who was showing off something on her phone. Madison was perched on the teacher's desk, sorting through a stack of papers and ignoring everyone. Their faculty adviser, Mr. Mulligan, was nowhere to be found. He had failed to show up so many times that most people had forgotten he had anything to do with the prom committee.

"Hey, Felicity," Cassie called. "Come check out the pageant dress I'm ordering!"

Felicity squeezed into the huddle between Savannah King and Topher Gleason, the only boy on the committee, to get a look at the dress. It looked more like a large baby-blue shower loofah than an article of clothing. "Wow, Cassie," she said. "That's . . . pretty amazing."

Cassie beamed. "I know, isn't it? Have you gotten yours yet?"

"Not yet. I'm going shopping this weekend with Haylie and Ivy."

Topher sighed dramatically. "Why can't boys be in the pageant? I'd make a *killer* Miss Scarlet." Felicity didn't doubt it. Topher had better legs than most of the girls in the school, and he knew it. The majority of his pants were so tight, they looked as if they'd been spray-painted on.

Savannah stroked Topher's shoulder. "Don't worry, Toph, you can dress up for prom."

"Prom will be nothing but a disappointment unless I can borrow Cassie's dress." Topher looked at Cassie with big, pleading eyes. "Cass? What do you think?"

"Honey, if you can fit into it, you can wear it," said Cassie, and everyone but Madison laughed.

Despite her ambivalence about the committee, Felicity was genuinely excited about prom night—she had never been to a formal event that didn't involve being judged. Brent was sure to look spectacular in his tux, and they were meeting Haylie, Ivy, and their dates beforehand for dinner at a fancy Italian restaurant. Post-prom, they were throwing a party in Haylie's backyard. Ivy was going with Darren, the captain of the boys' swim team, who had been quietly pursuing her for months. Haylie's date was Lorelei Griffin's older brother, Ryan, who was the drummer in a band called The Crucial Douches. Felicity hoped Haylie would dispose of him after prom. His band was shockingly bad, and she didn't want to have to feign enthusiasm for their screamy, atonal "songs."

"Guys, can we *please* have our meeting?" snapped Madison. "We have a lot to talk about, and I have to get to cheerleading practice." She sounded exasperated, as if this were the forty-fifth time she had called them to order instead of the first.

Felicity rolled her eyes and sat down next to Savannah and Kendall Forsythe, a senior from her art class. She tried to keep her mind from wandering as Madison ran through the items on her agenda, but it was a losing battle — she had no interest in deposits, dessert platters, printing costs, or sound systems. After forty-five minutes, Madison finally released them to meet with their subcommittees, and Felicity, Savannah, and Kendall headed to the art studio.

This year's theme was "Paint the Town Red," and Felicity had suggested a 1920s look. She'd designed an Art Deco–style cityscape backdrop to cover one of the gym walls, and the other three would be draped in gauzy red fabric she had borrowed from the drama department. They were renting replica 1920s streetlamps from a theatrical-supply company, and they planned to hang red paper lanterns between the basketball hoops and along the tops of the bleachers.

"God, I'm so glad you're in charge of the decorations this year," Kendall said as they unrolled the half-finished backdrop on the floor. "Last year was just embarrassing. The theme was 'Moulin Rouge,' but the dumb-ass strawbie designer made a New York City skyline *and* an Eiffel Tower and put them up on the same wall."

Savannah piled her long coppery hair on top of her head and stuck a pencil through it to keep it from falling into the paint. "How did a strawbie even get to be the designer in the first place?" she asked.

"Who knows? But it's not a mistake we'll be making again any time soon. Right, Felicity?" Kendall gave her a wide, friendly smile and offered her a paintbrush.

Felicity's stomach clenched. "Right," she said, accepting the brush. "Of course."

"Speaking of embarrassing, how did Ariel Scott get into the pageant?" Savannah asked. "Her hair is practically *blond*."

"They always put one strawbie in," Kendall said, echoing Ivy's words from Scarlet Sunday. "Jillian Wells competed last year, remember?"

"I don't get that at all. It's the Miss *Scarlet* Pageant. Hey, should I start painting this part at the bottom, Felicity?"

"Yeah, go ahead." Felicity tried to focus on painting, which usually soothed her, but it was impossible to relax. She couldn't very well stand up for Ariel, but joining the strawbie-bashing seemed equally awful. "Don't worry, Ariel won't win," she finally said.

"Damn right she won't. Not with us in the picture." Savannah rewarded her with a grin. "Hey, did I tell you guys I'm singing 'Red-Letter Day' by Invisible Stallion for my talent?"

Felicity stayed quiet as Savannah and Kendall chattered on. She wondered whether either of them would ask her why a bunch of brunettes had been sitting at her lunch table, but nobody brought it up—fifth period was eons in the past, and new gossip had already eclipsed the old. Felicity spoke up only to answer questions about the drop, which was taking shape exactly as she'd planned. The girls deferred to her opinions automatically, letting her artistic vision guide their hands.

If they only knew they were taking orders from another "dumb-ass strawbie designer," Felicity thought, her life would be over.

4

WEDNESDAY, MAY 5

Felicity was terrified to open her locker. She was staring at the metal door, trying to imagine what fresh hell might be lurking behind it, when Haylie and Ivy arrived.

"Are you okay?" Ivy asked, reaching for Felicity's mocha. "You look pale, even for you." That said a lot — Felicity's complexion was almost transparent. You could read the road map of her veins right through her skin without even trying.

"What? Oh, yeah, I'm fine. I just haven't been sleeping well." Felicity took a deep breath and spun the dial on her lock. Her hands were trembling so much that it took her three tries to get the combination right. When the lock finally clicked, she said a silent prayer and pulled open the door.

A little red envelope tumbled to the ground at her feet.

"Ooh, what's that?" Haylie asked, reaching for it.

"Nothing!" Felicity frantically snatched the envelope out of her friend's fingers and shoved it deep into her pocket.

For a moment, Haylie looked wounded, but then her eyes lit up. "Oh my God, do you have a *secret admirer*? What is Brent going to say?"

Felicity nearly laughed—what she had was pretty much the opposite of a secret admirer. "Trust me, it's nothing like that," she said. She shoved her books into her bag in record time, then slammed her locker shut much harder than necessary, as if the violence might scare away any future envelopes. "I have to go."

Haylie put a hand on her arm. "Hey, you're not mad, are you? I was just kidding about the secret admirer thing."

"No, it's not that. I just . . . I'll see you guys later." Felicity tried to smile, but she feared it was one of those forced, manic smiles that looked more crazy than happy. As she walked away, she heard Haylie say, "What is with her lately? She's been acting so weird."

Felicity locked herself in a bathroom stall, then clawed the envelope open with shaking fingers. Inside was another piece of creamy stationery.

Well done yesterday. You will continue to make overtures of friendship to every

54

> brunette you encounter. In addition, there
> is a CD in the art show submissions box
> containing a painting of hyenas. You will
> include the painting in the gallery show.
> Fail to do so, and you know what happens.

Seriously? Her blackmailer was using her to get a painting into the *student art show*? How absurdly petty. Felicity stuffed the note into the bottom of her bag, feeling much more relaxed for the moment. At least this was a demand she knew she could meet.

When she arrived in the art room after school, Jonathan was already there with the box of submission CDs. He gave her a big smile as she dropped her backpack and sat down next to him; he seemed a lot calmer in the sawdust-and-turpentine-scented classroom than he had been in the chaotic hallway.

"I hope some of this stuff is decent," he said as he slipped the first CD into the computer. "But I guess if it all sucks, we can just curate a whole show of horrible art, and then we can pretend it's really deep and profound and go around spouting pretentious art criticism all night. There's a whole museum in Massachusetts that does that, and people actually go."

Felicity laughed, surprised. She hadn't known Jonathan had a sense of humor hidden under his agitated exterior. "Honestly, I think that's what they do in most galleries," she said. "Can we wear berets? It'll make us look more official."

"Definitely. And black turtlenecks. They don't let you say things like 'The semiotics of this piece are so antediluvian' if you're not wearing a black turtleneck."

They spent the rest of the afternoon going through the CDs and choosing the best pieces to display in their own "gallery space," which comprised the school's two squash courts. Felicity's favorite submission was a photograph of a girl reclining in a bathtub full of Skittles. Even after staring at it for five full minutes, neither she nor Jonathan could tell whether it was Photoshopped.

Every time Jonathan inserted a new disc, Felicity wondered whether it would be the hyena picture. And when the painting finally made an appearance late in the afternoon, her stomach plummeted toward the floor. She had assumed it would be a realistic depiction of wildlife, but nothing could have been further from the truth.

As advertised, the piece featured a group of five slobbering hyenas, but each of them was dressed in a garish formal gown trimmed with ruffles, sequins, and lace. They were fighting over a sparkly tiara on a velvet pillow, ropes of drool hanging from their gaping mouths. Each hyena's head was topped with red hair decorated with flowers and sparkly combs.

The painting was titled *Miss Scarlet,* and the dimensions were listed as seven by four feet.

Felicity wrapped her arms protectively around her stomach, suddenly afraid she might be sick. Jonathan snorted in disgust. "Are you kidding?" he said. "She can't have thought we'd actually put this in the show. This has to be some kind of joke, right?"

Felicity knew it wasn't. And as she looked at the painting more closely, she realized that the hairstyles on the hyenas weren't arbitrary. One of them had two buns secured with butterfly barrettes. Another wore its hair in a messy pixie cut. A third had long bangs swept to the side. Felicity's breath caught in her throat as she recognized herself and her two best friends.

"It's really well crafted for a joke," she said. "Looks like someone spent a lot of time on it." Her voice sounded strangled, and she took a big sip of her Diet Coke.

Jonathan shook his head. "This is ridiculous. I mean, I'm a guy, and I don't even have red hair, and *I'm* offended." He closed the window on the screen, and the picture disappeared.

Once it was out of sight, Felicity found it a little easier to focus, and something Jonathan had said suddenly registered. "Wait, you just said, '*She* can't have thought we'd actually put this in the show.' Do you know whose this is?"

"Yeah, it's Gabby Vaughn's. She's in my art class. She's been working on it all month. I bet you can imagine how much the rest of my class loved that."

Felicity's head was suddenly spinning, and she gripped the edge of the table. Here was concrete proof that Gabby was involved in the blackmail scheme. Though Felicity had been looking for this information all week, having it only made her feel worse. Any of the other girls could have been tormenting her based on speculation. But Gabby might very well have evidence of Felicity's strawbie status. She was by far the most dangerous adversary. Felicity wondered if she was working alone or if her friends were in on it.

"Hey, are you okay?" Jonathan's voice seemed to be coming from very far away.

"Yeah. Just . . . Can I see the painting again?"

Jonathan seemed reluctant, but he reopened the file, and Felicity stared at her hyena counterpart. The neon-orange dress it was wearing was so bright it made her brain throb. Even if she managed to confront Gabby tomorrow, the terms of the note were very clear: if this painting didn't appear on the list of winning pieces first thing in the morning, everyone would find out what she really was. For the moment, she had no choice but to obey.

Felicity swallowed hard. "I think we should include it," she said.

"What?" Jonathan stared at her, incredulous. "Really? I mean, don't you think it's kind of . . . vicious?"

"It doesn't bother me," she lied. She prayed he wouldn't see the truth on her face.

But Jonathan was too busy squirming to notice her false tone. A blush was creeping up his neck, and a bright red splotch blossomed high on each cheekbone. "But—I mean, Felicity, isn't that . . . isn't that supposed to be *you*?" With a pained look, he gestured to the center hyena. "I don't want to, you know, do that. To you."

Was it possible that a non-redhead could be so concerned about hurting her feelings? Jonathan seemed even more uncomfortable than she did. "I know it's not exactly flattering," she said. "But there are lots of people who don't like the pageant, and they should get to express their opinions. I think we should put it in the show."

They both stared at the painting on the screen for a long minute. Felicity examined the ropes of drool dripping from the Haylie hyena's gaping maw.

"You really think so?" Jonathan asked.

"Sure. Yeah. Art's supposed to be controversial, right?"

Jonathan was quiet for a moment. Then he said, "You're right. And I really respect that you think that and that you aren't, you know, taking this personally. I'm okay with putting it in if you are. But, Felicity?"

"Yeah?"

Jonathan's blush was intensifying, and his gaze dropped to the floor. "I just want to make sure—I want you to know that I don't think—um—*that*. About you." He gestured toward the hyenas.

Felicity's heart did a strange little flip. Hearing something so personal come out of Jonathan's mouth was disorienting, and she was speechless just long enough for the situation to become intensely awkward. Finally, she blurted out, "Well, I hope not. I make a pretty big effort to keep my drooling under control. At least in public."

Jonathan laughed, and the tension eased a little. He ejected the CD, and they moved on.

It took almost three hours to choose the twenty-eight best pieces. "Should we map out how we're going to arrange everything?" Felicity asked when they had finished.

"Sure. But we haven't seen each other's stuff yet. Do you want to do that now, so we have a complete idea of what we're working with?"

"Oh, right." Felicity had felt good about her sculpture earlier, when Ms. Kellogg had praised it in class. But now that it was time to show it to Jonathan, a swarm of butterflies seemed to have taken up residence in her stomach. She really wanted to earn her place in the art show — lately, she'd had a few too many reminders that she often got things she didn't deserve.

"I'll go first," she said quickly. Jonathan's painting was sure to be of Rembrandt quality, and her piece would probably look like third-grade macaroni art by comparison. Better to get it out of the way.

She collected her sculpture from the back of the art room, where she had tucked it under a protective drop cloth. She set it down in front of Jonathan and removed the fabric with a self-conscious little flourish. "It's called *Skin-Deep*." She could hardly bring herself to look at his face.

The piece was a self-portrait, created using a technique she'd invented that combined sculpture, photography, and papier-mâché. Felicity had built a life-sized wire sculpture of a seated female figure hugging her knees to her chest, her cheek resting against them as if she were pensive or exhausted. Then she had taken hundreds of digital photos of herself smiling, laughing, dancing, joyfully tossing her vivid hair. She had printed them on translucent paper and brushed them onto the frame with a glue mixture so they formed a skin. A small part of her hoped someone would see her piece and walk away with a deeper understanding of who she really was. But a larger part hoped nobody would look past the shiny outer layer.

Jonathan circled the sculpture slowly, taking it in from all angles. Then he crouched down, looked at it up close, and ran his finger gingerly over the figure's papier-mâché shoulder. Felicity's own shoulder tingled sympathetically.

It seemed like it had been way too long since either of them had spoken, and she grew increasingly anxious. Maybe Jonathan was trying to find a tactful way to tell her that the sculpture wasn't good enough for the show. "If you don't like it, I have other stuff," she finally said to break the silence. "I've mostly been working with this technique lately, but there are other things I could show you if —"

Jonathan stood up. "I love it," he said. It was the most declarative thing she'd ever heard him say.

Felicity felt her cheeks flood with heat. "Really?"

"It's so original. I've never seen anything like this. She's awesome." Felicity loved how Jonathan referred to the sculpture as "she" instead of "it." He crouched again and looked closely at the photographs. "Did you take all these yourself?"

"Yeah. It took forever."

He walked around the sculpture again. "I think—I mean, we don't have to do this if you don't want to, it's your piece—but I think we should put her up on a pedestal so people can see the photographs better. Otherwise, I'm worried they might miss the point."

So Jonathan got the point. Did that mean other people would, too? A spark of terror ran through Felicity as Jonathan looked up from the sculpture and stared intently into her face, as if a puzzle piece had just clicked into place in his mind. Exactly how much did he suddenly understand about her? Maybe she had revealed too much. Putting this work on display suddenly felt intensely personal, almost like stripping in public, and she had to fight the urge to throw the drop cloth back over it.

But Jonathan's gaze was kind and warm, respectful and supportive. There was no judgment in it at all. Felicity noticed that behind his glasses, his hazel eyes were flecked with green.

She nodded, then quickly looked away. "Can I see your painting?"

"Oh, yeah, sure. It's not nearly as interesting as this, though." Felicity followed him as he crossed the room and pulled a drop cloth off several canvases, which were leaning against each other, their faces to the wall. "I have a bunch of options, actually. I wasn't sure which one was best for the show, so I . . . Why don't I just show you all of them, and you can choose." Jonathan's hands were getting fluttery again as he prepared to spread out the paintings. Was he actually *nervous* about showing them to her? That didn't seem possible.

"I've been doing a lot of landscapes this semester," he said as he flipped the first canvas around. It was a painting of the most beautiful place Felicity had ever seen. In the background, huge, majestic rock formations reared their heads out of a stretch of turquoise ocean. There was a light sprinkling of boats in the water, and the foreground was filled with magenta flowers. Though the colors and the composition were gorgeous, the most striking thing about the painting was how confident and sure each brushstroke was. It was obvious that Jonathan hadn't painted over anything. He'd gotten it all right the first time.

"Oh, *wow*. Is that Hawaii?"

"It's Capri. It's this little island in Italy? My grandmother lives near there. I visited her over Christmas, and I did a ton of sketching. It's so — I don't know, I just love it there."

Jonathan flipped over more paintings of cliffs, water, and street scenes. Each piece looked like it belonged in a museum. But when he turned over the final canvas — a little smaller than the others, and less finished-looking — Felicity immediately knew that was the one she wanted in the show.

The subject of the painting was a girl about their age. She stood at a railing overlooking the ocean, her body turned toward the endless expanse of blue. Her long dark hair danced in the wind that whipped around her face, and she was trying to catch hold of it with her hand as she looked back over her shoulder at the viewer. Her eyes were warm and alert and a little mischievous, as if she were about to make a wry joke. It was obvious that Jonathan cared about this girl, whoever she was; the painting overflowed with tenderness.

"This one," Felicity said, pointing.

"Really? But all these other ones feel more finished to me. I mean, doesn't this one seem — "

"No," said Felicity. "This one is the best. Who is she?"

Jonathan rested his hand on the top of the canvas protectively. "This is Lucia," he said. His eyes got brighter just saying her name.

"Is she in Capri, too?"

"Yes." He looked at the painting like he wished he could reach right through it and grab the girl's hand. The expression on his face gave Felicity a peculiar little ache in her chest. She wanted to ask all kinds of questions about Lucia, but since she and Jonathan were just art class friends, not *real* friends, she felt that might be out of line.

"She's beautiful," Felicity told him. "She should definitely be in the show."

Jonathan looked at his painting for another minute, then nodded. "Okay. That's fine. If you think so." He gave the top of the canvas an affectionate pat.

Felicity and Jonathan covered their artwork, then wrote out a list of the chosen artists' student ID numbers, including Gabby's. Felicity posted the list on the studio door, and then they got to work figuring out where each piece would go in the "gallery."

But Felicity found it hard to concentrate. All she could think about was the expression on Jonathan's face as he'd looked at his painting of Lucia. There had been so much sweetness and longing in his expression. Nobody had ever looked at her that way.

She hadn't even known she wanted that kind of attention until now, but suddenly she wondered how she had ever managed to live without it.

That night, Felicity was sitting on her bed, doodling plans for her next sculpture in her sketchbook, when she heard rustling in the tree outside her window. Her heart started pounding; nobody had gotten around to fixing her screen since a squirrel had chewed through it and gotten into her bedroom last month. Felicity grabbed a heavy art book from her desk and held it up like a weapon, then sidled toward the window.

But it wasn't a squirrel—it was a football player. Just as Felicity reached the window, all 180 pounds of Brent tumbled over the sill headfirst and landed directly on top of her. She tried to scream, but all the air had been knocked from her body, and no sound came out. The book skidded ineffectually across the floor.

Felicity struggled out from under her boyfriend. "God, Brent, you scared the crap out of me."

He grinned. "Sorry, babe. I wanted to surprise you. I didn't think you'd be right there."

"You either have to call first or use the front door, okay?"

"I can't use the front. If your mom knows I'm here, she won't let us close your door, and I wanna be alone with you." He flopped down on her polka-dotted bedspread with his shoes on and held out his arms. "C'mere. I didn't mean to freak you out."

Felicity made sure her door was shut tightly, then went over and sat on the bed. Brent pulled her down next to him and kissed her, then wrapped both arms around her and settled her head onto his chest. She allowed herself to be embraced, and despite her annoyance, she felt herself relaxing. Her head fit so perfectly into the little dip next to his collarbone. Their legs tangled together in a reassuring, familiar way. One of Brent's hands rested on her hip, and the other twined through her hair. She closed her eyes and listened to the slow, even thump of his heart.

It was nice, just lying there with him. Brent was perfect when he wasn't talking, and for a little while, Felicity felt safe and comfortable and content. But soon she felt his breathing start to deepen, and she realized he was falling asleep. She knew he had good reason to be tired — he got up super early for football practice, and he often went to the gym after school, too. But now she wasn't sure whether he'd been seeking a girlfriend or a body pillow when he'd climbed through her window.

She squirmed around and repositioned her head, hoping the movement would wake him. "We picked the pieces for the art show today," she said, a little louder than necessary.

Brent's yawn was so wide it made Felicity think of a snake preparing to swallow its prey whole. "Oh yeah?" he mumbled.

She told him about the submissions—with the exception of the hyenas, of course—and he made noises that indicated he was listening as he stroked her hair. But when she was done talking, he just yawned again and said, "You smell so good."

She wasn't sure why she still tried to talk about art with Brent. He had never made an insightful comment on the subject or even asked a question. Felicity always told herself that he wasn't uninterested in what she did. He was the kind of person who thought in sports metaphors, and he just didn't know what to ask. Unfortunately, these rationalizations didn't make her feel any better today. Spending the afternoon with someone who understood art—and seemed to understand *her* just from looking at what she'd created—had been such a new and enlightening experience. It made Brent's disinterest seem even more unsatisfying by comparison.

She wished she could at least tell her boyfriend about the hyenas, which she couldn't seem to banish from her mind. What should she say to Gabby tomorrow? Would she be able to shut down the blackmail scheme before the rest of the school saw her and her best friends depicted as mangy scavengers? If she managed to get her blackmailers to back off, how could she pull the painting from the show without making Jonathan think she was a coward?

But of course, she couldn't talk about any of that. She sighed. "What's up with you?" she asked, hoping Brent would come up with a good story to distract her.

"Not too much. Carson and I totally slaughtered Tim and Damien at two-on-two basketball in PE. And Carson and Damien made this bet that whoever lost had to drink six cartons of chocolate milk in ten minutes at lunch. Damien almost did it, but he puked in the courtyard after five. It was so hilarious."

This wasn't really the kind of story Felicity had in mind, so she interrupted her boyfriend with a slow, soft kiss. Brent responded eagerly, and within moments, he was running his hands all over her body. Felicity closed her eyes, relieved to be able to switch off her brain for a while.

Half an hour later, she snapped back to reality at the sound of her mom's voice shouting from downstairs. "Felicity! I need you to take out the recycling!"

She swore under her breath. "Give me a couple minutes, Mom!"

"*Now*, Felicity. If you put it off any longer, I'm coming up there and dumping these cans in your bed!"

Felicity scrambled to her feet, flushed and disheveled. She couldn't have her mom bursting in while Brent was there. "You have to go before she finds you," she whispered, tugging her T-shirt back into place.

Brent groaned, but he didn't argue. "See you tomorrow," he said. He kissed her one last time. "You are seriously so awesome."

"Felicity, you have thirty seconds to get down here!" shouted Ginger.

"See you," Felicity whispered. "Come on, you have to go *now*."

Brent's exit was much more graceful than his entrance. As he started down the tree, Felicity dashed to the mirror and smoothed her rumpled hair and clothes. She hoped her mom wouldn't notice how pink her cheeks were.

Feeling a tiny bit hollow, she watched from the window as Brent sprinted across the lawn and out the back gate.

5

THURSDAY, MAY 6

Felicity arrived at school the next day prepared for battle. She had once seen a nature documentary about what to do if you encounter an animal predator while hiking, and she had decided to follow the same protocol regarding Gabby: Make yourself look as large and threatening as possible. Make a lot of noise. Whatever you do, don't show your fear. *Gabby is a mountain lion,* she told herself as she walked down the hall. *Convince her that you're dangerous prey, and she'll find someone else to eat.*

When Felicity opened her locker, there were no little red envelopes in sight, and she smiled. It seemed like a good omen.

Gabby arrived at her own locker five minutes later,

70

and Felicity's heartbeat accelerated as she watched her enemy rummage around for her books. She took a deep breath. Just as Gabby moved to close the door, Felicity looped her arm through her adversary's in what she hoped looked like a friendly way. "Hey, Gabby," she chirped.

Gabby looked surprised, but before she could pull away, Felicity dug in her nails and steered her toward the nearest bathroom. "I need to talk to you," she hissed.

The bathroom was mercifully empty. Felicity checked each stall for feet, just to make sure, then leaned against the door and wedged it closed with her heel. She didn't want this conversation interrupted by giggling freshmen eager to redo their lip gloss, and being in control of the only exit made her feel safer. Gabby lolled against the sinks across the room, looking totally unintimidated.

"I assume these are from you," Felicity said in her best authoritative voice, pulling the three little red envelopes from her pocket.

"Impressive detective work." Gabby surveyed her nails and picked at some chipped polish on her pinkie. "Took you long enough."

It was incredibly annoying that she seemed so relaxed. Felicity wished she could move closer and shake the notes in Gabby's face, like they sometimes did on cop shows, but she worried the gesture might come off as ridiculous.

"Why would you write this?" she snapped instead. "It's obviously not true. You know my hair's been the same color my entire life. You've been in my class since second grade."

"Just because it's always been the same doesn't mean it's real. It's that sandalwood perfume you wear that finally tipped me off. For years, every time you walked by, I always thought, God, that smells so familiar, what does that remind me of? And then a couple weeks ago, my mom came home from work smelling the same way, and I finally put it together. It hides the smell of the dye, right?"

Felicity breathed a little more easily. If that was all Gabby had to go on, it might not be so hard to make this whole situation go away. "Are you serious?" she snorted. "*That's* your proof? That I wear the same perfume as your *mom*? I know this might be hard to believe, Gabby, but sometimes, *different people like the same smells*." She made a face of exaggerated shock.

Gabby rolled her eyes. "Oh, give it up, Felicity. I can see your roots."

Felicity's smile died on her lips, and she struggled against the wave of terror that crashed through her. It took every bit of her strength to resist rushing to the mirror, but she reminded herself sternly that this was reality, not The Dream. She had been to Rouge-o-Rama four days ago, so she couldn't possibly have roots. Gabby had to be bluffing.

"You think I'm going to fall for that?" she said. "This whole thing is ridiculous. You can't have roots unless you dye your hair. Which I *don't*."

Gabby shrugged. "Say what you want. But I think

my mom missed a little spot this time. Right about here." She pointed to her left temple.

She looked so serious that Felicity's mask of calm began to crumble. What if Rose really *had* missed a spot? There was a first time for everything. Before she could restrain herself, she was across the room, inspecting her hairline in the mirror. Everything looked fine, and for a moment all she felt was relief. Then Gabby snickered, and Felicity realized she'd been tricked.

"I don't have any roots, you bitch," she snapped. She stalked back to the door, her face flaming with fury.

"No, you don't. But you obviously thought you did, which kind of proves my point. Plus, I've seen you leaving the salon. Unless you just like to hang out in supply closets for fun."

Felicity felt unbelievably betrayed. Rose had told her there was *no way* anyone could know who came to Rouge-o-Rama. And yet here Felicity was, rendered completely powerless by the stylist's own daughter. "How do you even know where the salon is?" she sputtered. "It's supposed to be *secret*. Does your mom know you spy on her clients?"

"Of course not. But she keeps a set of blueprints for the salon at home from when she helped renovate it. It's right there in her office with the key to the appointment-book code names. She even has her work calendar synced to her home computer. She didn't make it very hard for me to spy."

"Isn't it illegal that you looked at that stuff? Like, invasion of privacy or something?"

"Sometimes you have to break the rules to get information, Felicity. Do *you* always follow the rules?"

Felicity felt her face grow even hotter. Though she hadn't technically broken any rules, her whole life as a redhead was one big lie. She was much worse than Gabby, really. *You have to get a grip,* she told herself. *Don't lie down and let the mountain lion eat you.*

She squared her shoulders. "It's not like anyone would believe you if you told them my hair color was fake. I'm a celebrity around here right now, with the pageant coming up. You couldn't even get a rumor started. Everyone would think you were just jealous of me. You probably are."

Gabby adopted the tone one might use to explain something to a dim-witted kindergartener. "Felicity, have you *seen* how rumors spread in this school? *Everyone* would believe me. And even if they didn't, they'd still tell everyone they knew."

That was a distressingly valid point. Felicity's popularity was no match for the Scarletville High rumor mill. Everyone was always hungry for a scandal, and a disgraced pageant contestant was even more exciting than a potential winner.

She slumped against the door, her bravado gone. "Does anyone else know? Did you tell your friends?"

"No, not yet."

That was a relief. "Are you going to?" She hated the desperation in her voice.

"I haven't decided. Do you have any convincing reasons why I shouldn't?"

74

Felicity had hoped she wouldn't have to resort to groveling, but it was clearly time to abandon her pride. "Seriously, Gabby, I'll do anything you want. This absolutely cannot get out, or my life will be over. What can I do for you? Do you want money? Do you want me to try to get you into the pageant? I could probably get my mom to pull some strings."

But Gabby just laughed. "*That's* what you think I want? To be in the *pageant*?"

It did sound a little ridiculous, but Felicity didn't know what else she could offer. Social status didn't come with actual power. "I don't *know* what you want. I don't know why you're doing this to me!"

"I'm not doing anything to you. You're the one dyeing your hair. All I did was find out about it."

Gabby was definitely doing something to her, and that something was called blackmail. But Felicity fought the urge to argue. "Okay, so you don't want to be in the pageant. That's fine. What *do* you want? You just tell me, and I'll work on getting it for you."

Gabby gestured to the little red envelopes, which Felicity was still clutching in a death grip. "I've been very clear about what I want. And you've done such a good job of following my instructions so far." She gave Felicity a condescending little smile. "I'm so looking forward to seeing my painting on the wall of your art show."

Felicity closed her eyes and rubbed her temples as she imagined what would happen when Haylie and Ivy saw the painting . . . and when her *mom* saw it. "Gabby,

I'm not opposed to what you painted on principle, and I really do think you're talented. But people know I'm curating the show, so if I include something offensive, it reflects badly on me. If the pageant judges see your painting, it could jeopardize my chances of winning. Can't I give you something a little less . . . *public*?"

Gabby raised one eyebrow, obviously amused. "What do I care if you win the pageant? How does that affect me?"

"Look, I'm totally happy to put another one of your paintings in the show instead. Maybe you have something more accessible?"

"I don't want another painting in the show. I want this painting in the show."

"What if I included *two* of your other paintings? Nobody else has two submissions."

Gabby chuckled. "Nice try, but the hyenas are what I'm offering. Take them or leave them. And you know what happens if you leave them." When she smiled, it reminded Felicity of the face Ivy's cat made just before he eviscerated a mouse he'd been batting.

She knew she'd have to hang the painting after all. But maybe the backlash wouldn't be *that* bad; it was just a piece of student art. If her friends confronted her about it, she could always say it was Jonathan's choice. "Fine," she said. "Bring the painting to the squash courts on Tuesday, when we're hanging the show."

"Fabulous. I look forward to it."

The first bell rang. Hoping it would soften her tormentor up a little, Felicity tried to smile and said, "You know, Gabby, I really don't have a problem with you."

"Of course you don't have a problem with me. You don't even see me." Gabby grabbed her bag and slung it over her shoulder. "We're done here."

"So you won't tell anyone?"

"For now." She gestured for Felicity to move out of her way.

Felicity stepped away from the door, hating that Gabby was so clearly in charge. Her enemy paused in the doorway and looked back at her. "By the way, your life will not 'be over' if this gets out. Don't be so melodramatic. You may have noticed that my hair is brown, and amazingly enough I'm still very much alive."

With that, she let the door swing shut behind her, leaving Felicity with only her shame for company.

6

Saturday was dress shopping day, and Felicity woke in a flurry of excitement. Playing dress-up had always been one of her favorite things. Ginger had wanted to take her shopping, but Felicity had begged for permission to look for dresses with her friends. "Let me surprise you this time," she'd wheedled. "You've taught me so much. You'll see, I'm going to choose the perfect dress."

Ginger had gotten teary-eyed at how grown-up her little girl was, and then, to Felicity's great joy, she had agreed—and handed over her credit card. Felicity had been astonished by her mom's generosity. She had seen a cell phone bill on the counter just that morning, stamped PAST DUE in big red letters; she knew they couldn't afford anything extravagant. Money had been especially tight lately. But Ginger had waved away Felicity's concern. "This is the most important thing we could spend our money on," she had said. "Go get a dress that will win you that prize money and it'll all be worth it."

Haylie sat in the front beside Felicity as they sped toward Iowa City, a stack of formal-wear catalogs in her lap and a huge smile on her face. Ivy huddled in the back, scowling at the cornfields out the window. It seemed impossible that anyone could be in a bad mood on such a beautiful day, but Ivy was dedicated to being annoyed, and she wasn't about to let gorgeous weather get in her way. She had even brought along her calculus book, a monstrous, twelve-hundred-page symbol of her refusal to have fun. Felicity wondered, as she so often did, how Haylie and Ivy managed to stay friends. They'd had almost nothing in common since Ivy had renounced everything "girly" at the beginning of seventh grade. Though there was a lot to be said for having known someone since preschool, Felicity sometimes feared she was the only glue holding her friends together.

As they sped past the sign at the town limit that proclaimed YOU ARE NOW LEAVING THE RED ZONE, Haylie turned in her seat to watch it recede. Felicity could tell that her friend was a little uncomfortable — none of them left the safety of Scarletville very often. "We need a plan of attack," she announced to distract Haylie from her anxiety.

Haylie turned back around. "I think we should hit

the boutiques first, and if we don't find anything, we can go to the mall. Though we should probably just go to Cedar Rapids or Des Moines if we don't find good stuff at the small stores. Department-store dresses always look so cheap."

"Hays, I'm sure there are great dresses for all of us in Iowa City," Felicity said. She didn't have the gas money to drive any farther.

"All I'm saying is that it's important to look our best. This is our last pageant. If I don't find the perfect gown here, I'm not going to buy something second-rate just to be done with it."

"I am," Ivy chimed in. "I'll wear a dress made out of a potato sack if that's what's convenient. Listen, if I find something to wear right away, I'm just gonna go to a coffee shop to study for my math test, okay?"

Haylie looked stricken. "No, you're not! You have to help us find *our* dresses!"

In the rearview mirror, Felicity saw a pained expression flicker across Ivy's face. "Haylie, you do understand that shopping for dresses is the most torturous activity I can imagine, right?"

"We know," Felicity said. "We really appreciate that you're doing this. And that you're doing the pageant at all."

"If you shop with us the whole day, we'll let you pick all the movies for our sleepover tonight," Haylie coaxed.

"All of them? No conditions?"

"No slasher flicks," Felicity said. "Remember that

time we watched *The Red Hand of Death* and Haylie attacked me in the middle of the night when I got up to pee?"

"Fine. No slasher flicks." Ivy settled back into her seat looking slightly mollified.

Haylie directed Felicity through the streets of Iowa City until they arrived at the first boutique, Lulu Levine. The two-story brick building was painted flamingo pink, and the sign out front urged passersby to INDULGE YOUR INNER DIVA! Ivy stared at the shop and rattled off a string of profanities before Felicity ushered her firmly through the door.

If a burlesque theater and an antique store had a baby together, the offspring would look like the interior of Lulu Levine. The three girls gazed around with a mix of horror and fascination — every surface was covered with pink sparkles, distressed gold paint, or mirrors. The wallpaper sported textured leopard spots, and the countertops were crowded with china figurines of cherubs and baby animals. All the furniture was strangely undersized, as if it had been harvested before it was done growing.

When Felicity caught sight of Yolanda, she had to bite her tongue to keep from laughing. The shop owner's clothes appeared to have been sewn from the interior decorator's discarded fabric scraps. She wore heart-shaped sunglasses and at least fifteen strands of pink glass beads, and her bright red hair was teased into a massive mushroom cloud. She was holding a mug in each hand, and when she saw Haylie, she gasped and sloshed coffee over both bangle-clad wrists. "Oh my goddess! It's Haylie Adams!"

Felicity and Ivy exchanged a mortified look and mouthed, "Oh my *goddess*?" but Haylie didn't miss a beat. "Hi, Yolanda, it's good to see you!" she said. "These are my best friends, Felicity and Ivy. We're looking for pageant gowns!"

Yolanda put down her coffees and squeezed Haylie tightly. "Your darling mom told me you were competing in Miss Scarlet! Congratulations, sweet pea! What an achievement!" When Haylie finally managed to escape, Yolanda shook Felicity's and Ivy's hands with painful enthusiasm. Felicity gaped at her jeweled skull-and-crossbones ring, which was the size of an Oreo.

"Tell me *exactly* what you're looking for!" Yolanda said, and Haylie promptly pulled out her catalogs. As she described her dream dress, using wild hand gestures, Felicity started drifting through the clothing racks. Ivy trailed her reluctantly.

"I don't even know where to start," Ivy said. She picked up a turquoise velvet sleeve with two fingers, holding it as if it might be infested with fleas.

"Here, I'll help you. Let's look for stuff for you first, and we'll deal with my dress later, okay? Give me some guidelines."

"No pink. No white. No sequins. Nothing that makes me look like a layer cake or a bridesmaid in Barbie's dream wedding."

"Got it." Felicity dug through a rack for a minute and held up a blue chiffon dress. "How about this?"

Ivy wrinkled her nose. "Too ballroom dancer."

"All right, what about this one?" Felicity offered a black gown covered with gold flowers.

"That looks like my grandmother's couch upholstery."

"Yeah, you're right." She pulled out a sparkly green dress and held it up next to Ivy's face. "This color looks nice with your eyes."

"I'd look like the Little Mermaid in that."

"Ivy, you have to try on *something*."

Ivy rolled her eyes. "Fine. Just pick stuff out, and I'll put it on. You guys can dress me up like the pliable little doll that I am."

Haylie had finished explaining her criteria to Yolanda, and they both came over to join the search. Yolanda peered at the scowling Ivy with concern. "What's the matter, honeybunch?"

"Ivy hates shopping," Haylie and Felicity explained in unison.

"Tell me what you want, and if it's here, I'll find it, sweet thing. That's my job."

Ivy repeated her guidelines. Yolanda assessed her carefully over her sunglasses, then ordered Ivy to take off her hoodie. She pulled a neon-pink tape measure out of her cleavage, took a few quick measurements, and beamed. "I know just the thing," she said as she bustled off.

Ivy flopped down on a puffy ottoman printed with

giant peonies. "I'm going to end up looking like a drag queen, aren't I?"

"Don't worry. Yolanda's really good at this," Haylie promised.

"As good as she is at decorating?"

"Just wait. You'll see." Haylie started purposefully plowing through the racks.

A few minutes later, Yolanda returned. "Voilà," she said, presenting a dress to Ivy with a flourish.

The gown was silvery blue-gray, pleated and draped in a way that looked almost Grecian. There was some silver embroidery around the edges, but for the most part, it was simple and understated. Ivy's eyes widened. "Wow," she said. "That's actually . . . not bad at all."

"It's perfect," Felicity said as Haylie bounced up and down and clapped. "Put it on!"

As Ivy disappeared into one of the Pepto-Bismol-colored fitting rooms, Felicity asked, "How did you do that? Ivy hates *all* dresses."

Yolanda shrugged, her beads clinking together. "I'm good at reading people's energy. I thought that dress would complement Ivy's aura. Oh no, babycakes," she said, snatching a purple sequined sheath out of Haylie's hands. "Your chakras clash with that color."

When Ivy stepped out of the fitting room, obviously uncomfortable but also grudgingly pleased, Felicity's jaw almost hit the ground. For the first time since elementary school, Ivy looked like a girl. It was fascinating.

"Ives, you look *awesome*!" Felicity said.

"How does it feel?" asked Yolanda. "Are you comfortable? Is it the right length? Will you be able to walk in it in heels?"

"It's good," Ivy said. "I'll take it."

Haylie's eyes widened. "But it's the first dress! I mean, it's great, but don't you want to try—"

"No. It's good. I'm done." Ivy shut herself back into the fitting room.

Things didn't go so quickly for Felicity and Haylie. Yolanda brought them gown after gown that "matched their chakras," but none of them seemed like The One. After an hour of scouring the store, Yolanda ran out of dresses to offer. "I guess it wasn't meant to be today, chickadees," she said as she rang up Ivy's purchase. "At least the universe smiled on one of you."

"It's all right, Yolanda," Haylie said. "You were so helpful."

"You're a superhero," Ivy declared. "Hopefully I won't ever need another dress, but if I do, I'm coming back here."

"Aw, thanks, boo-boo." Yolanda handed Ivy the dress and took a huge gulp of one of her cold, stale coffees. "You girls have a great day, now. Haylie, say hi to your adorable momsie for me. May the goddess be with you, now and always."

"You too," Felicity said, trying to keep a straight face. Ivy unsuccessfully tried to stifle a snort.

Four stores later, neither Felicity nor Haylie had a dress, and Ivy had long ago grown tired of playing games on her phone. "Can't you two just *pick* something?" she moaned as they approached boutique number five. "It's just a dress. It really doesn't matter that much!"

"Easy for you to say, Little Miss The-First-Thing-I-Tried-On-Was-Perfect," Haylie snapped.

Felicity was just opening her mouth to soothe her friends when she saw The Dress. It was royal blue, her favorite color, with a full, sweeping skirt and a small train. The top was a halter, and there was a delicate pattern of sparkly silver flowers that started at the right strap and meandered down across the left hip. She knew without a doubt that it was meant to be hers.

She approached the gown reverently. It was just as beautiful up close, and the fabric felt silky and expensive between her fingers. Though it was a little pricier than she'd hoped, it wasn't unreasonable. She turned to call her friends over, but Haylie was already by her side, her eyes the size of hubcaps. "Oh my God," she gasped. "It's the perfect dress!"

"I know!" Felicity clawed through the hangers until she found the gown in her size. Only when she had it in her hands did she realize that Haylie was searching through the rack with equal enthusiasm. "Hays, it's okay, I found one."

Haylie looked at the dress Felicity was holding, perplexed. "That's a size six."

"Well, yeah. That's my size."

Haylie pulled a size two off the rack and hugged it to her chest, comprehension slowly dawning on her face. "Oh no. *You* want this one?"

Felicity stared at her friend across the rack of identical gowns, and Haylie stared back. Of all the dresses in Iowa City, how could they fall in love with the same one? Felicity tried to tell herself it was just a dress. Surely she could find another, and it would make Haylie so happy to have this one. But she couldn't make herself back down. She needed that prize money far more than Haylie did. She had to look her very best for this competition, and she knew she could do that in this gown.

She tried to think of something articulate to say, but all she came up with was "Well, this totally sucks."

"Why don't we both try it on?" Haylie suggested. "Whichever one of us looks better in it gets it. And the other one has to promise not to be upset. It's just a dress, right?"

"How will we decide who looks better?"

Felicity and Haylie both turned to Ivy, who said, "Oh, *hell* no. I am *not* getting involved in this." She was out of the store so fast it was as if she had vaporized.

Haylie sighed as she watched Ivy retreat. "I guess we can decide for ourselves, right? We're always honest with each other."

Felicity thought of all the times she'd lied to Haylie in small ways over the past few weeks. *I can't come over — I have to pick up the twins. I only let Gabby sit at our lunch table because I felt bad for her. I put sandalwood oil in my hair because I love how it smells. Nothing's wrong, I'm just tired.* A huge wave of guilt crashed over her. But those lies couldn't be helped. They were for her protection. This time, she would be forthright.

"Of course. I'm sure we can be impartial," she said.

They found the fitting rooms in the back of the store, each of them carrying her dress as if it were a precious relic. There were two blondes and a brunette waiting in line, and Haylie shoved right past them. "Um, excuse you," one of the blondes snapped. "There's a line."

Haylie stared at her. "But we're red—" she began before Felicity grabbed her shoulder and gently pulled her back.

"Sorry," Felicity said to the girls. Even at home in Scarletville, she tried not to cut lines, though redheads who did usually weren't frowned upon.

The blonde eyed Haylie's Scarletville High School Dance Troupe T-shirt with disgust, then turned away. "Scarletville girls," she muttered to her friend. "They think they're God's gift to the universe."

"*Someone* needs to learn her place," Haylie whispered, and Felicity's stomach twisted. She gave a noncommittal smile in response.

They only had to wait a few minutes before two fitting rooms opened up. Just before Haylie closed her door, she turned to Felicity and said, "Listen, I really don't want us to fight about this dress, okay? So if either of us starts getting mad or upset, nobody gets it, and we'll both find something else to wear. Deal?" She stuck out her tiny manicured hand.

Felicity was touched; she could see in her friend's eyes how much she wanted the dress. "Deal," she agreed, then shut the door behind her.

The dress felt alive in her hands as Felicity unzipped it, stepped inside, and pulled the silky fabric up around her body. There was an unexpected slit in the skirt that reached the middle of her thigh, just high enough to be sexy but low enough to be classy. When she zipped it and tied the halter top, the gown embraced her like an old friend. She turned around to look in the mirror, and her heart fluttered when she saw her reflection. Her very best self was smiling back at her.

"How's it going in there?" called Haylie.

"Good. You?"

There was a little pause. "Good. You ready to come out?"

"Yeah, are you?"

"Yeah."

Felicity stood with her hand on the doorknob for a long moment. Until she saw Haylie, she could pretend this dress was hers. She glanced back at her reflection one last time, admiring how the fabric hugged her body as if it had been made for her. But she heard Haylie's door creaking open, and she knew it was time to face her friend.

She took a deep breath and stepped out of the dressing room.

For a full fifteen seconds, the girls appraised each other in silence. Haylie looked beautiful in the gown, but she was a little too short for it. The slit in the skirt hit her leg in a weird place, and three inches of silky fabric puddled around her feet. But those things could be corrected with a little tailoring. A voice in the back of Felicity's mind whispered, *Give up the dress. Haylie deserves this more than you, you big artie fake.*

She opened her mouth to tell Haylie how beautiful she looked, but her friend cut her off before she could say a word. "You look better in it," she announced. "It's meant for someone taller. You win. It's yours." Though she was clearly disappointed, she sounded sincere.

A strange mixture of guilt and joy suffused Felicity, and she struggled to keep her voice even. "Are you sure? You look really great in it, too."

"Not as good as you. It's okay, Felicity. I want you to have it. It's your perfect dress, not mine."

If Haylie really *wanted* her to have it, maybe it was okay to accept it after all. Maybe the universe was trying to tell her something. She'd show everyone she deserved it. She would win that crown, earn that prize money, use it to move her family to a redder neighborhood, just like her mom wanted. She would do this dress justice.

Felicity swooped in and hugged Haylie, squeezing her so hard she squeaked like a rubber chew toy. "Thank you thank you thank you thank you," she said. "We're going to find *your* perfect dress, even if we have to drive all the way to Des Moines."

After Haylie retreated to her fitting room, Felicity did a silent happy dance, jumping in circles and shaking her butt. The most beautiful dress in the world was hers. She could barely stand to take it off and change back into her jeans. From the fitting room, she texted

Brent and her mom that she'd found the perfect pageant gown.

A minute later, she received responses from both of them:

BRENT: cool. bet you look hott.

MOM: BABY I AM SO EXCITED FOR YOU CANT WAIT TO
SEE IT LOVE MOM.

Haylie didn't find anything suitable at the fifth boutique, but the sixth store had a promising selection. As Ivy napped on a bench outside the door, Felicity scurried back and forth between the racks and the fitting rooms, fetching Haylie new sizes and colors. At last they found a backless teal gown with just the right amount of sparkle and sophistication for Haylie. Felicity saw her friend's eyes light up as she gazed at her own reflection, and she knew Haylie had finally found her perfect gown.

Speeding down the highway back to Scarletville with her two best friends and her new dress, Felicity was perfectly content. Her garment bag swayed gently on the hook in the backseat, and every time she glimpsed it in the rearview mirror, a little jolt of excitement coursed through her.

As they sped past the sign informing them that they were entering the Red Zone, Haylie asked, "Hey, when's the prom court nomination assembly? It's got to be really soon, right?"

Students at Scarletville High had been electing their

prom royalty in the same ritualized way since the school was founded. All the juniors and seniors attended the assembly, where students stood up one by one and announced their nominations for king and queen. Each nomination had to be seconded, and each person was only allowed to nominate *or* second for one boy and one girl. Then the names of all the nominees went on a ballot, which everyone received during prom week. The top five winners comprised the prom court, and the king and queen were announced on prom night.

"The assembly's on Friday," Felicity said. "Madison's going to talk about it during announcements on Monday."

Haylie squealed and bounced in her seat. "Ooh, yay! I'll nominate you if you nominate me, okay? And Brent can second for you, and Ivy can second for me. Is that all right, Ives? I assume you don't want to be nominated."

Ivy snorted. "No, that's okay. I'm willing to make this enormous sacrifice for you."

"Sounds great," Felicity said. A senior almost always won for prom queen, but it was a status symbol even to be nominated. It would be a nice boost to her red cred.

They stopped at Hy-Vee for staples on the way home: Twizzlers, Sour Patch Kids, Doritos, microwave popcorn, and a tub of cookie dough ice cream. Finally, they arrived at Haylie's house, where they changed into pajamas, sprawled on the squishy couches in the living room, and immersed themselves in sugar and mindless entertainment.

By the time they had demolished the junk food and watched three horrible B movies about oversized insects, it was nearly two in the morning. Felicity lay on the floor next to Haylie, her hair spread out on the carpet like seaweed and her feet propped on the couch next to Ivy's head. A single lamp glowed softly in the corner of the dark peaceful room. Felicity was in a sugar-and-salt-induced daze that made her feel queasy, jittery, and exhausted in equal parts, but she was happy. She had almost forgotten what it was like to relax. This day with her friends had been so blissfully normal, and it felt like a gift, with her perfect dress shining on top like a giant bow.

Just as she was drifting toward sleep, she heard Haylie say, "Can I ask you something?"

"Me? Yeah, okay."

"What's been up with you lately? You've been acting so weird at school."

Felicity's brain registered that this was a dangerous question, but her body was too tired to react with much alarm. "What do you mean? Weird how?"

"Sort of twitchy and jumpy, like you think someone's following you. And why are you suddenly talking to brunettes all the time? You're going to start getting a reputation if you keep doing that." Haylie nudged Ivy's head with her toes. "Don't you think, Ives?"

Ivy yawned. "Hmm? Oh, yeah. We've been kind of worried about you."

"What is this, some kind of intervention?" Felicity tried to keep her tone light.

She felt Haylie shake her head. "We're not trying to put you on the spot or anything. But maybe we can help if you tell us what's wrong."

Felicity desperately wanted to spill the whole story, but she knew she couldn't. "I don't know. Nothing. Everything."

"Well, that's specific," said Ivy.

Felicity had to give them something. She chose her words carefully, trying to lie as little as possible. "I just feel like . . . I don't know. There's a lot going on all of a sudden, and I feel like maybe I don't deserve everything I'm getting. The pageant and the art show and you guys and Brent and everything. I just keep thinking I'm going to get . . . exposed as a fraud or something. Like maybe I'm not really this person everyone thinks I am. And when they realize they've made a mistake, I'm going to lose it all."

"You'll never lose us," said Haylie. "We're your best friends."

"I know what you mean, though," Ivy said. "It's super stressful dealing with so much stuff at once."

You have no idea what I mean, thought Felicity. But she just said, "Yeah, it is."

Haylie rolled toward her and rested her head against Felicity's shoulder. "You *totally* deserve everything you've got, silly. You're a smart, talented, gorgeous redhead, and you can't fake that stuff. It's not like you're in the art show and the pageant by accident. You got picked 'cause you're the best."

"Unlike me, who's in the pageant one hundred percent by accident," Ivy said, smacking Haylie on the leg. "If someone's a fraud, it's me."

Haylie kicked her back. "Shut up! This isn't about you. Felicity, I promise you don't have to worry. You're so amazing! And everyone will forgive you if you're not perfect all the time. Nobody expects that."

Felicity nodded, even though she knew nobody in Scarletville would forgive her if they found out what she really was: a cheater and a liar and a *secret strawbie*. But she just leaned her head against Haylie's and doubled her resolve to do everything Gabby demanded of her. She couldn't lose her friends' faith in her, no matter what it cost.

7

As promised, Gabby delivered her hyena painting to the squash courts the day Jonathan and Felicity hung the art show. Her canvas was absolutely enormous—it required fifteen heavy-duty adhesive strips to affix it to the wall—and the colors were even brighter than they had appeared on the CD. Some of the neon paint had glitter in it, lending it an extra kitschy touch. Though Felicity hung it in the most inconspicuous location possible, it still screamed for attention. To her dismay, there was no conceivable way it would escape anyone's notice.

But by the time the art show actually opened, Felicity had seen the painting so many times that she had grown used to it. She was grudgingly shocked to find that the longer she looked at it, the funnier it became.

In addition to being a talented artist, Gabby was clearly very observant. She had captured the little wrinkle that always appeared between Haylie's eyebrows when she was concentrating hard, and the Lorelei Griffin hyena wore its dress off the shoulder to reveal a pink bra strap, just as the real Lorelei often wore her shirts. Felicity started to realize that the painting wasn't meant to be cruel. It was simply a satire, and it was a good one.

Felicity showed up half an hour early for the gallery opening to help set up the refreshments. Ms. Kellogg was already there when she arrived, teetering on insanely high heels as she cut cheese into little cubes. The cheese was flecked with some sort of herb, which made it look fancy and intriguing.

Ms. Kellogg looked fancy, too. Her shoes had sparkly buckles the size of golf balls, and her strawberry-blond hair was swept up in a complicated twist. Felicity wasn't sure exactly what her own natural hair color was, but judging from her baby pictures, it was probably about the same shade as her teacher's. A lot of students blatantly disrespected teachers who weren't redheads, but Ms. Kellogg's hair color made Felicity feel a connection to her.

"Hey," Ms. Kellogg called when Felicity entered the room. "You look fantastic!"

"Thanks." Felicity smoothed the skirt of her little black dress and smiled. She was probably overdressed, but it couldn't hurt to look *too* good. Besides, she wanted this art show to seem authentic, and she'd seen enough movies to know that you were supposed to wear little black dresses to gallery openings. Since Ms. Kellogg was wearing a cocktail dress, too, she felt like she'd made the right choice. Her teacher had gone to school in New York City, the heart of the art world, so she probably knew what she was doing.

"I'm really impressed by what you guys have done with the show," Ms. Kellogg continued as she peeled the plastic wrap off a wedge of Brie. "It looks very professional. And your sculpture is so, so beautiful. Have you considered applying to art school next year, like Jonathan?"

Felicity had always assumed she'd go to Scarletville Community College, like her mom, but lately she'd started imagining what it might be like to go to art school instead. This was the first time she had heard someone else voice the possibility, and her heart gave a little flutter. The prospect of creating beautiful things as a job was so thrilling that it almost seemed dangerous to consider. "Could I really do that, do you think?" she asked tentatively.

"Oh, absolutely! You're very talented. I think you'd thrive there."

Felicity felt a bubble of happiness expanding in her chest. Ms. Kellogg didn't give compliments unless she really meant them. There was no redhead privilege going on here, and Felicity felt like she'd finally done something worthy of praise. "Thank you so much," she said. "Where is Jonathan going?"

"The Art Institute of Chicago. He really deserves it — I've never seen a portfolio like that from an eighteen-year-old. I'm surprised he hasn't mentioned it. He's the first student from Scarletville ever to get in there."

"We don't really talk about personal stuff," Felicity said. "I mean, we're friendly and everything, but we're not *friends* friends."

"That's too bad. I think you two have a lot in common."

As if on cue, Jonathan hurried into the room. He was wearing a blazer over a band T-shirt, jeans, and Converse sneakers, which made Felicity wonder if she was overdressed after all. "Hey," he said. "Sorry I'm late."

"Speak of the devil." Ms. Kellogg popped a cheese cube into her mouth. "I was just telling Felicity how awesome the show looks. You guys really have an eye for this."

"Thanks," Jonathan said. "It was fun. Working with Felicity and everything." He gave her a quick, shy smile.

They had just finished arranging the crackers and cookies on platters when the first artists and parents arrived, and Ms. Kellogg went into hostess mode, shaking hands and raving about how talented her students were. Felicity stood alone by the food table, nervously tugging on the hem of her dress. The show was out of her hands now. Her sculpture was sitting on a pedestal in the other room, waiting to reveal her secrets. And everyone was about to see the hyena painting, including her mom and her best friends. Felicity wiped her damp palms on her skirt, praying she wouldn't have to take too much of the blame.

Jonathan appeared next to her, holding out a champagne flute filled with sparkling cider. "To controversial art," he said, as if he had read her mind.

She took the glass and clinked it against his. Despite his awkwardness, she felt a little calmer with him by her side. "It looks good, doesn't it?" she asked.

It might have been her imagination, but she thought she caught his eyes dipping down to the low neckline of her dress for a moment. "It looks awesome," he said.

The St. Johns were among the first to arrive, their approach heralded by Andy's and Tyler's voices echoing down the hall. They were belting out their favorite song, which was about slimy fish guts. Felicity smiled as she heard her mom trying in vain to quiet them.

"LISSY!" Andy shouted when he caught sight of her, his voice amplified to three times its normal volume by the squash court. He barreled into her side, and Felicity nearly spilled her cider all over Jonathan's shirt. Tyler burrowed into her other side, and she gulped down her drink so she'd have an arm free to hug each twin.

"You like the fish guts song, right?" Tyler asked. "Mom hates it."

"I think it's the most disgusting song *ever*," Felicity told him.

"Disgusting is awesome," Andy proclaimed. Jonathan laughed, and Andy beamed.

"These are my brothers," Felicity said. "Guys, this is my friend Jonathan." The word "friend" came out of her mouth effortlessly, before she had time to think about it.

100

Jonathan smiled at the twins. "*I* like the fish guts song," he said, immediately securing their eternal loyalty. They slipped out from under Felicity's arms and gravitated toward him like planets orbiting a star.

"Hi, baby," Ginger called, her heels clopping loudly on the shiny hardwood floor. She planted a kiss on Felicity's temple, then glanced around at the walls. "Oh *wow*, look what you've done! This looks so professional, Felicity! I can see why it took so much time away from practicing for the pageant."

Felicity bit back her annoyance at the double-edged compliment. Her mom rarely showed any support at all for her art, and she knew she'd have to take what she could get. "I'm really glad you guys came," she said.

"Mom, look! *Cookies!*" Andy rushed to the refreshments table as if he'd never seen food before, Tyler close at his heels.

"Maybe that'll keep them occupied long enough for me to take a quick look around," Ginger said. "We can only stay for a few minutes. Can you keep an eye on them?"

"Yeah, sure. My sculpture's in the other room, if you want to see it," Felicity said. "This is Jonathan, by the way. He curated the show with me."

Ginger looked surprised to find Jonathan standing two feet from her, as if her eyes were unable to focus properly without something red to latch onto. "Oh, nice to meet you," she said dismissively before bustling off to do a quick circuit of the room.

Felicity hoped Jonathan hadn't made the connection

between his hair color and Ginger's rudeness. "Sorry, I think she's pretty distracted. My brothers can be really exhausting," she said.

"Don't worry. I have two sisters and a brother. I know how it goes." Jonathan drained the last of his cider and watched Felicity's brothers investigate how many cookies they could stuff into their mouths at once. "So, there's this gallery in Des Moines that's exhibiting a bunch of huge sculptures, and I saw a couple on the website, and they looked like they had some papier-mâché parts. So I thought, you know, you might be interested."

"Yeah, that sounds cool. Thanks. I'll check it out."

"Actually, a couple of friends and I were thinking about driving down to see them. If you wanted, maybe you could, um, come with us . . . ?"

Before Felicity could answer, she heard a low whistle behind her, similar to the wolf whistles she sometimes got walking past construction sites in shorts. When she turned around, indignant, she discovered Brent leaning against the doorjamb. "Wow, babe, you look hot," he said, giving her the same look of hungry appreciation he usually reserved for the chocolate caramel clusters at Crimson Confections.

Felicity gave Jonathan an apologetic smile and went to hug her boyfriend. She resented the wolf whistle, but the fact that he was actually here canceled out some of her annoyance. Although she'd told him about the art show countless times, she had never expected him to show up. She put her arms around his neck and let him run his hands over her hips, and she heard Jonathan's footsteps retreating behind her.

The moment Brent released her, he shot a dirty look at Jonathan across the room. "What were you talking about with that guy?"

"Jonathan? He was just telling me about this gallery in Des Moines."

"Looked like he was asking you out or something."

"What? No! Of course not. I mean, he invited me to go see this exhibit with him and his friends, but that's not the same as *asking me out*."

Brent's jaw stiffened, as if he were trying to bite through a stick of stale beef jerky. "He looked all nervous."

"He always looks like that. It has nothing to do with me."

"But you're not going with him, right?"

"I haven't decided. He just asked three seconds ago." Felicity reached out and touched Brent's cheek. "Hey, I won't go if you don't want me to, okay? It's really not a big deal." But even as the words came out of her mouth, she heard how wrong they sounded. If she wanted to go to the gallery, she should go. Brent shouldn't be allowed to tell her what to do.

"You want to go to the gallery with me instead?" she teased, trying to lighten the mood. "Then I won't have to go with Jonathan."

Brent opened his mouth to respond, but having to choose between two horrors—allowing his girlfriend to go out with another guy or driving all the way to Des

Moines to see *art*—left him speechless. Felicity laughed, unable to stay mad at him when he looked so clueless. "Why don't we walk around?" she suggested. "I'll show you my sculpture."

"Yeah, okay." Brent squeezed her butt. "This dress is seriously awesome. You should wear stuff like this all the time."

She led Brent across the hall to her sculpture. Her mom was already there, circling it slowly and inspecting all the tiny pictures up close. As soon as Brent saw her, he stood up a little straighter and quickly moved his hand up to Felicity's waist. "Hi, Mrs. St. John, how're you doing tonight?" he asked, morphing into a wholesome all-American boy. Brent had always had a way with parents.

"I'm great, Brent, honey. Thanks for asking." Ginger wound a strand of coppery hair around her finger and batted her eyelashes, and Felicity had to stifle the urge to gag. She *really* wished her mother wouldn't flirt with her boyfriend. Then again, Ginger would probably flirt with a Christmas tree if it had a red wig perched on the top.

"What do you think of the sculpture, Mom?" Felicity asked, trying to redirect her mother's attention.

"Oh, Felicity, it's just *wonderful*. Look at all these tiny pictures of you! It must have taken you ages to glue them on here. And you look so gorgeous in all of them!" Ginger peered closely at an image on the sculpture's knee. "Can I have a copy of this one for my desk at work, baby? Your hair looks so striking. You should start using this as a head shot."

Felicity wasn't surprised that her mom was fixated on the sculpture's bright shiny skin and couldn't see the piece as a whole, but she was disappointed nonetheless. "Okay. I'll make you a copy. But you're not really supposed to look at the photos separately. It all goes together."

"It's such a great shot of you, though. They all are. My beautiful girl. I'm so proud of you." Felicity's mom beamed at her.

Brent was taking cues from Ginger and looking at the individual photos from a few inches away. "This is really awesome, Lissy," he said.

"Thanks." In an attempt to give them both a clue, she said, "It's called *Skin-Deep*."

Brent nodded. "Oh, 'cause the pictures, like, make a skin? That's cool." He walked around and looked at the back of the sculpture's head. "I can't believe you made this. It totally looks like a real artist did it."

Felicity assumed Brent had meant to compliment her, but the comment still stung. "I *am* a real artist, Brent."

"No, I mean . . . you know what I mean. Like, a professional."

A burst of her brothers' laughter drifted across the hall, and Ginger straightened up. "Did you leave the boys alone?"

"I'll go check on them." Felicity headed for the other

room, eager to put as much distance as possible between her mom, her boyfriend, and herself.

The boys were by the food table, right where she'd left them, deep in conversation with Jonathan. "Do you know what we're going to be when we grow up?" she heard Andy demand as she approached.

Jonathan furrowed his brow in mock concentration. "Let's see. Firefighters?"

"No!"

"Hairdressers?"

Andy opened his eyes wide in horror. "Eew, *no!*"

"What, then?"

"Paleontologists! We're gonna discover new kinds of dinosaurs, and then we're gonna be famous. And then we're gonna buy planes with red lightning on the wings!"

"Sounds awesome," Jonathan said. "I'm going to be a painter. Will you fly me to my art shows in your planes?"

Tyler looked panicked. "We don't know how yet!"

Felicity laughed. "Thanks for watching the boys. I was supposed to be doing that."

"Hey, don't worry about it. They're great." Jonathan held out his hands, and the twins slapped his palms, each trying to outdo the other in enthusiasm.

Felicity was just starting to feel relaxed again when she spotted Gabby across the squash court. She was standing near the hyenas and wearing a bright orange dress that no redhead could possibly pull off—if Felicity put it on, she'd look like a safety cone. But it looked elegant against Gabby's long dark hair, which was loose around her shoulders. It was almost as if she were flaunting the fact that her hair *wasn't* red.

When she saw Felicity, she gave a little nod, then held up her phone. Felicity had no idea what she was trying to signal, and she shot Gabby a confused look. Gabby rolled her eyes, then pointed back and forth between the phone and Felicity.

Oh — Gabby wanted her to check her phone. She dug it out of her sequined handbag and found a text.

Unknown number: meet me in the bathroom by the weight room, 2 minutes.

Felicity felt her stomach plummet. She already had enough on her plate tonight — she really didn't need the added stress of another confrontation with Gabby. How had Gabby even gotten her phone number? She tried to act normal as she handed the twins off to her mom, then excused herself and headed toward the weight room.

All four of the faucets in the bathroom were dripping, creating an eerie soundscape. Felicity considered trying to turn them off, but the plumbing in this bathroom was notoriously sketchy, and she was afraid to touch the knobs in case one of them sprayed her dry-clean-only dress. Instead, she leaned against the wall farthest from the sinks and waited for her enemy. Her heart tripped along as if it were trying to match the uneven dripping of the water.

Gabby finally arrived, her dress glaring like a road flare against the gloom. She seemed to be in a good mood and gave Felicity an uncharacteristically wide smile. "The show looks good," she said.

Felicity tried to seem relaxed. "Yeah, I'm happy with how it turned out."

"So, the hyenas didn't ruin your life after all. Imagine that." Gabby wedged her heel against the door, blocking it shut.

"Actually, you might not believe this, but I kind of like your painting, now that I've had a chance to really look at it," Felicity said. "It's clever."

"Thanks. I like your piece, too, for what it's worth. It's very . . . enlightening."

Felicity blushed as she realized Gabby was the only person at the show who completely understood her sculpture. Jonathan got the basic idea, but it took on a whole different meaning for someone who knew about her hair. "Thanks," she muttered.

"So, let me get to the point," Gabby said. "You'll be nominating me for prom queen at the assembly tomorrow."

Felicity felt the blood drain from her face, and the room suddenly felt colder. "*What?* But I promised I'd nominate Haylie, and we only get one nomination each!"

"You're a smart girl. I'm sure you'll figure something out."

There were plenty of other people who would be willing to nominate Haylie. She had lots of devoted friends. But Felicity knew she would never be able to explain nominating Gabby. Her recent behavior had already made Haylie suspicious; this would only confirm that something strange was going on. Besides, pulling a stunt like that would be terrible for her red cred. Brunettes were rarely nominated for prom queen at all, and they were *never* nominated by redheads. "Can't you get one of your own friends to nominate you? I don't see why it has to be me."

Gabby shrugged. "You don't have to understand it. You just have to do it."

Felicity was suddenly struck with an idea, and a single ray of hope pierced through her panic. She squared her shoulders and looked Gabby right in the eye. "If you make me do this, I'll tell your mom you're blackmailing her clients," she said. "She'll never let you get away with it. She's legally bound to protect our secrets."

To Felicity's horror, Gabby just laughed. "First of all, I'm not blackmailing her *clients*, plural. I'm blackmailing you. And my mom would never believe you. I'll just tell her you're spreading malicious rumors about me because you hate brunettes. Who do you think she's going to trust? Her artie client, who pays her to lie, or her own daughter?"

"I can prove it. I still have those notes you put in my locker. She'll recognize your handwriting."

Gabby's look hardened. "Felicity, if you make my life difficult in any way, I will make sure my mom drops you as a client."

Felicity almost snapped back, "If you do that, I'll tell everyone your mom runs the salon," but she quickly realized she could never follow through on that threat.

What would she do without Rose? Dye her own hair? She had no idea how to mix the right shade of red. How would she explain it when she screwed up and her hair changed color overnight?

If Gabby turned Rose against her, it would all be over. Felicity opened her mouth but found she had nothing more to say.

Gabby gave her a toxic little smile. "That's what I thought." She turned to go.

"Nobody's going to vote for you for prom queen, you know," Felicity called after her. "I don't understand why you'd even want to be nominated. SHS has never had a brunette prom queen, not even once. People are just going to laugh at you."

Gabby's eyebrows jumped up in surprise. "I don't think I'm going to *win*. I'm not delusional. This isn't about *winning*."

"Then what's it about? Making my life miserable? Can't you at least tell me what I did to deserve this? I mean, I've never bullied you or teased you or anything, and there are plenty of other people who have. So why are you taking it out on me? I'm sorry for whatever I did, if that's what you need to hear."

"You didn't *do* anything." As Gabby pushed the door open, Felicity could have sworn an expression of pity flickered across her face. "This isn't about you, either."

The door swung shut, and Felicity stood alone in the gloomy bathroom, wondering what Gabby could possibly mean. How could this *not* be about her? The whole point of blackmail was to control people and extort things from them. Gabby had the control thing down, but why would she bother to extort things that didn't even benefit her? Her chances of being prom queen were lower than her chances of spontaneously combusting. There had to be an ulterior motive, and Felicity had no idea what it could be.

Her hands balled into fists as a wave of fury swept through her. She was sick of letting Gabby walk all over her for reasons she didn't understand. If Gabby's vendetta wasn't personal, that made things even worse. It was one thing to pay for your mistakes and quite another to suffer when you were totally innocent.

She had to fight back somehow. Maybe she could counter with blackmail of her own. Gabby had to have a secret — everyone had *something* to hide. But there was nothing she could do before first period tomorrow. If Felicity didn't cooperate at the assembly, Gabby would tell everyone she was a strawbie, and her life would be over. It was as simple as that.

For now, there was a more pressing issue at hand: what was she going to tell Haylie? Could she concoct a story about how prom committee members weren't allowed to make nominations? No, her lie would be exposed the moment Madison Banks nominated one of her fellow cheerleaders. Should she go straight to Ivy and ask her to nominate Haylie instead? Ivy was less likely to get angry, but she'd probably ask a lot of unanswerable questions.

Felicity knew that if she didn't leave the bathroom soon, her mom would start to worry and come looking for her. She'd have to think of a solution while circulating through the art show. So she put on her pageant smile and made her way back out into the crowd, her head spinning with questions.

When she returned to the squash courts, Felicity was greeted with the strange sight of her teacher talking to her mom. Ginger's eyes looked a little glazed, and she was gazing slightly past Ms. Kellogg, as if she were searching for a more interesting focal point. Felicity paused just outside the door, where she could listen to their conversation without being spotted. "I hope you know how talented she is," she heard her teacher say. "Her sculpture shows so much artistic promise."

"Mm-hmm." Ginger leaned down and busied herself with brushing cookie crumbs off of Tyler's face.

"She should definitely think about pursuing art as a career. She seems interested, and I'd be happy to help with her art school applications when—"

"Thanks," Ginger said, cutting her off. "We really have to be going."

"Oh. Of course. Well, if you and Felicity would like to meet with me sometime and discuss options, just let me know. Here's my card."

Ginger walked away with a sour look on her face, both twins trailing behind her. "Oh, there you are, baby. I was just coming to look for you. I need to get the boys home."

"Sure," Felicity said. "Were you talking to Ms. Kellogg in there?"

112

Ginger rolled her eyes. "That woman has a lot of nerve, telling me what you should do with your future. I'm your *mother*. I'm the one who knows what's best for you, not some strawbie from God-knows-where."

Felicity swallowed hard. She hated contradicting her mom, but the topic had already been broached—she might as well go all in. "Actually . . . I think I might be interested in art school."

"Baby, that's totally impractical. You need to study something that will prepare you for a real job. And even if it made sense, you know we could never afford it. Scarletville Community College is a very respectable school, and that beautiful hair will get you in tuition-free."

"But that's what financial aid is for. Lots of people can't afford school and still manage to go."

Ginger's look darkened. "Felicity St. John, this family does not accept charity from *anyone*. If you want to move up in the world, you have to do it yourself. I grew up with practically nothing, but I worked my fingers to the bone, and I bettered myself, and I made sure I could provide my children with a good life. So don't you dare throw it all back in my face by acting like a spoiled brat who expects everything to be handed to her on a silver platter."

Ginger's words stung, but Felicity tried not to show it. "I don't expect that, Mom. And if you'd let me get a job, I could—"

"Your job is to prepare for the pageant. That's the

most important thing. So from now on, I need to see you focusing on that. This art show has been nothing but an enormous distraction. You have to keep your eye on what really matters, Felicity." She started propelling the twins toward the exit, signaling that the conversation was over. "I'll see you at home. Come on, boys."

Felicity stood in the hall, listening to the fading clicks of her mother's heels and willing herself not to cry. It didn't surprise her that her mom had shot down her dream without even considering it, but that didn't make it hurt less. All her mother cared about was the stupid pageant and the stupid crown and the stupid title and the stupid prize money—

Wait. The prize money. Felicity had always assumed that if she were crowned Miss Scarlet, she'd turn her winnings over to her mom. But she'd have no legal obligation to do that. She would turn eighteen just a week after the pageant, and then she'd have total control over the money. She'd have options. It wouldn't be enough to pay for art school, but it would be a good start.

Since she was a little kid, her mom had been telling her that winning the pageant could change the whole course of her life. Now, for the first time, that actually felt true.

Felicity returned to the squash courts with her mind reeling. She was so distracted that she almost walked right by Haylie and Ivy, who were parked in front of the hyena painting, talking in intense whispers. Felicity took a deep breath and joined them. "Hey, guys. I'm so glad you came," she said, trying to sound as upbeat as possible.

Ivy smiled, but Haylie's expression was less than welcoming. "Did you personally pick out everything in this show?" she asked.

"Me and Jonathan, yeah."

"Was *this* seriously the best thing that got submitted?" Haylie pointed angrily at the hyenas. "You didn't have *any* other options?"

"No, I mean . . . yeah, there were other options. But this is actually pretty impressive."

Haylie looked outraged. "How is this good? This is *so* offensive! Did you not notice that the drooling hyena is supposed to be *me*?"

Felicity had seen this conversation coming, but watching Haylie react this way was more upsetting than she'd expected. "Of course I noticed. All of us are in it. But, Hays, it's just a satire, not a personal insult. If you can get past the concept, it's actually really funny."

"Get past the concept? The concept is *me*! I don't understand how you could let her represent us this way in public so close to the pageant!"

"People always say there's no such thing as bad publicity," Ivy chimed in.

"Haylie, I swear I'm not trying to sabotage us," Felicity said. "You know I care about the pageant."

"That's why I don't get how you could do this! Or did you just choose it 'cause it's Gabby's? What is *up* with you and Gabby lately, anyway?"

Felicity struggled to keep her voice even. "What are

115

you talking about? Nothing's up with us. I barely know her. And Jonathan and I picked the pieces blind. Try to separate yourself and actually look at it, Hays. It's really clever. She got all the little details right. Look at how Lorelei's bra strap is hanging out of her dress. Look at how my bangs are falling in my eyes like they always do. And look at that hideous paisley dress she put Ivy in. It's kind of hilarious."

"It is," Ivy agreed. "I'm not Gabby's biggest fan, but she's obviously talented."

"It's just a commentary. We all know there are people who don't like the pageant. They should get to express themselves, too." That came out sounding more patronizing than Felicity had intended, so she added, "Come on, look at the insane beehive hairdo on Lorelei. Tell me that's not awesome."

Haylie's face softened a little as she inspected the towering mass of hair. "Yeah, okay. That part's kind of funny. What do you think Lorelei will do when she sees it?"

"Are you kidding? There's no way Lorelei's going to come to the art show." Ivy grabbed Haylie's arm and steered her away from the painting. "Come on, let's go see Felicity's sculpture."

"You're not mad at me, are you?" Felicity asked Haylie. "I would never offend you on purpose. You know that, right?"

"I guess," Haylie said grudgingly.

Felicity knew it was nothing compared to how she

would sound tomorrow after the nomination assembly. *You have to tell her,* a little voice in the back of her head commanded. *The longer you wait, the worse it's going to be.* But when Haylie gave her a small, fragile smile, Felicity knew she couldn't hurt her friend again right now. Two blows in five minutes might be too much for Haylie's goodwill to withstand.

As soon as they reached the doorway of the second room, Ivy broke into a grin. "Oh wow, that's yours, isn't it?" She hurried over to the sculpture. "Felicity, this is *so awesome*."

"Thanks." Felicity felt her cheeks flush with pride.

"It's amazing," Haylie agreed. "So much better than Gabby's. How did you make it? Is this papier-mâché?"

As Felicity described the process, her friends circled her sculpture, looking at it from every angle, from close up and far away, just as Jonathan had. When she was done explaining, Haylie looked at the label on the stat-ue's pedestal. "*Skin-Deep.* This is what you were talking about the other night, right? How you're afraid people think you're something you're not?"

Felicity wanted to kiss her. "Yeah, exactly. My mom and Brent totally didn't get it."

"How could they not get it?" Ivy asked. "The title makes it really clear."

After such an emotionally taxing night, her friends' support and understanding made Felicity's eyes well up. "Thanks, guys," she said, hoping they wouldn't no-tice the catch in her voice.

"For what?"

"For . . . getting me, I guess. For understanding my sculpture."

Ivy and Haylie exchanged perplexed looks. "Of course we get you," Ivy said. "We're your best friends."

Felicity smiled at them, but she couldn't help wondering if they'd still be her best friends by this time tomorrow.

118

Part Two

"You'd find it easier to be bad than good if you had red hair," said Anne reproachfully. "People who haven't red hair don't know what trouble is."
— L. M. Montgomery, *Anne of Green Gables*

Part Two

You'd find it easier to be bad than good if you had red hair," said Anne reproachfully. "People who haven't red hair don't know what trouble is."

—L. M. Montgomery, *Anne of Green Gables*

8

Felicity got to school half an hour early on the day of the assembly and headed straight for the auditorium in an effort to avoid her friends. So she was dismayed when the first person she saw was Haylie, waiting just outside the auditorium doors. At the sight of her friend's excited face, Felicity's guilt wrapped around her lungs like an anaconda and squeezed tightly. *Tell her, tell her, tell her,* the guiltaconda demanded. *This is your last chance.*

"Hey!" Haylie cried, throwing her arms around Felicity. "Ready to get nominated?"

"Absolutely." Felicity swallowed hard. "Why're you here so early?"

"Vanessa wanted to talk to me about the final order for the dance show. It's so ridiculous—we've already changed it like eight times. And now I can't even find her." Haylie shrugged. "So, is your mom excited that you're getting nominated for prom queen? Mine was totally freaking out this morning."

Felicity knew she had to explain what was about to happen. Haylie would be furious, but at least she'd be prepared. Maybe she could even find someone else to nominate her. Felicity struggled to take a deep breath. "Haylie, there's something—"

"Felicity, is that you?" Madison's voice echoed through the empty auditorium. "Come help me with this banner."

Haylie giggled at Felicity's expression, interpreting her distress as hatred for Madison. "Go! It's fine. We'll talk later, when we're both prom queen nominees!" With an ache in her stomach, Felicity watched her friend go. After this assembly was over, Haylie might never smile at her again.

Felicity tried to make up for her impending betrayal by being extra helpful to Madison—maybe everything would balance out in the grand, karmic scheme of things. They hung the PAINT THE TOWN RED banner, set up the prom committee's chairs on the stage, and unwrapped the red roses they'd present to all the female nominees. By the time they had finished setting up and the rest of the committee had arrived, students were trickling in, chattering excitedly and making last-minute nomination plans. Felicity sat down onstage and watched Haylie and Ivy enter the room, followed closely by Gabby. All three of them waved at her, and she wondered if it was possible to throw up without having eaten anything.

When everyone was assembled, Madison stepped up to the podium and beamed at the applauding crowd as if her heart were full of puppies and bonbons. "Thanks, everyone!" she chirped. "Welcome to this year's prom court nomination assembly! Let's start with the girls. I'll begin. I, Madison Banks, nominate Georgia Kellerman for prom queen."

"I, Chelsea Barrington, second the nomination for Georgia!" called another cheerleader.

Georgia stood up and smiled as if she had just been nominated for an Academy Award. "Thank you *so* much. I accept your nomination." Everyone cheered as she did her shampoo-commercial walk up to the stage, received her rose from Madison, and performed a little curtsey.

Felicity was so nervous she could barely pay attention to the five cheerleaders who were nominated next. She prayed someone would come to her rescue and nominate Haylie; then she could claim she had decided to nominate Gabby at the last minute as an act of charity. But everyone was too busy nominating their own best friends to pay attention to hers.

The world seemed to slow down and recede when she finally saw Haylie stand up and say, "I, Haylie Adams, nominate Felicity St. John for prom queen."

Across the auditorium, Brent stood. "I, Brent Sanderson, second the nomination for Felicity." He grinned and gave her a thumbs-up.

Felicity's legs took control, and before she knew it, she was standing. Her whole body trembled slightly, but she hoped it didn't show. "I, Felicity St. John, thank you and accept your nomination," she heard herself saying. Savannah smiled and passed her a rose, and there was a roar of applause. Felicity could barely distinguish it from the ringing in her ears.

Now was the moment. She had to get it over with before she chickened out. She looked at Haylie, who was preparing to make her way down the aisle and accept her own rose. Her little freckled face was radiant with anticipation. Gabby, who was sitting two rows behind her, stared at Felicity expectantly.

Do it, her eyes said. *Do it now. Or else.*

"Felicity? Does the fact that you're still standing mean you'd like to nominate someone?" asked Madison, the sweetness in her voice edged with annoyance.

Felicity took a deep breath.

"Yes. I, Felicity St. John, nominate Gabrielle Vaughn for prom queen."

The sound of one person drawing in her breath is almost inaudible. But the sound of three hundred students drawing their collective breath was surprisingly loud. There was a moment of silence following the gasp, and then the whole room broke out in whispers and laughter. Felicity forced herself to look at her friends, then wished she hadn't. Haylie looked stricken, and she was gripping Ivy's hand as if she were afraid she might drown. Felicity mouthed, "I'm sorry," but there was no way Haylie could read her lips at this distance.

Madison banged her clipboard on the lectern, and the noise subsided. "Everyone, please settle down," she called, sounding more like the sharp-tongued Madison Felicity was used to. "Would anyone like to second Felicity's nomination for . . . um . . . Gabrielle Vaughn?" She seemed to have trouble saying the name out loud.

Marina stood up. "I, Marina Rios, second the nomination for Gabby."

Gabby stood and looked around the auditorium with a beatific smile. She seemed oblivious to the fact that the entire junior and senior classes were staring at her with shock and horror. "I, Gabrielle Vaughn, accept your nominations. Thanks, Felicity and Marina." There was a feeble smattering of applause as Gabby approached the stage and pried a rose from the hand of flabbergasted Kendall. She nodded at Felicity before she walked away.

Felicity collapsed into her chair. It was done. Her secret was safe. But she didn't feel the relief she had expected.

Gabby wasn't even back in her seat before Ivy jumped up and announced, "I, Ivy Locklear, nominate Haylie Adams for prom queen." She shot Felicity a cutting look. Vanessa Caldwell, who was in the dance troupe with Haylie, seconded the nomination. When Haylie stood up to accept, she looked composed, but Felicity had known her long enough to recognize the slight catch in her voice. It was obvious how hurt she was.

It wasn't until Haylie was a few feet from the stage

that Felicity realized it was her turn to present a rose. She chose the prettiest flower in the box and offered it to her friend, her eyes full of apologies. But Haylie refused to look at her as she snatched the rose away, raking a thorn across Felicity's thumb.

The rest of the assembly was a blur. Felicity didn't even remember to nominate Brent until Gretchen Williams, who had been trying to steal him for the last six months, did it first. She considered leaving school immediately after the assembly, but she doubted she could slip out of the building unnoticed.

She was right. As soon as the assembly ended, a stormy-faced Haylie was on her feet and pushing through the crowd toward the stage. Ivy followed in her wake, also looking grim. Felicity left the rest of the prom committee to clean up and hurried off the stage before Haylie reached her. The last thing she wanted was for their confrontation to turn into a show.

Haylie ripped into her the moment she was within shouting range. "So, there's nothing going on with you and Gabby, right, Felicity? Is that why you just chose her over me in front of the entire freaking *school*? What is *wrong* with you?"

Everyone in the immediate vicinity paused to listen, their eyes fever-bright with curiosity. There was nothing Scarletville High liked better than a good scandal. Felicity grabbed Haylie's shoulder and tried to steer her toward the exit at the side of the auditorium, but Haylie jerked away. "Don't touch me!" she snapped.

"Can we please talk about this somewhere else?"

Felicity begged. "I don't want to do this with a hundred people listening."

"You know what? I don't care how many people hear what I have to say, because I'm *right*." There was a chorus of "Oooooohs" from the eavesdroppers, and Felicity's ears and cheeks started to burn.

She lowered her voice. "Yes, trust me, I know you're right. What I did absolutely sucked, and I'm the worst friend ever, and I'm so, so sorry. But seriously, I can't talk about this in here, okay? Will you please just come out in the hall with me?"

"Fine." Haylie pushed past Felicity and headed for the side door, and Ivy started after her. Felicity took a few deep breaths, trying to keep from crying. Then she followed her friends into the passage along the side of the auditorium.

The door slammed behind them, and everything went perfectly quiet. Ivy leaned against the wall behind Haylie with her arms folded across her chest. Though she didn't speak, the steely expression on her face left no doubt about whose side she was on.

"What the hell just happened?" Haylie demanded. "Is there a *reason* you humiliated me in there, or was that just your way of trying to get ahead?"

"Get ahead? Ahead in what?"

"I don't know! People's opinions! The pageant! Whatever it is that's making you act like a total *crazy person*! Let me give you some advice, Felicity: shooting down your friends in public is *not* going to make people like you more!"

127

Felicity had no idea where to begin. "I wasn't trying to humiliate you," she started. "I would never hurt you on purpose, and I'm not trying to get ahead. I tried to tell you what I was going to do before the assembly, but I just . . . I didn't think you'd understand, and I knew you'd be totally pissed at me."

"I *am* totally pissed at you, and I *don't* understand!" Tears were spilling down Haylie's cheeks now. "You're supposed to be my best friend, and you *promised* you'd nominate me. I've *always* been there for you. I even let you have the perfect pageant gown! You know how much that meant to me, and I gave it to you, even though you're my competition and you're already *so* much more likely to win than me —"

"Haylie, this isn't about —"

"And then you go and hang a massive picture of me as a hyena in the art show, and then you give my nomination to that bitch, who you claim you're not even friends with!"

"I'm *not* friends with her!" Felicity protested. "I didn't want to nominate her!"

"But you *did* nominate her! It's not like anyone was forcing you! So what the hell is going on? Do you secretly hate me or something?"

There were only two possible courses of action: Felicity could tell Haylie and Ivy she was being blackmailed, or she could refuse to tell them what was going on and look totally heartless. For a moment, she seriously considered spilling her secret. But if anyone else overheard her, the news would spread faster than a viral video. She'd become a social outcast in five seconds flat, and she'd probably be kicked out of the pageant, for which her mom would never forgive her. Plus, winning that prize money was her only ticket out of Scarletville, her only chance to have the life she really wanted.

Telling the truth just wasn't an option.

Four accusing eyes stared Felicity down.

"No, Hays, I don't hate you at all. And I do have a reason for what I did, but I can't tell you what it is. I'm so sorry." Both Haylie and Ivy gaped at her, incredulous. "It has nothing to do with you, I swear. You just got caught in the cross fire. I wish more than anything that I could take it all back, or at least explain it to you, but I just . . . can't."

"What do you mean, you can't? We tell each other everything. You don't trust us all of a sudden?"

"I do trust you. But I . . . I can't talk about it right now."

Haylie and Ivy stared at her, and she stared back. Nobody spoke, and in that silence Felicity felt something break between her and her best friends. Finally, Ivy said, "If you have nothing else to say for yourself, I think we're done here. You can come find us when you're ready to be honest." She took Haylie's arm and pulled her gently but firmly toward the door. "Come on, Hays. We have English."

Felicity followed them. "You still got nominated," she said to Haylie, her voice full of desperation. "I was sure you would be. I never would have left you stranded."

Haylie whirled around and shot Felicity a furious,

wounded look. "Getting nominated wasn't the point," she said. "Georgia's obviously going to win. I just wanted to be nominated by *you*." She followed Ivy into the hall.

"I'm so sorry," whispered Felicity, but it was too late. The only response she got was the slam of the door.

9

he rest of the day was a little slice of hell.
When the bell rang for lunch, Felicity headed for her usual table in the cafeteria, ready to apologize, plead, and prostrate herself at Haylie's feet. But she stopped short halfway across the room when Ivy caught her eye and gave her the patented Locklear Look of Death. Haylie stiffened, clearly aware she was there, but she kept her back turned and showed no signs of yielding. It was too early for forgiveness.

Felicity sighed and looked around for somewhere else to sit. She usually didn't mind that she and Brent had different lunch periods, but she really could have used him today. She needed a big hug and some un-conditional adoration.

"Felicity! Over here!" She turned around and saw

131

a table overflowing with sophomore girls, an explosion of flat-ironed red hair, miniskirts, and fur-topped boots. They were indistinguishable from one another; if one of them had mugged Felicity, she couldn't have picked the perpetrator out of a lineup. A few of them beamed and waved, and the rest giggled in unison. Felicity waved back halfheartedly and retreated a few steps.

"Is it true that you totally trashed Haylie Adams at the assembly this morning?" the bravest one called. Another chorus of giggles followed.

It was unbelievable how fast information spread. Felicity had never spoken to any of these girls, yet here they were, discussing her personal business. "No, of course not," she snapped.

"It's okay, we get it," another clone said. "She's your competition now, right?"

"I'm not going to discuss this with you." Felicity turned to leave.

As she walked away, one of the girls called, "Do you want to sit with us? We really love your outfit!"

"We hope you win the pageant!"

Felicity breathed a sigh of relief when she spotted an empty seat between Kendall and Savannah. "Do you mind if I sit here?" she asked, already sliding into the chair.

"Of course not." Kendall scooted her bag over to make room. "How're you holding up?"

"Haylie's still pissed at you, huh?" Savannah said. "She'll get over it."

Felicity unwrapped her sandwich and took an angry

bite. "Is anyone talking about *anything* besides me and Haylie? I just got grilled by a bunch of sophomores I don't even know."

Kendall shrugged. "All you pageant girls are like royalty right now. Of course people are going to dissect everything you do. Every entry we got for the lit mag this quarter was about the pageant except one. We're having an entire pageant-themed issue."

"What's the other one about?"

"I'm not actually sure. Cocaine, maybe? But it also could have been about skiing."

A smiling Gabby passed their table, and the very sight of her made Felicity's stomach twist into a pretzel. The moment she was out of earshot, Savannah leaned in close. "What you did this morning was really ballsy, by the way. Are you trying to make some sort of statement? Or are you guys actually friends?"

"No, we are *not* friends." Felicity glanced over at the table across the room where her real friends were laughing at a joke she'd never hear. A pang of sadness and anger stabbed through her.

"Why'd you do it, then?"

Felicity sighed. "I'm sorry, but could we not talk about it? It's been a really awful morning."

Savannah and Kendall seemed disappointed, but to Felicity's relief, the conversation quickly turned to Miss Scarlet gossip. Jessie Parish was allegedly having her dress custom-made at a shop in Des Moines, financed by her wealthy Southern grandmother, who wanted Jessie to be a debutante. Savannah wondered whether it would be boring to wear white orchids in her hair for both the prom and the pageant. Kendall had heard that Ariel was going to wear the same dress for both events, a plan everyone found outrageous. When Savannah shrugged and said, "Well, let's be honest, how much can you really expect from a strawbie?" everyone laughed, and Felicity had to stuff her mouth with sandwich to disguise her reaction. That was exactly how people would see her if they ever found out about her hair. And that was why she had to protect her secret at all costs, no matter what she had to trade for Gabby's silence.

But as she watched Haylie and Ivy sharing their daily pack of Skittles, a tiny splinter of doubt started working its way through her resolve. How much more lying and betrayal could she stand? At some point, would protecting herself stop being worth it?

Felicity tried Haylie's cell three times on Friday night, but the calls went straight to voice mail. She could barely stand to listen to the outgoing message, which Haylie had recorded while the two of them were together at the mall. She and Haylie had been friends since preschool, and they had never had a major fight. Was it possible to destroy a fourteen-year relationship with one mistake?

When she finally managed to fall asleep, things got even worse—for the first time, Felicity had The Dream twice in one night. After waking to the sound of her own screams at two a.m. and again at four-forty-five, she lay awake for what seemed like an eternity, wondering how she could gain the upper hand with Gabby. She finally brought her ancient laptop into bed with her, signed into RedNet—Scarletville's social networking site for redheads—and sifted through hundreds of photos from parties and school events. Just one shot of Gabby drinking, smoking, or hooking up with someone embarrassing might give her a bit of leverage. But nobody on RedNet socialized with brunettes, so Gabby didn't appear in a single picture.

Felicity finally drifted off at dawn, only to be ripped from her peaceful cocoon of sleep two hours later, when her mom burst into her bedroom. "Rise and shine, morning glory!" Ginger chirped. "We have work to do!"

Felicity opened one eye, then quickly shut it against the assault of sunlight that stabbed through her brain like a shish kebab skewer. "What?"

"I'm giving you a pageant coaching session this morning, remember? We've got to whip that tap routine of yours into shape if you're going to win. You've been letting the pageant fall by the wayside, and it's time to make it your first priority! Up, up, up, lazybones!" She smacked Felicity's butt.

Felicity groaned in protest and sat up, pushing her tangled mass of hair out of her face. "Isn't it unfair to the other girls if you give me special private coaching?"

"Oh, don't worry about that. I already handled it."

"What does *that* mean?"

"Well, if you must know, I took a hundred dollars

135

out of your bank account. That way, you can just say you hired me if it becomes an issue. Anyone can pay me to coach them, so it's totally aboveboard."

Felicity stared at her mom in horror. "That's all my Christmas money! I was going to go to Cadmium Paints and—"

"Felicity, this is more important than whatever else you were going to spend it on, okay? If you win the pageant, I'll happily give it all back. Now, get up and get your tap shoes. I'll make you a blueberry waffle."

Felicity dragged herself out of bed, enveloped in a fog of resentment. Her mother became a drill sergeant when she was in pageant-coaching mode, and Felicity wasn't prepared to deal with that or with her tap routine on just a few hours of sleep. The routine itself wasn't the problem—the choreography was impressive, and it showcased her abilities well. But the music her mom had forced on her was another story.

In a moment of nostalgia, Ginger had insisted that Felicity dance to the same song she had used for her own tap routine in the pageant twenty-five years ago. Seventeen-year-old Ginger had tapped to a big-band classic called "Red Is the Color of My Heart," sung by jazz legend Ella-Mae Finch. Everyone knew the song, which often played in department stores and dentists' offices, but Felicity didn't know anyone besides her mother who actually *liked* it. It was maudlin and saccharine, exactly the opposite of Felicity's personality. She had put up a fight, but Ginger was persistent and had talked of almost nothing else for ten days straight.

Finally, Felicity had chosen surrender over losing her mind.

At Ginger's urging, she had learned the routine over winter break, long before Miss Scarlet applications were due. Somewhere in the back of her mind, she still knew the choreography, but it was hard to practice when Ella-Mae's crooning made her wish she were deaf. The last time she'd given the routine more than a cursory run-through was weeks ago, and she knew her mom wasn't going to be happy when she discovered how much Felicity had been slacking.

Felicity dressed in a tank top and yoga pants and stumbled downstairs. Before she'd even finished her waffle, Ginger whisked her plate away and announced, "Time to get started! Go on down to the basement. I'm going to make sure the boys are okay helping Victor in the yard, and then I'll meet you downstairs."

Felicity shivered as she descended into the clammy air of the basement. The room smelled vaguely of cat litter, though they hadn't had a cat since she was in seventh grade. The sunlit living room would have made a cheerier rehearsal space, but she couldn't very well tap on the carpeting. Soon Ginger appeared with a sunny smile on her face. She cued up Felicity's music on her iPod, which she connected to the speakers. "You ready, baby?" she asked.

"As ready as I'm going to be." Felicity struck her first pose.

The opening trumpet riff began, and she started dancing, trying to block out Ella-Mae's voice and concentrate on the steps. Ginger, on the other hand, swayed to the music with a blissful expression on her face and hummed along:

Red is the color of my kissable lips,
and red is the color of my heart.
Red is the color of the pain I endure
whenever life keeps us apart.
Red is the color of my passion for you,
it's been this way right from the start.
Red is the color of my sizzlin'-hot love,
and red is the color of my heart.

Felicity's muscle memory kicked in, and at first the routine went surprisingly well. But when she reached the difficult series of Maxie Ford turns near the middle of the second verse, she stumbled and lost her place. Ginger clapped to emphasize the downbeat and shouted, "Shuffle ball change! Cincinnati flam! Come on, Felicity, pick it up!" But once Felicity lost the flow, she had a hard time getting back into her groove. Even when Ginger started tapping along with her, she didn't get back on track until close to the end of the song. Her last sets of scissor wings were crisp and impressive, but when she struck her final pose, she wasn't surprised to find her mother scowling at her.

The fog of resentment receded, and panic rushed in to take its place. She should have practiced more, regardless of what she thought of Ella-Mae. If she performed like that at the pageant, her art school dream would be dead in the water faster than she could say "national redhead sanctuary." Plus, she had made her mother furious, and she wasn't about to get away with it.

"What was *that*?" Ginger demanded. "Have you been practicing at *all*? God, Felicity, I'd have kept a much closer eye on you if I'd known things had gotten this bad! You are *really* far behind, and you're going to have to work your little butt off to get back in the running!" She massaged her temples.

Felicity squirmed, amazed at how small her mom could make her feel. "Mom, it's going to be fine. I'll work harder. I'm just a little rusty, that's all. But the pageant's not for two weeks, so I have plenty of time to get it perfect, and I will. I swear I'm not going to embarrass you."

"You'd better not. How does it look if the pageant director's own daughter can't even stumble through a three-minute routine?" She thumped the table where the speakers were sitting for emphasis. "Jesus, you can do *so* much better than that, and you know it. You could win if you just *worked* harder! But you have to want it, Felicity. The judges have to see that fire in you. Do you want to win? Do you care at all about helping this family, after everything I've sacrificed for you? Or are you just going to let this prize slip right through your fingers? Because if you're not willing to work, I'm wasting my time trying to help you."

Felicity looked deep into her mother's eyes and saw

the fear that lurked behind the anger. It wasn't just her own dream that was on the line. Ginger had put everything she had into preparing her daughter to be Miss Scarlet. And now that dream was crumbling to pieces, and it was all Felicity's fault.

Felicity swallowed hard. "I want to win," she said.

"Good. Then let's get to work."

If there was one thing Ginger knew how to do, it was whip a pageant girl into shape. For more than a decade, nearly all the pageant mothers in town had hired her to coach their girls. But business was lagging this season, as all the other parents feared Ginger might sabotage their daughters in favor of her own. As Felicity practiced her Maxie Ford turns over and over, she cursed the fact that she was being subjected to twelve girls' worth of attention. But she also had to admit that her mom's methods worked wonders. Two hours later, she was drenched in sweat, and her tap routine was flawless.

"That's enough for now," Ginger finally said. "Let's take a quick break, and then we'll work on your walks and poses and your personal introduction. Go get the rest of your competition shoes." She handed Felicity a water bottle and a towel, then patted her sweaty back. "You really pulled it together, baby. I'm proud of you."

"Thanks," Felicity said. Much as she hated to admit it, her mom's approval made her feel better.

While Ginger checked on the twins, Felicity went up to her room to retrieve her heels—black ones for her personal introduction, red ones to go with her swimsuit, and silver ones to match her evening gown. She also checked her voice mail, but there were no messages, and her email in-box was empty, too. She tried not to let it bother her too much; Haylie probably just needed some time to cool down. But Felicity couldn't help feeling as if she had done permanent damage to their friendship.

She returned to the basement, buckled her first pair of shoes, and spent the next hour practicing her poses and pageant walks—bouncy and energetic for the swimsuit portion, smooth and elegant for the evening wear competition. Ginger hovered and buzzed around her like an annoying dragonfly, adjusting Felicity's body by millimeters and saying, "Feel that? See how that tiny head tilt makes such a difference?" It all felt pretty much the same to Felicity, but she tried her best to remember each angle and posture. Then she practiced her thirty-second introduction over and over as her mom corrected her inflection and pacing, told her when to pause and smile, and reminded her over and over how important first impressions were. She didn't seem to remember that several of the judges had known Felicity since her birth.

Finally, Ginger nodded with satisfaction. "Good job. I just want to do one last thing, and then we'll be done. Can you put your tailcoat on and try your tap routine one more time? I brought it down for you."

Felicity was exhausted, and the last thing she wanted to do was repeat her routine. "Why? It's not like it's any different with the jacket."

"Just put it on, baby." Ginger pointed at a chair in the corner, and Felicity noticed for the first time that her costume was draped over the back.

"Why is it in plastic?" she asked, suddenly suspicious.

"It's just a little surprise for you. Go on, take a look!"

Felicity approached the chair with apprehension. She had chosen her tap costume because it was simple and classic: a short black jacket with tails, a black sequined tank top, black pants with tuxedo stripes, and a silver belt. It wasn't nearly flashy enough for Ginger's taste, and Felicity was terrified of what her mom might have done to it. But when she peered down at the jacket, it looked exactly the same as it always had. What was her mom so excited about?

"Look at the back!" Ginger urged.

Felicity picked up the jacket and flipped it over.

The back of her simple, no-frills tailcoat was now decorated with an enormous red heart made of tiny, sparkly jewels. It looked like something Topher Gleason might wear to a Valentine's Day dance. Felicity was speechless with dismay. "Wow," she choked out.

"Isn't it *amazing*? Linda at the tailor did such a wonderful job. I knew you would love it. It spices up the outfit so much, don't you think? This'll really make you stand out to the judges, especially because it matches your music. Try it on!"

There was no use resisting. Felicity freed the costume from its plastic sheath and slipped it on over her tank top. Her mom squealed with delight when she turned around and displayed her bejeweled back.

"It's perfect," Ginger declared, squeezing her. "Perfect for my winner."

Felicity submitted to the hug. "Thanks, Mom," she said with as much enthusiasm as she could muster. "It was really nice of you to do this." She tried not to think about how much money her mom had probably spent on this jacket.

"It was my pleasure. Now do the routine for me one more time. I want to see how the jacket looks when you dance."

So Felicity sighed, laced her tap shoes back up, and did the routine again, the heart on her back winking and sparkling in the light.

143

10

MONDAY, MAY 17

When Felicity got to school, Ivy was waiting at her
locker alone. Felicity held out her coffee cup to see
if the morning routine was still intact, and she was relieved when Ivy reached for it with no hesitation. Her
friend took her customary gulp and handed the cup
back with a sigh. "Felicity, this has to stop."

"What, the coffee? I only have one cup a day."

Ivy frowned. "No, not the coffee. You and Haylie
have to make up. All she did the entire weekend was
obsess over why you didn't nominate her for prom
queen. I can't listen to it for one more second or I'm going to puncture my own eardrums with a fork."

So Haylie's fury was subsiding—that was good
news. Angry Haylie was impossible to reason with, but

hurt Haylie just needed love and validation, things Felicity could easily provide. "I tried calling her seven or eight times to apologize, but she never got back to me," Felicity said. "I assumed she was still too pissed to talk."

"She is. But she also keeps saying she thinks we're losing you and that you don't like us anymore. She's afraid you're still going to be fighting by prom and that 'everything will be ruined.' And she made me go shopping for pageant shoes with her for three hours. Seriously, Felicity, you have to do something."

"I hate that we're not speaking, too, but I can't talk to her if she won't listen. Will you tell her I really want to work things out whenever she's ready?"

"Yeah, I'll tell her." Ivy was quiet for a minute as she picked at the fraying sleeve of her hoodie. "Hey, Felicity?"

"Yeah?"

"Why *didn't* you nominate her?"

The prospect of thinking up another lie made Felicity feel heavy. "I . . . I really can't talk about it. I'm sorry, Ives. Can you just trust me when I say that it had nothing to do with Haylie? And that I feel awful about it and wouldn't have done it if there had been another option?"

Ivy shrugged. "I just don't get how something like that is unavoidable. Are you in trouble or something?"

"Well . . . kind of." It was both frightening and comforting to say that out loud for the first time. "But I'm handling it."

145

"Trouble like 'I plagiarized my English paper,' or trouble like 'I have six dismembered bodies in the trunk of my car'?"

"Closer to the first one. But it's nothing like that."

"Does it have to do with Gabby? Did she force you into this somehow?"

Felicity swallowed hard. "I . . . I mean, I really can't . . ."

"Okay, I get it. You can't say. But is there anything I can do to help?"

"Thanks, Ives, but I don't think so. It's just something I have to work out on my own."

"If you say so. But if you need me, just ask." The first bell rang, and Ivy turned to go. "I have to get to physics."

"Okay. I'm really sorry you and Haylie got caught up in this. And I'm extra sorry you had to go shoe shopping."

"It was horrible, Felicity. It was worse than that day with the bikinis freshman year." She shuddered at the memory. "See you at lunch, maybe?"

Felicity was so relieved to be welcomed back to her usual table that she felt as if she might levitate, but then she remembered her prom committee meeting. The juniors and seniors were voting for prom king and queen this morning. "Crap, I have to count ballots at lunch," she said.

"Okay. Hey, I have a swim meet at four-thirty, if you and Haylie want to come. Maybe you could talk."

"Yeah, that's a good idea. Tell her I'll meet her there."

"Cool. Later."

As she was closing her locker, Haylie's friend Vanessa passed by with a few other girls from the dance troupe. "Hey, Vanessa!" Felicity called.

Vanessa's face hardened when she spotted Felicity. She gestured for her friends to go on without her. "What's up?" she said with a tight smile.

"Listen, I was hoping you could text some of the dance troupe girls and tell them to vote for Haylie today. If we all vote for her, maybe we can bump out some of the cheerleaders and—"

"Way ahead of you," Vanessa interrupted. "A bunch of us are already voting for her. I thought you'd be voting for yourself, though."

"Haylie cares about it more than I do. I just want her to have a chance."

Vanessa's expression softened. "That's cool of you," she said. "I'll text the girls again to make sure, okay?"

"Thanks. That'd be great."

Felicity made it to History of Redheadedness just as the bell was ringing. Mr. Cavender was standing at the front of the room, next to the large poster that proclaimed YOUR MC1R GENE IS YOUR MOST PRECIOUS RESOURCE! He was holding a stack of hot-pink ballots by the corners, as if he were afraid the color might rub off on his hands.

"Good morning, future leaders of America," he said. "Before we continue talking about Queen Elizabeth the First, I'm going to distribute your prom court ballots. Please vote for one boy and one girl. The top five nominees will be posted outside the main office after school."

When Felicity got her ballot, she checked the box next to Haylie's name. Then she folded the paper in half and slipped it into the envelope on Mr. Cavender's desk, awash in the calm that comes from finally doing the right thing.

The prom committee congregated at lunch to count the votes. Madison tallied the scores on the dry-erase board as the count from each classroom was verified, making hash marks next to the nominees' names. The votes seemed scattered at first, but by the time half the ballots had been counted, patterns started to emerge. Felicity was pleased to see that Haylie was doing well.

Unfortunately, her own total was just a little bit higher, and it was still creeping upward.

Felicity's stomach thrashed as if she'd eaten live eels for lunch instead of a peanut butter sandwich. Being on the prom court would be a perfect bolster to her red cred. Her mind flooded with images of herself walking in the prom court procession and spinning around the floor in Brent's strong arms during the special prom court dance. But if she beat out Haylie for a spot on the court, it would look as if she really had been trying to get ahead, and then it would be impossible to repair their friendship.

Felicity didn't need to be on the prom court. She needed Haylie back.

It was time for more drastic measures.

She surreptitiously angled her desk away from the

rest of the committee, then set her paper lunch bag in her lap. Whenever she found a ballot with a checkmark next to her name, she quietly folded it up and slipped it into the bag. Her palms started to sweat, and she jumped at every sound, terrified someone might catch her—throwing a vote was a big deal, and she'd likely be tossed off the committee. But everyone was busy counting, and nobody looked her way, even when she shoved the bag full of ballots deep into her backpack. When the bell announced the end of the period, she said a silent prayer that she had managed to remove herself from the running. She spun around and looked at the whiteboard.

The hash marks were gone, and the names of the top five girls and boys were written in pink dry-erase marker. Georgia Kellerman was in the top five, of course, as was Holly Lancaster, last year's Miss Scarlet runner-up. Emily Dutton, a senior in the dance troupe, had snagged the third slot. Felicity was thrilled to see that Haylie's name was fourth on the list.

The fifth name was Gabby's.

It didn't seem possible. There had never been a brunette on the prom court before. Maybe someone else had been cheating, too? But no one on the prom committee would throw the vote in Gabby's favor. All the blondes and brunettes in the school must have banded together and voted for her while the many redheads on the ballot split the redhead vote. Madison was staring at the board, dumbstruck and furious that a brunette had beaten her out. Felicity quietly gathered her things and slipped away before Madison remembered that Gabby's presence on the ballot was her fault.

The hallways were absolute chaos at the end of the day as everyone swarmed the main office. Felicity's locker was in the opposite direction, and she had to use her heavy backpack as a battering ram to push her way through the crowd. In addition to the tears and screams of joy that always accompanied a prom court announcement, Gabby's name sailed around on an undercurrent of incredulous whispers. Felicity was mortified when she heard her own name in the same sentence as her adversary's again and again. She ducked her head and kept walking, hoping nobody would notice her and start asking impossible questions. Ivy's swim meet didn't start for another hour, but she headed to the pool early to hide from the rumor mill.

Ivy spotted Felicity in the bleachers as soon as she emerged from the locker room. She jogged up the tiled stairs, adjusting her SHS Rubies swim cap. "Hey," she called. "I'm glad you made it."

"Do you know if Haylie's coming?"

Ivy started doing lunges and windmilling her arms. "I think so. I want to congratulate her on making the prom court. She's going to be insanely happy. Sorry you didn't make it, though. At least Bitchzilla Banks didn't either."

Felicity shrugged. "Whatever, it's totally fine. I don't care at all. I voted for Haylie."

"Good. Me too." Ivy smiled. To Felicity's great relief, she didn't mention Gabby.

"What are you swimming today?"

"Just freestyle, one hundred, and four hundred. Coach is putting Grace in for butterfly, but she's going to regret it. Bethany Chase from St. Sebastian is going to kick her ass."

"Good luck, Ives. You're going to do great."

"Thanks. See you after." Ivy jogged back down the stairs, positioned her goggles, and did a perfect, splashless dive into the pool for some warm-up laps.

Ivy was already up on her starting block when Haylie slid onto the bleachers next to Felicity. Her cheeks were pink, and she was breathing hard, as if she'd been running. "Hey," she said. "The dance troupe meeting went late. I didn't miss Ivy, did I?"

Felicity's eyes swept over her friend, looking for signs of anger or resentment. But Haylie just looked like Haylie. "No, she's just starting now. That's her in lane three."

The starting tone sounded, and Ivy launched into the water. Felicity and Haylie both leapt to their feet, screaming and jumping up and down as Ivy streaked through the water. She flip-turned at the far end and sped back toward her starting point. With all the splashing, it was hard to tell who was in the lead, but there wasn't much time for suspense—the race was over in less than two minutes. Ivy took first place by half a second. As she hopped out of the water and pumped her fist, Haylie jumped on Felicity for a victory hug, and Felicity squeezed her back, her heart expanding.

But after a few seconds, Haylie abruptly let go and

sank back down onto her seat. She seemed to have just remembered that they hadn't spoken in three days. "So, I guess we should talk," she said.

"Yeah, probably."

To her surprise, instead of berating her, Haylie said, "Vanessa told me you were campaigning for me this morning."

"Yeah. I really wanted you to be on the prom court."

"You didn't have to do that. It was nice of you."

"I did it because I wanted to, Hays, not 'cause I had to. You deserve it more than I do. I'm super excited that you made it. You beat out tons of seniors."

Haylie gave her a shy grin. "I'm really excited, too. But it sucks that you won't be up there with me."

"It's fine. I seriously don't care that much. I voted for you."

"Really? You did?"

"Really."

"So . . . you're not mad at me?"

"No. God, of course not. You're the one who should be pissed at *me*. Why would I be mad at you?"

"I don't know, but I was sure I'd done something wrong, and that's why you didn't nominate me." Haylie nervously twisted the delicate gold ring she wore on her middle finger. "I still think it's weird that you won't tell me what's going on. I mean, you're obviously not trying to shoot me down like I thought, but I don't get what you *are* trying to do."

"I know. It's complicated."

"Ivy says you're in trouble."

"I'm not really in *trouble*." Felicity sighed. "I didn't do anything illegal or anything. I just . . . I've got some stuff going on that I can't talk about. But I promise it has nothing to do with you."

"Is it stuff at home?"

"Not really. Just something I have to work out."

Haylie was quiet for a minute. "Are you going to be all right?"

Felicity had no idea if she was going to be all right. People were gossiping about her and Gabby, and she still didn't have a solid plan to take her rival down. But she just said, "Yeah. I'm going to be fine." She reached out and linked her pinky through Haylie's like they used to do when they were eight years old, and she was relieved when Haylie didn't pull away. "I missed you, Hays."

"You too."

Haylie kept hold of her finger, and together they watched Bethany Chase obliterate Ivy's teammate in the hundred-meter butterfly.

11

To Felicity's dismay, people continued to talk about Gabby and the prom court throughout school on Tuesday. But on Wednesday, a senior on the football team was suspended for selling pot in the parking lot, and just like that, the prom court was old news.

By the time the last bell rang, Felicity was in high spirits. She hadn't heard anyone whisper her name or Gabby's all day. She was back in her best friend's good graces. Brent was planning to sneak through her window for an after-dinner visit. And tomorrow, when she went to Rouge-o-Rama, she planned to gather some good dirt on Gabby by pumping Rose for embarrassing childhood stories. If all went well, she'd finally have some ammunition of her own when her enemy initiated the next battle.

Felicity stopped at her locker, then headed for the squash courts to meet Jonathan and take down the art show. He was already there, struggling to remove Gabby's enormous painting from the wall. Felicity rushed over to help—taking down the hyenas felt symbolic of the way she hoped to take down their creator.

"Oh, hey, thanks," Jonathan said as they lowered the canvas to the ground. "This thing is ridiculously huge. How's it going?"

"Great. Everything's going great. How're you?"

He nodded enthusiastically. "Pretty good, pretty good. Busy. I feel like there's so much stuff I have to get done before graduation."

"God, that's only three weeks away, isn't it? Thinking about leaving must be so weird." Felicity removed the Skittles photograph from the wall and started peeling the adhesive strips off the back. "You going to prom?"

"Sort of. I mean, yeah, but I'm just bringing my sister Marissa. She's a freshman, and this senior asked her, but my mom won't let her go out with older guys. And it's not like I had a date to bring, so she's using me as her cover. It's fine. I'm not really into the whole limo-corsage-souvenir-photos thing anyway." Felicity glanced at the portrait of Lucia across the room, wondering if a transatlantic love affair was what stood in the way of Jonathan taking a real date to his senior prom.

Jonathan moved on to the next painting. "Oh, so I wanted to ask you—"

He broke off midsentence when Gabby walked into

the room. Her presence altered the very quality of the air, thickening it and sucking out all the oxygen, but Jonathan didn't seem to notice. He just said, "Oh, hey, Gabby, you here to pick up your painting?"

"Yeah, I thought I'd take it now so you don't have to lug it back to the art room. I know it's kind of unwieldy." She smiled her hungry-cat smile. "Felicity, would you help me carry this to my car, please?"

Felicity's good mood shattered. When Jonathan saw her face, he said, "It's okay, I can help you, Gabby."

"No, you look busy. Felicity can do it. Right?" Gabby picked up one end of her painting and waited for Felicity to grab the other. With extreme reluctance, she took it.

"I'll be right back," she said.

Gabby didn't speak as she led Felicity through the gym wing. When they reached the bathroom by the weight room, she abruptly stopped walking, and Felicity crashed into the canvas, the corner jabbing her painfully in the ribs. "You can just lean this against the wall," Gabby said. "We're going in there."

"I thought we were going to your car."

It was amazing how small and stupid Gabby could make her feel with just one scornful look. "I don't *really* need help carrying this, Felicity. I just need to talk to you, and I didn't want to do it in front of Jonathan. Now get inside."

Felicity did as she was told, but her heart was in her throat. One more day, one conversation with Rose, would have left her ready to fight back. But she didn't have one more day. And that meant that yet again, she was completely unprepared.

"So, what do you want from me this time?" Felicity asked when Gabby had blocked the bathroom door shut. "A blood sacrifice? My firstborn child?"

Gabby crossed her arms. "Actually, I'm going to need your prom date."

"I'm sorry, you need my *what*?"

"Your prom date. Brent. You know, tall redheaded muscular guy? Kind of dopey?"

Felicity couldn't believe she'd heard Gabby right. "But what do you need Brent for?"

"Why is this hard for you to understand? I just told you. I need him as my prom date."

Gabby couldn't possibly be serious—it was just too ridiculous. Felicity's nervous laugh echoed off the tile walls. "Brent's not going to take you to prom," she said. "That's insane."

Gabby shrugged, totally unconcerned. "He will if you tell him he has to. He wouldn't dare disobey you. The guy has the mental capacity of a collie."

"But he can't take you. He's taking me. Everything's already arranged. Besides, he has no interest in brunettes. I can't force him to like you, Gabby."

"He doesn't have to *like* me. He just has to take me to prom. Good thing arrangements can always be changed."

"What if I can't get him to agree?" Felicity choked out.

"Then everyone finds out about your hair color

157

before the end of the night. Just think how exciting it'll be. Everyone loves a good prom scandal."

This wasn't a joke — Gabby really wanted to take her beautiful, adoring date away. An image of Brent doing the prom court dance with her enemy sprang to mind, and Felicity started to feel sick. She stood very still, trying not to hyperventilate as she watched her prom night go up in flames. Her mom snapping photos of her and Brent, groomed and primped and grinning — gone. The moment Brent would wrap his strong arms around her and pull her close for the first slow dance of the evening — gone. The after-party at Haylie's, followed by a whole night of sleeping with her head resting on her boyfriend's chest — all of it gone in an instant.

Of course, it was technically possible to go to prom by herself. But no redhead ever showed up without a date. That alone could undermine her red cred. And how could she ever hold her head up if Brent was right there in the same room with another girl? Whispers and pitying looks would follow her all night. *Did you see how Felicity's sexy boyfriend ditched her? And for a brunette, of all people. What kind of girl can't hang on to her boyfriend on prom night?*

They would wonder why he had left her. And if they tried hard enough, maybe they'd find out.

Tears of fury and frustration pricked at the corners of Felicity's eyes, and she dug her nails into her palms and tried to concentrate on the pain. No matter what happened, she couldn't let Gabby see her cry. "You won't get away with this," she hissed. "You can't just go around terrorizing people and expect there not to be any consequences."

Gabby smirked at her. "Ooh, I'm paralyzed with fear."

"I'm serious. You're not the only one who can spread rumors. I could have the whole school talking about you in a second if I wanted to."

"What could you possibly have on me, Felicity?"

"Why should I tell you?" Felicity held her head high, hoping Gabby couldn't tell she was grasping at straws. "I could say anything—it wouldn't even have to be true. I could tell everyone you're pregnant. Or that you've been texting naked photos of yourself to the football team. Nobody around here even cares if the gossip they spread is real."

She expected to see fear flicker across Gabby's face, but instead her enemy broke into a radiant smile. "Oh, that's perfect," she said, more to herself than to Felicity.

"What? I'm serious. I'll do it unless you leave me alone."

"Fine. Do it. I dare you. Tell them I cheated on my SATs. Tell them I have an after-school job at the strip club on I-80. Tell them I'm a crack addict. I can't wait to see what people will believe." Gabby picked up her bag and turned to go. "And in the meantime, have your boy toy call me so we can make arrangements. I'll be wearing red, so a corsage of red roses would look nice."

Felicity stared at the closing door, more confused

than ever. Gabby wasn't just being stoic—she seemed genuinely delighted at the prospect of having her character defamed. If Felicity went ahead and spread malicious rumors about her, it seemed she'd be playing directly into her enemy's hands. Was Gabby really so desperate for attention that she'd stoop to this? What could she possibly be trying to achieve?

Of course, this meant that Felicity had only two choices: give up her boyfriend on prom night, or give up her secret, her shot at winning the pageant, and her dream of going to art school.

Her tears finally spilled over.

She let herself cry quietly for a few minutes, then gathered a wad of toilet paper and patted her eyes dry. Personal crisis or not, she had to go back to the squash courts. The art show had to come down, and she couldn't make Jonathan do all the work himself. She inspected her face in the mirror. Her eyes were a little red and her mascara was a bit smeared, but she didn't look too awful. It was possible Jonathan wouldn't notice anything was wrong as long as she kept her distance. She took a few deep, calming breaths and tried to rearrange her mouth into a convincing smile.

Unfortunately, Ms. Kellogg had arrived in her absence to help take down the show, and she waved Felicity over immediately. "Do you have nails?" she called. "I can't peel off these sticky strips."

"Yeah, I can do it." Felicity tried to keep her tearstained face averted as she picked the adhesive off a painting. "Where's Jonathan?"

"He's carrying stuff back to the art room. Hey, are you okay? What's the matter?"

"Nothing. I'm fine." Felicity sounded about as convincing as she had when she was six and tried to blame the cat for the crayon drawings on her bedroom walls.

Ms. Kellogg gently tilted Felicity's chin up and looked into her bloodshot eyes, and Felicity didn't fight her. "You want to talk about it?"

She did. More than anything, she wanted to spill out the whole story. Ms. Kellogg was a strawbie herself. She would understand. But the words stuck in her throat like a glob of peanut butter, and she couldn't get them out.

Instead she said, "Can I ask you a personal question?"

"Of course. Anything at all."

Felicity looked back down at her hands. "I hope this doesn't sound rude, but . . . do you ever wish you were a real redhead?"

Ms. Kellogg laughed, a quick, surprised cascade of notes. It wasn't the reaction Felicity had been expecting. "Felicity, I know this will sound weird to you, but everywhere except Scarletville, I *am* a real redhead."

"What? But you're a— I mean, your hair's strawberry-blond. It's totally different."

"That's not really a distinction the rest of the world makes. When I was growing up in Philadelphia, I got called Pippi Longstocking and Carrot Top all through grade school. I had the reddest hair in my class. I had this photography professor at NYU who used to talk about my 'Pre-Raphaelite copper locks' all the time. I feel like a redhead, and I've always considered myself one."

Felicity looked at the strawberry waves falling around her teacher's shoulders. She couldn't imagine a strawbie getting called Carrot Top. It just didn't make any sense. "But why'd you move to Scarletville if you knew your hair would look less red here?"

"Teach for America sent me here. It was a total coincidence. And then Principal Atkins hired me full-time when I was done with my assignment. My hair color has never factored into my decisions at all. This is just what I look like, and I don't really have the time or energy to be self-conscious about it."

Felicity couldn't fathom the concept of a person's hair color being unimportant. Rarely did an hour go by when she didn't think about her own.

"Huh," she said. It was less than articulate, but it was all her addled brain could manage.

Ms. Kellogg reached out and tucked a lock of Felicity's vibrant hair behind her ear. "Just wait till you get out into the world, Felicity. I think you'll be surprised by how big it is."

As Ms. Kellogg moved on to the next painting, Felicity knelt there on the floor, trying to make sense of her teacher's words. It felt like her world had just stirred in its sleep, stretched, and settled back down in a different position, taking up a little more space than before.

Felicity had been looking forward to her rendezvous with Brent all day, but now the prospect of seeing him filled her with dread. By the time he texted that he was coming up the tree, she was so nervous she felt sick; the spaghetti she'd eaten for dinner seemed to be braiding itself around her organs. She had worked out what she would say to him, but she wasn't sure she could successfully force the words out of her mouth. For a moment, she considered telling him she couldn't hang out after all. But this conversation would have to happen eventually, or there would be unspeakable consequences. If Brent found out Felicity was a strawbie, he'd probably break up with her, and she'd lose him forever. This way, she'd only have to give him up for one night.

She texted back and told him to come up.

A few minutes later, Brent slid through the window. He paused just long enough to say hello before he swept Felicity up in his arms like a Disney prince rescuing a damsel in distress. Then his mouth was on hers, urgent and thrilling, and everything ceased to exist except for his tongue and his wintergreen breath and his strong hands running up her back. The speech she had so carefully prepared flew from her mind like a pigeon in the path of a rampaging toddler.

After a few blissful minutes, they fumbled toward the bed, struggling out of their shirts on the way, and fell into each other's arms on top of the covers. Felicity's heart was beating so quickly it felt like a continuous hum in her chest. She pressed against Brent, wishing they could melt together. Even with no space between them, he didn't feel close enough.

Just then, Felicity heard her brothers race down the hall, screaming something about a plane crash. She froze with her mouth an inch from Brent's and waited for them to move on. "Can we keep going?" Brent whispered against her lips.

"Hang on a second," she whispered back. "I don't want my brothers to come in here."

"No, I mean, can we keep *going*." Brent pressed his hips against hers for clarification.

Felicity's entire body was begging, *Yes, yes, yes, just do it already!* But the screaming and banging outside the door made her reluctant to plunge into uncharted waters. She wanted her first time to be slow and tender and romantic, not a quick, illicit whirlwind punctuated by seven-year-old voices.

"Babe, we can't do it with them in the hall," she whispered. "My door doesn't even lock, and I'd get in so much trouble if anyone found out you were here."

Brent gave a low moan that was one part frustration and one part assent. He kissed slowly up Felicity's neck, and when he reached her ear, he whispered, "Maybe we could do it on prom night. We could get a hotel room, if you wanted. It would be really romantic."

When Felicity heard the words "prom night," her entire body shut down. She tried to roll away from Brent, but he grabbed her shoulder and gently turned her toward him. "Hey," he whispered. "We don't have to, if you don't want. I just thought—"

"No, it's not that." Felicity struggled to a sitting position. Her shirt was across the room, so she gathered the

164

covers up against her chest. Still breathless, she said, "I have to talk to you about something."

"Now?" Brent's expression was incredulous.

"I know. I'm sorry, but—" She couldn't go any further. Brent looked at her, an adorable crinkle of confusion between his eyebrows. He was breathing hard, too, and the waistband of his chili-pepper-patterned boxers was sticking out of his jeans. He was so trusting, so vulnerable, and he wanted her so much. How could she possibly do what she was about to do?

She reached out and touched his face, and he leaned into her hand like an affectionate dog. "I need you to do something for me," she said.

Brent's worried look disappeared, and a grin took its place. "Ooh, okay. Is it kinky? 'Cause if it is, I'm up for—"

"No, not that kind of thing." Felicity took a deep breath. "I need you to take Gabby Vaughn to prom."

"What? Why? But I . . . How am I supposed to take both of you?"

"No, I mean, I need you to take her instead of me."

Brent looked deeply wounded, and he drew back from her. "You don't want to go to prom with me?"

"I *do*. I want more than *anything* to go to prom with you." Felicity was suddenly afraid she was going to cry again.

"Then I don't get it. Why do you want me to take Gabby? You're not—Lissy, you're not breaking up with me, are you?"

"*No.* No. Of course not. It's just . . . it's a hazing

thing. For the prom committee. I want to be in charge next year, but Madison wants it, too, and I have to prove I care the most by doing something really self-sacrificing." Felicity looked down at her polka-dotted duvet, unable to lie directly to Brent's face. "Nobody asked Gabby to prom, even though she's on the court, and giving you up is . . . pretty much the most self-sacrificing thing I could think of."

"What's Madison doing?"

"I don't know. But I'm sure whatever she comes up with won't be as bad as this."

Brent stared at her, blinking slowly. "You're still going to *come* to prom, right?"

"Yeah, I'll still come. But Gabby has to be your date."

"Do I have to hang out with her the whole time? I don't have to do the prom court dance with her, do I?"

"I think you do, babe. If you'll do this for me, I mean." Felicity grabbed his hand and held on tightly. "I'm so sorry. I know how much this sucks. I'm really upset about it." Voicing her emotions out loud made them more real, and a tear trailed down her cheek.

Brent wiped it away with his thumb. "If I do it, will you get what you want?"

Felicity thought about all the things she wanted. She longed for a perfect, fairy-tale prom night that would leave her with stars in her eyes and Brent in her bed. But much more than that, she wanted safety. She needed to be certain that Gabby wouldn't bring her entire redheaded existence to a screeching halt just when the pageant prize money was within her reach. And that meant her secret had to stay a secret.

"Yes," she said. "This will help me get what I want."

Brent sighed. "Fine. I guess I'll do it."

"And there's one more thing — nobody can find out I asked you to do this. So if anyone wants to know why you're with Gabby, tell them it's a community service thing for one of the athletic scholarships. Okay? Can you do that?"

He shrugged, defeated. "If that's what you want."

Felicity threw her arms around him, pressing her heart to his, and he cradled her against him. All the breathless, fluttery, expectant feelings from just a few minutes before had faded, but Felicity felt a flood of genuine affection for Brent that was more intense than ever. "Thank you," she whispered.

And that was when Andy and Tyler burst through her door.

Felicity shrieked and grabbed a pillow to cover her chest. "Guys, you have to leave," she hissed.

"Why?" Andy demanded. "What are you doing? Why aren't you wearing shirts?"

"Um, we were —"

" — having a wrestling match," Brent supplied.

Felicity stared at her boyfriend, surprised by his uncharacteristic display of quick thinking. "Right," she said. "People in ancient times always wrestled with their clothes off."

"Oh." Her brothers nodded solemnly, filing this

information away for later use. Felicity was sure there'd be naked twin wrestling on the living room rug within the week.

Brent handed Felicity her shirt, and she tugged it on, then knelt down in front of her brothers. "Listen, guys, you can't tell Mom you saw us wrestling, okay? There's no wrestling allowed in the house, and I'll get in really big trouble. I'll buy each of you a whole bag of jelly beans if you can keep it a secret. But you really have to promise."

Tyler looked skeptical. "Will there be lots of red ones?"

"*Tons* of red ones. As many as you want."

Her brothers looked at each other, then nodded. "Okay." They ran out the door with their model airplanes and resumed their game as if nothing had happened.

Brent pulled on his shirt and got up to go. Their romantic mood was utterly destroyed, and he and Felicity had nothing more to say to each other. Though he didn't seem angry, he was sullen and subdued, and the good-bye kiss he gave her was halfhearted at best.

It was only when she was alone that the reality of the situation hit Felicity full-force. She, who hadn't been without a date to a school function since she was twelve, was about to attend the most important event of the year *alone*. She had done so much thankless work on the prom committee to make sure everything was perfect and magical, and now she wouldn't even get to share in the rewards. No matter what the decorations looked like or how beautiful her dress was, she would have a horrible evening. Plus, she knew that these humiliating demands would just keep coming until she figured out Gabby's mysterious endgame and found a way to shut it down.

She texted Gabby:

It's done.

And then she collapsed on her bed and cried stormy, furious tears.

A few minutes later, her mom tapped on her door. "Baby, are you okay? Can I come in?"

"Yes," Felicity choked out.

Her mom was beside her on the bed in an instant, rubbing her back and making soothing sounds. "Tell me what happened."

"Brent's taking someone else to prom," Felicity sobbed. "Now I have to go alone, and I'm going to look so stupid, and everyone's going to laugh at me."

"He's taking someone else? Did you break up?"

Felicity sniffled. "No. I don't think so. It's all really confusing."

"How could he do this to you? Brent adores you. And he's such a good boy."

He *was* a good guy, and none of this was his fault. Felicity thought of the hurt on his face when she told him she wouldn't be his date, so similar to the expression on Haylie's face when she had nominated Gabby for prom queen. Keeping her secret safe had seemed like the most important thing in the world, but she had

169

caused so much pain to the people she cared about. They were the ones who deserved sympathy, not her. Thinking about that just made her cry harder.

"I'm so sorry, sweetheart," her mom said, misinterpreting the fresh flood of tears. "I know how hard it is when someone breaks your heart. Is there anything I can do?"

Felicity was about to say no, but it suddenly occurred to her that maybe there *was* something Ginger could do. Maybe it wasn't necessary for her to carry this burden alone. The blackmail was starting to spiral out of control now, and it would be such a relief to tell someone what she was going through, to ask for help. Her mom was smart and competent. She would know exactly what to do, and together maybe they could finally end Gabby's reign of terror.

She sat up and faced her mom. "I need your help," she said.

"Of course, baby. Anything for my girl."

Felicity swallowed hard, and then all the words she'd been keeping back came spilling out in a rush. "I'm being blackmailed," she said. "Gabby Vaughn—Rose's daughter—somehow she found out about . . . about my hair, and she's been forcing me to do all this horrible stuff, like nominating her for prom queen when I was supposed to nominate Haylie, and hanging her super-offensive painting in the art show, and now she's making me manipulate Brent into taking her to prom. And I've tried to fight back, but nothing works because she doesn't even seem to care about her own reputation.

She has all the power, and I can't figure out what she wants from me or why she hates me so much, and I have no idea what to do."

When Felicity met her mom's eyes, she expected to find sympathy and compassion there. She was totally unprepared for the cold, hard look of panic she saw instead. "Has Gabby told anyone?" Ginger asked.

"I . . . No, I don't think so."

"Oh, thank God." Her mom took a deep, shaky breath and put a hand to her heart. "How long has this been going on?"

"Since just after Scarlet Sunday. Two and a half weeks."

"And she still hasn't spread it around. That's good. That's really good."

"But she's only keeping it a secret so I'll do whatever she wants, and . . . Mom, it's just been *awful*. She's making me hurt my friends, and it's not like I can explain to them what's going on, and I never feel safe, and I'm afraid I'm going to lose everyone." Two more tears trailed down Felicity's cheeks and dripped onto her jeans.

Ginger's face softened, and she took Felicity's hand. Felicity waited for the soothing words she'd been craving for weeks: *This must be so awful for you. I'm glad you came to me. We'll figure out a way to make it all stop.*

"I know this is hard, baby," Ginger said. "But sometimes we have to make sacrifices for the things that are really important. You've been doing such a good job of handling this . . . inconvenience so far. You're my

171

strong girl, and I know you can do whatever it takes to keep Gabby quiet and protect this family."

Felicity stared at her mom. "What?"

"There's nothing more important than keeping your secret. If this gets out, it'll destroy our whole family's reputation. But if you do what she wants, everything stays under wraps."

Felicity couldn't believe what she was hearing. She pulled her hand away. "But . . . she's destroying my life, Mom. Aren't you going to help me?"

"Baby, I *am* helping you! I only want what's best for you. I know it seems like Gabby's ruining your life, but everything will get so much worse if you give her a reason to expose you. In the long run, it doesn't matter who you nominate for prom queen or whether you have a date to one dance. But if your secret gets out, nobody will ever respect you again. You'll get thrown out of the pageant before you even have a chance at that prize money. I could even lose my job—you know how the mayor feels about arties. And then how would I support you? I'm just trying to give you the safe, happy life you deserve, but you have to do your part. And for now, that means following Gabby's instructions."

Felicity felt as if she'd been kicked in the stomach. "For how long? Forever?"

"Nothing lasts forever. It'll only be a year before Gabby goes to college somewhere else and forgets all about you. And then everything will go back to normal."

A *year*? There was no way she could survive this for a year—she'd hardly been able to get through a few weeks. "But there must be another way," she choked. "Some way we can fight her."

Ginger shook her head sadly. "I understand why you want that, but you can't antagonize her. It's way too dangerous when she holds your entire future in her hands like this. I need you to be strong and find a way to make this work. It's your job to protect all of us. Can you do that?"

Felicity wanted to burst into tears again, to throw things, to scream, *You're my mother! You're supposed to love me! Why won't you help me?* But she knew that was useless. Her mom did love her—of course she did. But she loved the daughter she'd created, the popular redhead and pageant hopeful. She wasn't about to let the strawberry-blond daughter she'd been given get in the way.

"Felicity? Can you do that?"

Felicity nodded, knowing there was no other answer.

"That's my brave girl."

Ginger reached out and pulled her daughter into a hug. Her arms were warm and strong, but for the first time, Felicity found no comfort in her embrace. Asking for help had been a huge mistake. Nobody was ever going to help her.

She would have to handle this alone.

12

The prom committee spent all of Saturday preparing the gym for its night of glory. Felicity and Kendall hung their painted cityscape backdrop and artfully draped the bleachers in red fabric. Topher perched atop an A-frame ladder on a rolling base and hung strings of paper lanterns, belting out "The Red, Red Rose of Love" as Cassie wheeled him from place to place. Savannah helped the yearbook photographers with their photo booth, and the rest of the girls set up clusters of small tables and chairs around the perimeter of the room. Madison spent the entire morning ordering everyone around, unwilling to touch anything in case she chipped her manicure.

Felicity couldn't concentrate at all. She hadn't been

able to focus on much of anything since the painful conversation she'd had with her mom three days ago. Plus, she still hadn't told Haylie and Ivy that she no longer had a prom date, and that secret had been weighing on her as well. Of course, they'd discover what was going on soon enough, when she showed up to dinner alone. And the rest of the school would see Brent walk into this very room with Gabby on his arm just a few short hours later.

"Felicity!" Kendall was waving a hand in front of her face.

"What? Sorry, I was thinking about something else."

"Obviously." Kendall gave the fabric over the bleachers a final tug. "I was just going to say that I thought this looked good. What do you think? Should we go get the streetlamps from the drama room?"

"Yeah, sure. It looks great."

"So, what are you guys doing before prom?" Kendall asked as they walked down the hall. "Jeremy and I are going to that French bistro on Thorne Street. We had to make the reservation back in January. They have this thing called a *croque monsieur*. French food is so classy."

"That'll be great," Felicity said, trying to sound enthusiastic. She'd had the *croque monsieur* at that bistro, and she couldn't figure out how it was supposed to be different from a regular grilled ham-and-cheese sandwich. "I'm going to Mamma Leoni's with Haylie and Ivy and their dates."

"Oooh, I *love* Mamma Leoni's! Have you had the pesto tortellini? It's totally to die for."

As Kendall wrestled the first streetlamp onto the dolly, Felicity's phone beeped.

HAYLIE: how's it going? u ok to do photos @ my house before dinner?

Everything was running smoothly in the gym, and the prom committee would probably be done setting up in two or three hours. But what was the point of taking photos without Brent? Felicity didn't need her fifth-wheel status documented for everyone on RedNet to see.

FELICITY: running a little behind. not sure I'll make it for photos. meet you at the restaurant.
HAYLIE: :(:(:(

Felicity stuffed her phone back into her pocket, relieved that her torturous evening would be slightly shorter.

When everyone had finished their assigned tasks, Topher turned off the overhead lights and switched on the lanterns, streetlamps, and Christmas lights around the makeshift stage for a test run. Felicity knew she should be pleased by what she'd accomplished—the gym looked every bit as magical as she had hoped—but nothing about prom felt exciting anymore. As Kendall led a round of applause for her, their esteemed designer, she tried to memorize the expressions of respect on her classmates' faces. She'd need to remember them later, when she was alone on the sidelines, the object of everyone's pity.

Felicity had seen enough prom movies to know that the preparty primping was supposed to be one of the best parts. She went through all the motions, hoping to feel some of that delicious anticipation bubbling up inside her. But now that she had no date, the whole thing just seemed pointless. When she slipped on her vintage thrift-store dress—black with tiny white polka dots and a full skirt supported by frothy red petticoats—it didn't make her feel playful and vivacious, as it had the day she bought it. At the time, she had imagined how Brent would react when he saw her in it. But now the only one he'd be reacting to was Gabby.

When Felicity dragged herself into the kitchen to say good-bye to her mom, Ginger gave a dramatic gasp and clasped her hands to her heart. "Oh, baby, *look* at you! You're so *beautiful*!" She grabbed the camera off the kitchen counter and ushered Felicity toward the back door. "Come outside, I need photos!"

Felicity grudgingly followed her mom into the yard and endured a few minutes of posing, trying to cover her sadness with elegance and poise. When the camera battery finally ran out, Ginger hugged her good-bye. "Have a fabulous time," she said. "Don't get drunk, don't do drugs, and don't get pregnant."

"Mom, who's going to get me pregnant? I don't even have a date."

"I'm your mother. I have to say it." Ginger kissed her on the cheek and whispered, "I love you. I know this is hard for you, but you're doing the right thing. Hold that beautiful head high." Felicity tried, but it was hard to smile through her dejection.

She arrived at Mamma Leoni's and parked across the street, in front of the fertility clinic that promised to "make those shy MC1R genes express themselves!" The hostess had already seated Haylie, Ryan, Ivy, and Darren at a table with two empty chairs. Haylie was radiant in a flowing shell-pink dress, an orchid corsage the size of a mango around her wrist. Ivy was decked out in a pin-striped suit with tails, and she and Darren had matching yellow rose boutonnieres. She looked absolutely perfect. Both of the boys seemed fidgety and uncomfortable in their rented tuxes, and looking at them sent a pang of longing through Felicity. She had no doubt Brent would wear his tux as if it were a second skin.

Haylie jumped up with a shriek and pulled Felicity into an enthusiastic hug. "You look *amazing*!" she squealed. "God, I love that dress so much!"

"Yours too," Felicity said. "Nice suit, Ives."

Ivy grinned. "I don't see why I can't just wear this for the pageant."

"Doesn't she look awesome?" Darren agreed, running his hand through Ivy's spiky hair. Felicity waited for her to bat his hand away and toss out some clever, snarky comment, but Ivy just looked down at her bread plate and blushed a deep shade of raspberry.

Felicity tried to say hi to Haylie's date, but Ryan was busy inspecting his salad fork at very close range and didn't seem to notice that there was a new person at the table. When she leaned closer to see what was so fascinating, she caught a strong whiff of pot, and Ryan's whole personality suddenly made more sense. Every seven seconds or so, he jerked his head violently to the side to flip his shaggy, rock-star hair across his forehead, and Felicity wondered how long it would take for him to stab himself in the eye. She didn't see how he was going to make it through the prom court dance without embarrassing Haylie.

"Where's Brent?" asked Ivy, looking around. "Is he parking the car?"

Felicity shook her head. "Actually . . . can I talk to you guys alone for a second?"

"Sure." Haylie shot Ivy a worried glance, then headed for the bathroom at the back of the restaurant. Ivy and Felicity followed her, and the three of them squished into the tiny room.

"What's going on?" asked Ivy when the door was safely locked behind them.

Felicity swallowed hard. "Brent's not coming."

"What do you mean? He's not coming to dinner, or he's not going to prom?"

"He's going to prom. Just not with me."

Haylie's eyes widened. "Oh my God, Felicity, did you break up?"

"No, it's nothing like that. He just has to take someone else. It's not his fault, it's this community service thing for an athletic scholarship he wants. Some of the guys are taking brunettes who weren't invited. I told him it was okay, but I'm just . . . I'm really sad about it."

"Wow, that seriously sucks." Haylie rubbed Felicity's back. "When did you find out?"

"A few days ago."

"God, he could have at least given you some warning," Ivy said. "That's kind of a dick move. Who does he have to take? Is it someone horrible?"

Felicity took a deep breath. "He got matched with Gabby Vaughn."

Haylie and Ivy exchanged a long look, and Felicity's heart began to race. Her friends were clearly aware that something didn't quite add up. "Does this have to do with the trouble you were in before?" Haylie finally asked.

"What?"

"I mean, something's obviously going on with you and Gabby. I'd never even seen you speak to her before this month, and then she's suddenly at our lunch table, and her painting's in the art show, and then you nominated her for prom queen, and now this. Is she, like, blackmailing you or something?"

Felicity's heart was pounding so hard now that she felt slightly dizzy. She grabbed the edge of the sink for support and forced a laugh. "What? *Blackmailing* me? Of course not. And no, this doesn't have to do with any of that stuff. It's just a coincidence." She could tell her friends weren't buying her story. "Guys, come on. Don't look at me like that. I'm already having the suckiest prom night ever, and now you're making me feel like it's my fault."

Haylie slipped an arm around her waist. "Nobody thinks it's your fault. I'm so sorry this is happening to you, and we'll do everything we can to make sure you have fun tonight. Okay?"

"I'll punch Gabby in the face if it'll make you feel better," Ivy offered. "I'm small, but I'm scrappy. I could totally take her." She held up her tiny fists, and Felicity finally managed a weak smile.

"You ready to go back out?" Haylie asked. "I'm starving, and the pesto tortellini here is *so* good."

Felicity nodded and followed her friends back to the table. When the waiter came, she asked him to remove the sixth place setting.

Dinner was a blur. The threads of various conversations wove lazily around each other, but Felicity had trouble following any of them. She sat quietly at the table, mechanically moving her fork to her mouth, but her mind was a cyclone. What would happen when they got to prom and everyone saw Brent with Gabby? Would her classmates point and laugh at her, like they always did in The Dream? What if someone figured out this was a setup and there was no athletic scholarship? Was taking the blackmail lying down really the best way to protect her secret and her family? What if her mom was wrong? What if Felicity could make this all go away by landing one good strike on Gabby's weak point? But what *was* Gabby's weak point?

By the time the check had been paid and everyone

181

was ready to go, Felicity felt queasy and exhausted and headachy, and she wasn't sure she could go through with prom after all. Maybe she should just go home and hide under the covers. She closed her eyes and massaged her aching temples.

"Felicity?" Ivy said, gently shaking her shoulder. "Are you okay?"

"I don't feel very good," she said.

Ivy rubbed her back, a distinctly un-Ivy-like gesture, and Felicity realized she must look pretty terrible. "Are you going to throw up?"

"No, I don't think so. Just . . . I don't know. My head hurts and I'm kind of dizzy." She hoped Ivy would suggest she go home—if someone else said it first, it wouldn't count as chickening out.

"Tonight really isn't working out for you, huh? You probably shouldn't drive if you feel dizzy. Why don't you come with us, and someone can drop you back here to pick up your car after the party. If you're feeling really awful, I'll take you home sooner, okay?"

Felicity nodded and let Ivy lead her to the car, but even her friend's steady hand on her back couldn't chase away her dread.

Darren and Ivy kept up a steady stream of chatter all the way to the school, but the ride wasn't nearly long enough for Felicity to steel her nerves. Before she knew it, she was ordering her body to follow her friends across the parking lot, one red-heeled foot in front of the other. In moments, she was swept up into a flash

182

flood of rainbow-colored prom-goers. There was no escape now.

Felicity put on her most convincing smile and let herself be funneled through the door of the school. She produced her ticket, had her hand stamped, and then she was back in the gym. Her friends gasped and congratulated her on how beautiful the decorations looked, but she hardly heard the praise. All she could do was watch the door, waiting for Brent and Gabby to arrive.

That was hardly necessary—their entrance a few minutes later was impossible to miss. It affected the crowd like a lightning bolt, spreading crackles of electricity through the room. Every coiffed head snapped to attention as the couple glided through the doorway arm in arm. Brent was gorgeous and regal in his tux, and Gabby was resplendent in a backless satin gown the color of fresh blood. They left a trail of whispered fragments in their wake as they crossed the floor: "Did you see . . . ? But why are *they* . . . ? Isn't he supposed to be with . . . ?"

And then came the ubiquitous, "Where's Felicity? Does she know?"

Even with her advance knowledge of what was going to happen, Felicity was totally unprepared to see Brent and Gabby together in person. Watching her boyfriend with her nemesis was like having an open chest wound sprinkled with lemon juice and salt. The fact that they looked *good* together made things even worse. When Brent located Felicity in the crowd, his eyes were full of hurt and longing. Felicity's hand flew to her mouth, trying to trap her emotions before they turned into words.

When she finally tore her eyes away and looked around at the rest of her classmates, she saw her worst fears realized. Everyone was staring straight at her with pity, confusion, or suppressed delight on their faces. No one could have anticipated a prom scandal this delicious.

Cassie Brynne was suddenly by her side, digging her shellacked nails into Felicity's arm. "Oh my God, what is *he* doing with *her*?"

Felicity's first instinct was to pull away and tell Cassie to mind her own business. But then she realized she might be able to use Cassie, who had the biggest mouth in the school, to make the rumor mill work in her favor. "I know it looks dramatic, but it's really not," she said, rolling her eyes and trying to look nonchalant. "Brent's just with her because of this community service project. It's for an athletic scholarship."

"Taking brunettes to prom counts for community service?"

Felicity looked around, then leaned in as if she were confiding something nobody was supposed to know. That pretty much ensured the information would be all over the gym within minutes. "When the situation is *this* pathetic? Absolutely. I mean, Gabby somehow made it onto the court, but then nobody even asked her to prom. Can you imagine doing the prom court dance *alone*? How embarrassing would *that* be?"

Cassie nodded solemnly, her eyes wide. "Wow. Your boyfriend is *really* nice. But you must be so bummed that he's not with you!"

"I am. But he asked me for permission, and I said it was okay. Sometimes you have to give back to the community, you know? Help people less fortunate than you."

"You're right. Way to go, Felicity. You're totally an inspiration." Cassie beamed at her, then trotted off to join Savannah and Kendall. Felicity was pleased to see her gesturing at Brent and Gabby and talking a mile a minute. In the end, people wouldn't remember her as the pathetic one.

The DJ put on the first slow song of the evening, and the dance floor flooded with starry-eyed couples. On the other side of the gym, Felicity watched Gabby wrap herself around Brent like an evil little tourniquet, and the few bites of dinner she'd managed to swallow churned in her stomach. "I need to get out of here for a minute. I'm going outside," she told Ivy.

"Are you okay? Do you want me to come with you?"

Felicity would have liked the company. But Darren was tugging at Ivy, and she looked as if she wanted to give in to some long-dormant female instinct and slow-dance with him. Haylie was already entwined with Ryan, who was experimentally squeezing her butt. "No, I'll be fine," she said. "Go dance. I just need a minute alone."

The front lawn and the parking lot were full of people, so Felicity circled around to the empty soccer field at the back of the building. Her high heels sank into the soft ground the moment she left the path, so she kicked them off and abandoned them where they fell. She dug her toes into the cool damp field, closed her eyes, and breathed in the quiet night air, perfumed with the scent of newly cut grass. It was a relief to let the painful forced smile fade from her lips. The thump of the bass echoed from the gym, but otherwise, the only sounds were those of the occasional car and her own rustling petticoats. She started walking out across the dark field, glad to be free of her classmates' prying eyes.

By the time she'd reached the center of the field, far from the lights of the path, her petticoats were full of static and were bunching up around her hips. She glanced around to make sure she was alone, then reached up under her skirt and wrestled the frothy red fabric back into place. Just as she was adjusting the ruffles over her butt, she heard a noise and whipped around.

A guy stood on the path at the other end of the soccer field, staring out into the darkness.

Felicity quickly finished tugging her skirt back into place. How much had he seen? Was it someone from her class, or was it a teacher who could get her into trouble for being out here alone? She stood very still, hoping he hadn't noticed her.

The guy walked to the edge of the grass, then stooped to pick up her shoes, and she silently cursed herself for leaving them by the path. "Hello?" he called. "Is someone out there?"

The voice sounded familiar. She couldn't place it exactly, but it was definitely just a student. "I'm over here," she called back. "Those are mine."

He moved back and forth along the edge of the field, shielding his eyes and trying to see her better. Finally, he called, "Felicity? Is that you?"

It was no use hiding now. Felicity started trudging back toward the path with a sigh. "Yeah, it's me," she called back. She put her pageant smile in place and prepared to face yet another pitying look.

But when she got close enough to see the guy's face, she stopped, surprised. "Jonathan?"

He looked different in a tux. Most of the guys she had seen tonight looked younger than usual in their formal wear, like kids playing dress-up. But the tux had the opposite effect on Jonathan, lending him an unexpected air of maturity and sophistication. Felicity had never seen him look so comfortable in his skin. Her candy-apple-red shoes dangled from his fingertips.

"Hi," he said. He wasn't wearing his glasses, and Felicity noted with surprise how long his eyelashes were. Then he smiled, and it suddenly occurred to her that Jonathan Lyons was very attractive. How had she never seen that before?

She stepped into the light and reached out to take her shoes. As Jonathan's gaze swept over her, his face changed, as if someone had lit a match behind his eyes. "You look beautiful," he said. "I mean, I love your dress."

"Thanks," Felicity said. "You look really great, too."

She leaned over, brushed the wet grass from her feet, and slipped her shoes back on. "What are you doing out here?"

"It was loud in there. And hot. And I don't really do the whole dancing thing." He shrugged. "Wait, what are *you* doing out here? Where's Brent?"

It reassured her that there was at least one person here who hadn't witnessed her moment of humiliation. "He brought Gabby Vaughn instead of me," she said. "I'm surprised you haven't heard. Everyone's talking about it."

Jonathan's eyes widened. "He ditched you for *Gabby*? Really?"

"He didn't ditch me. It's a comm—" Felicity broke off just in time as she realized she couldn't use the community service story on a dateless brown-haired guy. "It's complicated. But yeah, he's in there with her right now. You can go look for yourself."

"I mean, I believe you. I just . . . I'm really surprised."

"You and everyone else. Best gossip of the year, apparently."

"Well, if it makes you feel any better, nobody was talking about you when I got here. Topher Gleason came in right behind me wearing this baby-blue dress that looked like a cloud. Everyone wanted to take photos with him. It was kind of amazing, actually." Felicity laughed despite herself—the fact that there was already fresh gossip cheered her up considerably.

Her phone beeped, and she pulled it out to find a new text.

Felicity sighed. "We should probably go back in. They're announcing the king and queen in a few minutes. Are you ready?"

"Honestly, I don't really care who the king and queen are. Do you?"

Felicity's reflex was to say, "Of course I do," but that wasn't really true. She had counted the ballots herself; she already knew Georgia Kellerman and Zach Masters had won. And she could certainly live without seeing her rival parading her boyfriend around like a prize poodle.

"No, actually," she said. "I don't care at all."

When Jonathan turned and looked her in the eye, the intensity of his gaze surprised her. "Hey, Felicity? I know this sounds kind of weird, and I don't want you to take it the wrong way, but . . . tonight kind of sucks. Do you want to get out of here?"

For a moment, Felicity was at a loss for words. People didn't just *leave* in the middle of prom. But when she thought about it, there was nothing Felicity wanted more than to escape from this horrible, humiliating night.

"Yes," she said. "I would *love* to get out of here."

189

13

Five minutes later, Felicity was sitting in the front seat of Jonathan's dark green pickup truck. As they roared out of the parking lot, a bubble of happiness and excitement expanded in her chest, leaving no room for the hopelessness she'd been wallowing in all evening. She felt as if she had gotten away with a crime and was fleeing the scene, gloriously unobserved.

A small part of her knew that if she were really a good friend, she would have stayed to watch Haylie in the prom court ceremony. But surely Haylie would understand that she couldn't possibly be in that room while the whole school watched her boyfriend dance with Gabby. If their roles were reversed, Felicity would let Haylie off the hook without question. So she sent an apologetic text telling her friend that she couldn't handle the ceremony, dashed off a similar one to Brent, then banished all thoughts of prom from her mind. Jonathan hadn't told her where they were going, but Felicity realized she didn't even care. Anywhere but Scarletville High was fine.

Jonathan drove with a little half smile on his face, tapping his fingers on the steering wheel in time with the music on the stereo. Felicity didn't recognize the song—it sounded like a love child of punk and pop, peppy and defiant in equal measures. It wasn't the sort of music she'd expect Jonathan to play, but she liked it a lot. "Who is this?" she asked.

"It's my friend Amy's band, Sharks in Heaven."

There was only one Amy in Jonathan's class, and she was the captain of the debate team. "Amy Riley?" Felicity asked skeptically.

Jonathan laughed. "That's a really funny image, but no, different Amy. She lives in Seattle. I met her at this summer arts program I went to in Boulder last year. What do you think of them?"

"They're really great." Felicity stuck her hand out the window to surf the air currents as they sped through the dark, then closed her eyes and let the music wrap around her. The combination of Amy's strong voice and the wind against her palm made her feel exhilarated and free. When the song's catchy chorus repeated, Felicity found herself humming along.

I won't be your cookie-cutter girl,
can't mix me from a recipe.

All the right ingredients in all the right proportions
sometimes make an anomaly.
I'd rather be a rock star than a groupie on the sidelines,
I look so much better with these blue streaks in my hair.
I'm not the perfect little princess you expected,
and if that means you can't handle me,
I don't care.

The lyrics were just right for her state of mind. "Hey, do you think you could burn me a copy of this?" she asked.

"Sure, no problem. I'll burn you the whole album."

Jonathan took the ramp onto the highway and sped past the YOU ARE NOW LEAVING THE RED ZONE sign. As they accelerated, the wind whipped through the car and peeled tendrils loose from Felicity's complicated updo. There was no point in fixing it—she wasn't going back to prom—so she pulled out all the pins and let her hair fall loose around her shoulders. "What was the arts program like?" she shouted over the rush of the air.

"It was amazing. Six weeks of pure awesome. We had class every morning in our own discipline, like music or dance or visual art or whatever, and then the afternoon was our studio time. I did a lot of my Art Institute portfolio there. You should have seen the supply room—it was like paint heaven. And there was a huge darkroom and digital printing labs and a big sculpture studio. You would have *loved* it. And every night, we'd share our work and talk about it. It was . . ." Jonathan

192

shook his head. "It's hard to even describe it. I had so many new ideas all the time, it felt like my brain was going to explode."

Felicity had never experienced anything like that, but now that she knew it was possible, she longed for it. "That sounds unbelievable."

"You could go," Jonathan said. "You should. It's called Tanglewilde. It's too late to apply for this year, but you should go next summer. Your stuff is definitely good enough to get you in."

Even though she knew she could never afford it, Jonathan's words ignited a warm glow deep in Felicity's center. "You think so?"

"Oh, for sure."

When Jonathan put his blinker on and took the exit for the next town, a sleepy little place called Caldner, Felicity could no longer contain her curiosity. "Where are we going?" she asked. "What's in Caldner?"

"You'll see. We're almost there."

She was growing more intrigued by the minute. In addition to wondering about their destination, she was fascinated by this new Jonathan. It seemed that slipping on a tux was all it took to transform him from Awkward School Jonathan to Confident SuperJonathan.

They turned onto a street lined with dark shuttered storefronts. It ended in a cul-de-sac, and Jonathan pulled the truck into the last parking space before the curve. "We're here," he said.

They were parked in front of the Caldner Public

Library. The breeze carried strains of muffled music and laughter, but Felicity couldn't find their source. "Umm . . . where are we, exactly?"

Jonathan hopped out of the car and came around to the passenger side. "Come on, you're gonna like this. I promise."

Felicity opened the door and slid out of the pickup amid a rustle of petticoats. The evening air had grown cool, and she realized she had left her wrap on a chair at the back of the gym. She shivered a little and hugged herself.

"Are you cold?" Jonathan asked. "Do you want my jacket?"

She smiled. "I'll be okay. Thanks, though."

"No, really, it's fine. You can have it." Jonathan shrugged out of his tux jacket and draped it gently around her shoulders. It was warm from his body and fit her much better than Brent's broad-shouldered one would have. She snuggled into it gratefully.

"Come on, it's this way." Jonathan led her around to the back of the library, where she spotted a turquoise house with a huge, flood-lit sign reading FRY ME TO THE MOON. People sat at brightly painted picnic tables all over the lawn, lit by strings of novelty lights shaped like jalapeño peppers and flamingos. Light poured from the windows, revealing an explosion of color and activity inside, and the air was full of the mouthwatering scent of french fries. Felicity hadn't eaten much of her dinner, but until that moment, she hadn't realized how hungry she was.

They walked across the lawn and up the weathered stairs, which listed to the left and felt as if they might collapse any second. When Jonathan pushed open the screen door, the smell of fries intensified, but the décor was so overwhelming that Felicity barely noticed. Neon-pink and lime-green shelves lined the walls, all of them crowded with Pez dispensers and action figures. The tables were draped in plastic shower curtains printed with cupcakes, sea creatures, and maps of the New York City subway system. In one corner, a five-foot-tall Lego sculpture of a carton of fries sat on a glittery pink throne. Colored lightbulbs dangled from the ceiling, a sky full of schizophrenic stars.

Felicity instantly fell head over heels in love with it all.

"I hope you like french fries," Jonathan said. He pointed at the wooden menu on the wall, which was hand-painted with lists of french fry varieties, dipping sauces, and milk shake flavors. If Felicity had been a cartoon character, her pupils would have turned into little hearts and started spinning.

There was another couple standing at the counter, and Felicity and Jonathan got in line behind them. The girl had a bright red ponytail, but Felicity didn't recognize her from school. Just as she was wondering why someone with hair so red would choose to live just outside of Scarletville, a tiny blonde wearing an apron hurried out from behind the counter and threw her arms around the redhead. "Oh my god, Sienna, you finally did it!" she squealed. "That color looks *amazing* on you!"

"Thanks!" The girl fingered the end of her coppery ponytail. "I'm still getting used to it, but I think I like it."

"I'm telling you, it's awesome. Where'd you have it done?"

"Live Free or Dye, over on Orchard."

Felicity suddenly realized what they were talking about, and she drew in her breath sharply. How could this Sienna girl *openly admit* to having dyed her hair? This was a public place, and anyone could be listening. Didn't she know that hair dye should only be discussed in whispers in the privacy of one's own home? Though the girl seemed totally at ease, Felicity flushed with embarrassment on her behalf. She had the urge to avert her gaze, as if the other redhead were doing a drunken striptease on the counter.

But at the same time, she couldn't stop staring. Because even to her expert eyes—eyes that looked at dyed red hair every single day of her life—this girl's hair color looked natural. And that meant there was someone right here in Caldner who was just as skilled with dye as Rose Vaughn.

Gabby had said she'd make her mom drop Felicity as a client if she refused to cooperate, but that threat was totally meaningless. Rouge-o-Rama wasn't the only option out there. The realization shocked Felicity so much that her knees felt a little weak.

"You okay?" Jonathan gently touched her shoulder.

"What? Yeah. Sure." Felicity realized the other couple had moved on and that she had been staring very intently into space. She tried to pull herself together.

The tiny blonde was back behind the register now, and she smiled radiantly when she saw Jonathan. "Hey, cutie! How are you? What're you all dolled up for? Who's your . . . um . . . *friend*?"

Jonathan grinned and looked at his shoes, and Felicity smiled to see a little glimpse of bashful School Jonathan peeking through the SuperJonathan exterior. "This is Felicity. She helped me escape from prom. Felicity, this is April, my brother's girlfriend."

April held out her hand. "Nice to meet you, Felicity. You have *such* gorgeous hair. Wow, two redheaded customers in a row. What are the odds?"

The question seemed ludicrous—at the stores and restaurants Felicity frequented, nearly *all* the customers were redheads. But as her eyes skimmed over the Fry Me to the Moon crowd, she had the startling realization that she and the ponytailed girl were the only redheads in the entire room. The lack of red made her feel a bit unsettled. "Crazy," she managed.

"Why'd you guys need to escape from *prom*?" April asked. "Isn't that usually a place people *want* to be?"

"Long story," Jonathan said. "And we're desperately in need of fries."

"Well, you're in the right place. What can I get for you?"

Felicity tried to focus on the menu, but it was overwhelming. There were at least twenty dipping sauces to choose from, and they all sounded equally delicious. She definitely needed some waffle fries, but was she in a jalapeño cheddar mood or a cinnamon barbecue mood? Maybe the spicy mayo was the way to go. Just as she was about to start asking questions, Jonathan said, "Well, since it's Felicity's first time, I think we better have one order of waffle fries with jalapeño cheddar and one order of sweet potato fries with cinnamon barbecue sauce." He turned to her. "Is that okay with you?"

Felicity's eyes widened. "How did you know what I wanted?"

"Trust me, those are the best. You want a milk shake?"

She was about to say she didn't need a milk shake, but she decided she deserved one after the night she'd had. "Yeah. Chocolate malt, please."

"Good call. I'll have the same thing."

Felicity opened her bag and reached for her wallet, but Jonathan stopped her hand. "Don't, um — I've got it."

Did that make this a date? Felicity instinctively looked around to make sure nobody was watching, but everyone who would gossip about her and Jonathan was back in Scarletville. "You don't have to do that," she said.

"I know. I want to."

April handed Jonathan his change. "Your order will be out in a few minutes," she said. Then she reached into her apron pocket, pulled out a hamburger-shaped windup toy, and presented it to Felicity with great solemnity. "This is for you, since it's your first time. Welcome to the Fry Me to the Moon family."

"Thanks," Felicity said. She wound up the hamburger, and it hopped crookedly across the counter. She found it more amusing than she should have, considering her age. She knew she should give it to her brothers when she got home, but she planned to keep it.

Jonathan led Felicity to a free table next to a mosaic of a pelican with its beak full of fries. Felicity chose a gold chair painted with pineapples, and Jonathan sat down across from her in a purple striped one. He looked more relaxed than she'd ever seen him. "So, you like this place?" he asked.

"I *love* it. How'd you find it? I never would have known this was here."

"I've been coming here pretty often since Jake and April started dating a couple years ago. It's pretty much the only place that stays open late, except for the truck stop on I-35, and that's not exactly my scene."

"Is that *anybody's* scene?"

"I think the football team goes there sometimes. They serve huge pieces of pie, and nobody cares if you act really rude and stupid." Jonathan's eyes suddenly widened. "Oh God, I'm sorry. I didn't mean Brent. I'm sure he's— I mean—"

Felicity considered defending her boyfriend's honor, but it was true—the football team's main pastimes were insulting each other and having eating and burping contests. "Don't worry, it's fine," she said. "You're totally right. That truck stop is awful."

Jonathan looked relieved. "Anyway, it's just nice

that I never run into anyone from Scarletville here, you know?"

"Do you really hate it there that much?" Of course, it made sense, now that she thought about it. The lack of redheads in Caldner made her feel uneasy, so the lack of brunettes in Scarletville must make Jonathan feel the same way.

"I don't *hate* it. It's just . . . I don't know. I guess it's not really my scene, either." Jonathan's hand reflexively flew up to fix his glasses, and when he remembered they weren't there, he smoothed down his hair instead. Just talking about Scarletville seemed to make his fidgety mannerisms rise to the surface, and Felicity was sorry she'd brought it up.

"You must be so excited about the Art Institute," she said, trying to steer him back into more comfortable territory.

"Oh yeah, definitely. I honestly can't even believe I got in."

"I'm not surprised at all. You're insanely talented. Ms. Kellogg told me she'd never seen a portfolio like yours."

Jonathan broke into a huge goofy grin. "She said that?"

"Yeah, when we were setting up for the art show."

"That's . . . Wow. That's awesome."

Their milk shakes arrived, and Felicity took a long sip of hers. It was absolutely perfect, thick enough that a spoon could stand up in the center but not so solid that she needed to make an embarrassing fish face to get it through the straw. As she closed her eyes to savor her next slurp, she heard Jonathan laugh. "Good, huh?"

She could hardly bring herself to remove the straw from her mouth. "This is the best thing I've ever tasted in my life."

"Just wait till you have the jalapeño cheddar fries."

She took another rapturous sip. "So, are you nervous about moving all the way to Chicago?"

Jonathan laughed. "All the way? It's only a five-hour drive."

Five hours sounded like an eternity to Felicity—Scarletville Community College was only fifteen minutes from her house. She wondered what it felt like to have the freedom to escape, to have some say in what your life would become. "My mom couldn't handle me being that far away," she said. "And it would suck not to be able to see my brothers. Won't you miss your family?"

"Sure. But it's not like it's hard to drive back and forth. It'll be fine. And Chicago's such a great city. I mean, I can go to the Art Institute and sketch every day if I want. They have a huge Impressionist collection. And there's so much live music and theater and stuff, and places that actually stay open past nine."

For the first time, Felicity really tried to imagine leaving Iowa, turning her back on everything she had ever known. She pictured herself walking down busy, unfamiliar city streets, getting lost in crowds of strangers who didn't think she was special, who couldn't care less what color her hair was. She'd be totally anonymous. At first, it seemed terrifying, almost impossible to fathom. But beneath her fear, she felt a current of electricity buzzing through her blood at the thought of starting over. Jonathan didn't look nervous at all as he talked about leaving everything behind. He looked as if his life were only just about to begin.

And just like that, as she watched him, Felicity's doubts began to fade. Leaving Scarletville and chasing her dream suddenly felt like something she could do. There was a whole new world waiting for her out there.

"What do your parents think about you leaving?" she asked.

"They're fine with the Chicago part, but they're not thrilled about the art school thing. They think I should do something more . . . I don't know, productive. Be a 'contributing member of society' or whatever." He made exaggerated air quotes around the words.

That sounded painfully familiar. "What do they want you to do instead?"

"They're both lawyers. Something like that, I guess. Or premed, or business." He wrinkled his nose, as if the word smelled like rotting fish guts. "The thing is, I think my dad actually gets it. He played bass in this band called Six-Fingered Man before he met my mom. But then they got married and had all of us, and he had to stop, and now he doesn't play at all anymore. When I

202

first told him I wanted to go to art school, his face kind of lit up, you know?"

Felicity knew. That was the same look her mom gave her every time they discussed the pageant.

Their baskets of fries arrived, and Felicity grabbed a waffle fry and dunked it in the jalapeño cheddar dip. True to Jonathan's word, the fry was glorious — just the right crispiness, just the right amount of salt and grease. "Oh my God, these are *ridiculously* good."

Jonathan laughed. "Try the other kind."

She complied. The barbecue sauce was sweet and salty and smoky and cinnamony all at once. It made her want to get up and dance. "That's it. I am never eating anything else for the rest of my life."

"Right there with you." Jonathan grabbed a fry and clinked it with Felicity's as if it were a champagne glass. "To not being at prom."

"Cheers." As she stuffed the fry into her mouth, Felicity realized she hadn't thought about Brent and Gabby since she had gotten into Jonathan's car. She was warm and happy and surrounded by delicious food smells, and she suddenly felt intensely grateful. "Hey, thanks for this," she said. "I was having a really awful night before you showed up."

"Thanks for coming with me. My night wasn't going so well, either."

"Why didn't you ask someone to prom who you actually wanted to go with? Your sister will have her own proms."

Jonathan played with his cuff link, suddenly unable to meet Felicity's eyes. "Well . . . the girl I really wanted to ask was—um—indisposed, I guess."

Of course. A wave of sympathy swept through her. She'd had to give up her boyfriend for one important night, but it would be infinitely worse to be in Jonathan's place, pining for someone who was all the way across the ocean. "That sucks. But I guess it's kind of hard to get to prom if you live on the other side of the world, right?"

Jonathan looked up, confused. "The other side of . . . what? What are you talking about?"

"Well, I mean, she's all the way in Capri, right?"

"Who is?"

"Lucia. Isn't that who—I mean, I thought . . ." Felicity let the sentence hang in the air, half finished.

Jonathan burst out laughing. "*Lucia?* Wow, *no*. Where'd you get that idea? Lucia's my best friend. She used to live across the street from me until her mom got a research grant to go to Italy. I would never— It's not like that at all."

"Oh." Felicity thought back on that day in the art studio, when he had looked so tenderly at his portrait of Lucia, as if he missed her more than anything. But of course you'd feel that way about your best friend. Jonathan had said nothing to imply that he liked her in any other way. Felicity had fabricated their entire romance. The realization sent a curious sensation through her, as if her heart were levitating.

"But then, who—" she started.

Jonathan shook his head and smiled. "Don't worry about it. So, the pageant's really soon, right? You must be excited."

Felicity reflexively plastered on her "I love competing" smile, but as she opened her mouth to give her usual cheerful answer, she realized she didn't have to lie right now. Jonathan had opened up to her about personal things, and he deserved the same level of forthrightness. She let the fake smile fade. "Honestly? Not really."

"How come? A lot of people think you're going to win. Jacob Sinclair from my math class set up this website where you can place bets on the contestants, and I heard that after Madison, the most money is on you."

Felicity stabbed at her shake with her straw. "Oh great. Now I feel like a racehorse."

"But at least you're a winning racehorse, right?"

"I guess." She shrugged. "Pageants just aren't my thing. When I'm up there competing, it just doesn't . . . it doesn't feel like *me*, you know? It's all just acting."

Jonathan nodded encouragingly, and she relaxed a little. Now that she had finally found a safe place to express herself, her words came spilling out like water from a broken dam. She told Jonathan about how her mom was obsessed with the pageant and had been pressuring her to win since preschool. She told him about the vomit-inducing Ella-Mae Finch song. She told him she had never really cared about competing and wished she could escape the life her mom had planned for her. Saying it all out loud for the first time made her feel like a helium balloon whose string had been cut, soaring dizzyingly upward.

"I totally get it," Jonathan said when she was finished. "You want your own life, not a rerun of hers. But she can't *make* you do the pageant. Why don't you just quit?"

"I can't. She'd never forgive me. Plus, there's a huge prize if you win, and I could really use the money."

Jonathan regarded her carefully as he chewed, his head cocked slightly to the side. "Hey, I don't know anything about pageants or anything, so feel free to ignore me. But what would happen if you just, you know, competed like yourself? If you didn't pretend to be someone else, or suck up to the judges, or use that horrible music? Could you just . . . act like you?"

Felicity shook her head. "That's not really how it works. The pageant's not about who you are, it's about how well you can play the game. I just have to suck it up and deal. It'll all be over in a week."

"Well, you know better than I do. I just think — I mean, you're an original person. You drive a bright green car with peace signs on it, and you make the most amazing art, and you don't always do what people expect you to do. Otherwise you'd be at prom, not here. It's just —" He shrugged. "I think you'd probably do really well either way."

"Thanks," Felicity said. Somehow, hearing him say that meant more to her than all the times her mom had told her that her routine looked perfect, all the times

206

Brent had told her she was hot. An unexpected lump rose in her throat, and she swallowed hard. "Hey, don't tell anyone what I said, okay? It's better if people think I'm excited about competing."

"What, you don't want me to write a feature story for journalism about your secret pageant aversion?" Jonathan smiled and offered her the last waffle fry. "I can see the headline now: 'Tiaras Hold No Sparkle For Beauty Pageant Hopeful.'"

Felicity giggled. "I didn't know you took journalism."

"Yeah, it's pretty fun."

"Is Gabby in your class?"

Jonathan rolled his eyes. "Yeah, but she's been totally slacking lately. She was supposed to be my partner for this project a few weeks ago, and then she bailed on me at the last second, so I had to do the whole thing myself. I heard she's working on some huge exposé for this internship application for the *Chicago Tribune*, and Mr. Armstrong likes her 'cause she writes for the paper, so he lets her do whatever she wants. She just sits there in the corner with her headphones on and works on it every day during class."

"An exposé? What kind of exposé?"

"I don't know, she won't tell anyone. It's some big secret thing. She says it's a case study, and if anyone knows what she's doing, it'll skew the results or something."

Jonathan kept talking, but Felicity wasn't paying attention anymore. A finger of cold was creeping down her spine. *A secret case study*. She had no idea what Gabby was writing or what she was trying to prove, but Felicity knew one thing beyond a doubt.

She was the case study.

She had spent so much time trying to figure out what Gabby had against her, what she had done to deserve the kind of treatment she was getting. But it wasn't personal. There was no grudge, no jealousy, no malice. Felicity was just a convenient lab rat, running through the maze Gabby had built for her. Gabby was ruining her life, hurting her friends, stealing her boyfriend, controlling her like a puppet, all for the sake of a stupid *internship application*.

Felicity felt something snap inside her, and her hands balled into fists under the table. Screw her mom's instructions about finding a way to make the blackmail work for her. She was done being compliant and letting her enemy destroy her world for no good reason.

It was time to take Gabby down.

As the ponytailed artie squeezed by their table on her way out the door, a plan came to Felicity all at once, fully formed and beautiful. The mayor had been trying for years to find Rouge-o-Rama and close its doors for good. And now that Felicity knew there were other places she could get her hair colored, it no longer mattered to her whether the salon's location remained a secret. If she had to drive to Caldner every few weeks, so be it. It would be a tiny price to pay if she got to see Mayor Redding run the Vaughns out of town. Plus, exposing the salon would destroy Gabby's credibility with everyone in Scarletville. Once the whole town knew the enormity of the secrets she'd been keeping, any rumor she spread about Felicity would just look like a desperate attempt at retaliation.

All Felicity needed was an audience with the mayor. So it was a good thing she'd see him at the pageant just one short week from today.

"Felicity? Everything okay?" Jonathan's voice seemed to be coming from miles away.

She took a deep breath and pulled herself back to reality. "Yeah," she said. "I'm great. Just . . . sad that the fries are gone."

"We can get more. Want to? You haven't tried the curly fries with curry ketchup yet."

Felicity's phone beeped, and she dug it out of her bag.

HAYLIE: WHERE ARE U? ivy & i are worried.
FELICITY: not coming back. i'm fine, don't worry.
have fun. talk to you tomorrow.
HAYLIE: WHERE DID U GO??? UR NOT COMING TO THE
PARTY???

"Are you sure everything's okay?" asked Jonathan.

Felicity turned off her phone and dropped it into her bag. "Everything's perfect," she said. "Curly fries sound amazing. It's on me this time."

Hours later, Felicity and Jonathan were deep in a heated discussion about whether painting a canvas one color constituted "making art" when they noticed that the staff of Fry Me to the Moon was wiping down tables and stacking chairs. The colored lightbulbs above their heads started winking out in sections. "Sorry, guys, we're closing," April called as she scrubbed the counter. "You're going to have to take your debate somewhere else."

It didn't seem possible that they'd been talking for four hours, but a chicken-shaped clock on the wall confirmed that it was one in the morning. Felicity stood up to put Jonathan's tux jacket back on, then groaned at the way her fry-filled stomach strained against her dress. "It's officially your fault if I'm too fat to fit in my pageant gown next week," she said.

"Don't even try to pretend it wasn't worth it." Jonathan held the door for her, gently touching the small of her back as he ushered her through. His hand lingered for just a moment longer than necessary, and Felicity found she didn't mind at all.

As she settled into the truck, she realized how exhausted she was from the stress of the day. She leaned her head against the window and closed her eyes as Jonathan drove back toward the highway. What seemed like moments later, he touched her shoulder, and she was shocked to see that they'd already reached the Scarletville town limits. "Am I taking you home, or is there a party you want to go to?" he asked.

Felicity didn't want her evening with Jonathan to end, but she couldn't very well show up at Haylie's party with him. "My car's in front of Mamma Leoni's," she said. "Can you just drop me off there?"

"Sure. Will you be okay driving, though? You seem really tired."

"I'll be fine, *Mom*," she teased. "My house is like four minutes away."

They reached Mamma Leoni's too quickly; Felicity wouldn't have minded another few hours of driving through the dark with him. "This is perfect," she said as Jonathan pulled up behind her car. "Thanks for the ride, and for taking me out."

"My pleasure. It was really fun." He tapped the stereo. "I'll bring you a CD on Monday."

"Awesome. I really love that cookie-cutter-girl song."

"That's my favorite, too." Jonathan put the truck in park, then turned to face her. His eyes reflected the streetlights, and they looked soft and vulnerable without the protective shield of his glasses. "Hey, Felicity?" he said. "I'm sorry your prom night didn't turn out like you wanted."

"Are you kidding? Nobody at prom got fries or milk shakes or one of these." Felicity pulled her windup hamburger out of her purse, and it feebly kicked its little plastic feet. "I had a great time. Seriously. I hope I was able to salvage your night a little bit, too."

Jonathan smiled. "Actually, my prom night was pretty much perfect."

For a minute, it looked like he might lean over and kiss her.

For a minute, somewhere deep down, Felicity hoped he would.

But he didn't. Instead, he reached out, took her

hand, and squeezed it gently. His palms were warm and dry and a little calloused, his fingers long and delicate. Somehow, holding hands with him seemed much more intimate than doing the same thing with Brent. "Good night, Felicity," he said quietly. "Sweet dreams."

She squeezed his hand in return, surprised by her reluctance to let go. "You too."

She didn't realize she still had Jonathan's jacket around her shoulders until she got home. Her mom and brothers were sleeping, so Felicity kicked off her heels just inside the door and tiptoed upstairs to her bedroom. She hung the jacket on the back of her desk chair, unzipped her dress, and left it on the floor where it fell. She didn't even bother to remove her makeup before she crawled into bed in her lobster-print pajamas.

Bits of the evening whirled through her mind when she closed her eyes: Jonathan laughing at a joke she'd made; Jonathan's eyes lighting up as he talked about art school; Jonathan driving through the night with that adorable half smile on his face; Jonathan squeezing her hand. Things he'd said played over and over, fitting themselves together like puzzle pieces.

"The girl I really wanted to ask was indisposed."

"Lucia's my best friend. It's not like that at all."

"Actually, my prom night was pretty much perfect."

She reached out and took hold of the cuff of his jacket, rubbing the fabric between her fingers. She was still holding on to it when she fell asleep.

14

Felicity slept until one in the afternoon. When she finally woke up, the house was silent, and she found a note on the kitchen counter explaining that her mom was out buying new sneakers for the twins. She was shuffling back up to her room with a bowl of cereal when her phone beeped.

BRENT: hey sexy u home? can I come up?

Felicity's heart did a strange little stutter that was half relief and half disappointment. The text indicated that Brent wasn't mad at her for the whole Gabby fiasco, which was reassuring. But he would probably expect her to make it all up to him now, and she was way too sleepy and confused to be in the mood. Last night had given her a lot to sort through; she had even thought about kissing someone else. But she couldn't tell Brent to go away when he had just sacrificed so much for her. So she told him everyone was out and that he should come around to the front door.

He rang the bell a minute later, and Felicity abandoned her cereal and let him in. She was about to apologize for her pajamas and messy hair, but Brent swept her up in his arms before she even had time to say hello. His embrace was warm and strong and familiar, and she relaxed into it. It suddenly seemed ridiculous that she had been having fluttery feelings for Jonathan when her body clearly craved no one but Brent. He pressed her up against the wall and kissed her hard, and all thoughts of last night melted away.

"Let's go to your room," he whispered against her neck, then took her by the hand and led her up the stairs.

As Felicity followed him, she realized this was the first time she and Brent had ever been alone in an empty house. She was surprised by how nervous she was all of a sudden. *I want this,* she told herself. *It's okay. I've wanted this for a while. Everything's going to be fine.*

The moment Brent entered her room, he froze, and Felicity crashed into his broad back. "What are you doing?" she giggled, her voice high and anxious. "Come on, let's go in." She pushed past him and reached out to pull him toward the bed, but she stopped when she saw his face, which had suddenly gone cold. "What's wrong, babe?" she asked.

"What is *that*?" Felicity had never heard Brent use

that tone before. There was hurt and confusion in it, but it was laced with a quiet anger that made the tiny hairs on the back of her neck stand up.

"What's what? What are you talking about?" She looked around, but nothing in the room seemed out of place.

"*That.*" Brent pointed accusingly at her desk chair. Jonathan's tux jacket was still hanging on the back. Oh *no*.

"It's a jacket," she said carefully.

"Yeah, I know that, Felicity. *Whose* jacket is it?"

She swallowed hard and reminded herself that she hadn't done anything wrong. She had eaten some fries with a friend. They had talked. He had driven her to her car. They hadn't even hugged. It had all been totally innocent.

"It's Jonathan's," she said.

"The guy who was hitting on you at the art show?" Brent's hands balled into fists at his sides. Felicity didn't think he would hurt her, but she had to fight the impulse to step out of his reach.

"He wasn't hitting on me. We were just having a conversation. Last night I went outside for some air, and I ran into him, and I was cold, so he gave me his jacket, and I forgot to give it back. It's just a jacket. It doesn't mean anything."

"I thought you'd gone to Haylie's when you disappeared last night," Brent said, as if he hadn't heard her. "But you didn't, did you? You came *here*, with *him*." It wasn't a question.

"I didn't, Brent! He's never been here. I just wanted to get away because everyone was staring at me. So Jonathan gave me a ride to my car, and I came home. By myself. That's it, that's the whole story. Okay?"

"He gave you a ride to your *car*? That doesn't even make sense. You couldn't walk to the parking lot?"

"It wasn't in the parking lot. It was in front of Mamma Leoni's. Ivy drove me from the restaurant to school. I was going to pick up my car today, after Haylie's party, but I didn't end up going to the party, so Jonathan gave me a ride." She reached out to touch Brent's shoulder. "Honestly. That's all that happened."

Brent jerked out of her reach and looked at her with eyes full of ice. "You seriously expect me to believe that? Why wouldn't you drive you own car to prom? That's the lamest excuse I've ever heard."

Felicity nearly laughed—she'd told so many lies lately, and Brent was fixated on the one part of her story that was totally true. "I swear to God I'm not making it up. Ask Ivy or Haylie."

"Oh yeah. Because I'll definitely get the truth out of your best friends." He rolled his eyes. "I'm not stupid, Felicity. I know you were lying to me all along. That whole 'prom committee hazing ritual' thing is complete crap. You made me take Gabby to prom so I'd look like a douche and you could run off with your other boyfriend."

"Brent, *no*. It's not like that at all!" She tried again to touch his arm, but he just backed away as if she had some contagious disease.

"I was trying to help you! Do you think I wanted to

216

go on a date with Gabby? And now I find out you've been cheating on me. How do you expect me to react to that?"

Righteous indignation rushed through Felicity. "I have *never* cheated on you," she said, her voice more forceful than before. "I would never do that. Don't you trust me at all?"

"Why would I trust you after this? Seriously, Felicity, do you think you're the only one in this relationship who's had other offers? Because I could have had anyone I wanted, any time. But I didn't, because all I wanted was you. I actually *cared* about you. But I guess that wasn't enough, since you ran off with some *brunette* behind my back."

Felicity gaped at the boy standing across from her. She knew every line of his body as well as she knew her own, but he suddenly seemed like a stranger. She and Brent had been together for more than a year, and he still didn't know her at all. Jonathan understood her better after four hours of conversation than Brent did after fifteen months.

She didn't love him. Right now, she didn't even *like* him. Brent was a safety net and an insurance policy, and she didn't need those things anymore. She could take care of herself.

"You know what, Brent?" she said. "It's over."

"What, you and him? You think that makes it okay that you — "

"No, not me and him. There is no me and him. I'm talking about me and you."

Brent stood perfectly still for a moment, looking so surprised that Felicity wondered if she'd made a mistake. But then the hardness returned to his eyes and he said, "Whatever, Felicity. I can do better."

He shoved past her and pounded down the stairs. Just as he reached the bottom, Felicity heard the front door open. "Oh, hi, honey," said her mom's voice.

"Good to see you, Mrs. S," Brent called before slamming the door behind him. Even after calling her a cheater, he still turned on the charm for her mother.

Ginger's quick footsteps clicked up the stairs. "We're back," she called. "Can't Brent stay and have lunch with us? I thought we could—" Then she stuck her head in the doorway and saw Felicity's murderous expression, and her cheerful words died on her lips. "Baby, what happened?"

"We broke up." Felicity wondered if she would fall apart as soon as she said the words out loud, but she didn't. Underneath her anger about the false accusations, she felt curiously calm about the whole thing.

She no longer had a boyfriend. And she didn't even care that much.

"Oh God, did he find out about your hair? Did Gabby tell him?"

"*No*, Mom. This isn't about my hair. Not everything is about my hair."

Ginger's face relaxed, and she reached out to embrace Felicity. "Oh, sweet thing, I'm so sorry you broke up. Do you want to tell me what happened? Do you think you might get back together?"

Felicity shook her head and tried to ignore the desperate hope in her mom's voice. "It's definitely over. He accused me of cheating."

"But you didn't really cheat, did you?"

"*No!* God, Mom! Of *course* not!" She squirmed out of her mother's grasp.

"I'm sorry, baby. I know you'd never do that. I'm just trying to get the facts straight."

Felicity was about to answer when her phone rang and Haylie's picture appeared on the screen. "I'm going to take this, okay? I'm fine, Mom, seriously."

"We'll talk about it when you get off the phone." Ginger backed out of the room slowly, clearly unable to process the fact that Felicity wasn't melting into a puddle of anguish. "I'll be right downstairs whenever you need me."

Felicity answered the phone, and it was a relief to hear Haylie's voice. "Hey, are you okay? Where have you been? I called your phone a bunch of times last night, but it just went straight to voice mail."

"Yeah, sorry. My phone's been acting weird." To deflect attention from her prom night activities, she said, "I just broke up with Brent. He accused me of cheating."

"What? *He* accused *you* of cheating after *he* took someone else to prom? God, what a loser! Hang on, Ivy wants to say something. I'm putting her on speaker."

There was a beeping sound, and then Ivy announced, "Brent's a douche canoe. I'll punch him in the teeth for you, if you want."

"I can't believe he called you a cheater," Haylie said.

"Seriously, does he think anybody's going to believe that? You're, like, the most honest person ever."

A bolt of guilt shot through Felicity. "I don't really want to talk about it. There's nothing to say anyway. It's just over, and it sucks. Tell me about the rest of prom. How was the party?"

"It was great, but we really missed you," Haylie said. "Well, I did, anyway. Ivy wasn't really aware of anything except Darren's tongue down her throat."

"You hooked up with Darren?" Felicity said. "That's awesome, Ives! He's liked you forever!"

"His tongue was not down my throat," Ivy protested. "And can we please discuss the fact that Haylie's delightful date found a butternut squash in the pantry and made a *bong* out of it?"

"He's really not that bad," Haylie said. "He's just creative."

"He's the poster child for why people shouldn't have babies," Ivy said, and Felicity let out a genuine laugh for the first time all day. A surge of love for her friends welled up in her.

"I'm sorry I wasn't there last night, guys," she said. "Everyone was staring at me and making me feel like a freak, and I couldn't handle it. I just had to get out of there."

"It's fine," Ivy said. "Seriously, don't worry about it. You did what you had to do. You should never have to be miserable if there's another option."

Felicity eyed Jonathan's jacket hanging on the back

220

of her chair. Last night she'd taken the other option, and it had only gotten her into trouble.

But then she remembered what Jonathan had said as they'd left the restaurant: *Don't even try to pretend it wasn't worth it.*

And even now, it was. Every single moment.

Part Three

It takes a red-headed woman to get a dirty job done.
—Bruce Springsteen, "Red-Headed Woman"

15

The first Miss Scarlet rehearsal was scheduled for Monday afternoon, and Felicity drove to school that morning in a car full of garment bags. All her outfits needed to be approved by the pageant committee before she wore them onstage on Saturday. Her shoes, her accessories, and a CD of "Red Is the Color of My Heart" were neatly packed in her duffel bag, which sat in the trunk next to Jonathan's tux jacket. Lugging all her pageant gear around made the competition seem real, and it also awakened Felicity's anxiety. For the first time, the daunting task before her seemed frightening rather than just distasteful. All her mom's hopes and dreams were riding on her success, and for a completely different reason, so were hers.

Jonathan was waiting by her locker when she

arrived at Scarletville High, wearing his school uniform of dorky glasses and a paint-spattered T-shirt and holding a CD in a plastic sleeve. "Is that for me?" Felicity called brightly.

He looked up and gave her a bashful smile. "Hey. Yeah. Here you go." There was a piece of notebook paper sticking out of the top, but when Felicity tried to pull it out, Jonathan stopped her. "Um, that's just the track list. Let me know what you think of the rest of the album?"

"Of course. Thanks so much. Oh, hey, I just remembered." She lowered her voice and glanced around to make sure nobody was listening. "I still have your tux jacket in my car. Sorry I forgot to give it back to you after . . . the other day."

"It's fine, don't worry about it. But I have to return it, so if you could leave it for me in the art room or something, that would be awesome." Jonathan's eyes darted around, as if he were casing the joint for a robbery. He seemed even more jittery than usual today. "I've gotta go, okay?"

"Sure." Felicity wanted to say all kinds of things about how much fun she'd had on Saturday night, but she just held up the CD and said, "I can't wait to listen to this."

As soon as Jonathan was gone, she pulled the notebook paper out of the plastic sleeve and unfolded it, eager to see the song titles. But it wasn't a track list at all. Written in Jonathan's neat, blocky print, the paper said:

Felicity,

Here's the Sharks in Heaven album I promised.
Hope you like it.

Thanks for making my prom night into something
I actually want to remember.

You are definitely not a cookie-cutter girl.

—Jonathan

Felicity's whole body felt warm as she folded the note into a tight square and tucked it into the front pocket of her jeans. All through the school day and the interminable pageant rehearsal, she was conscious of it nestled close to her hip. Just knowing it was there as she paraded around the stage in endless loops, practicing her pivot turns, poses, and walks, made her feel stronger and calmer. Over and over, her mom shouted, "Chins up! Shoulders back! Tummies tucked! Backs straight!" in an attempt to make her twelve pageant girls look uniform. It helped to know that someone out there appreciated her for being unique.

By the time Ginger reminded the girls to sign up for their sound check slots on Thursday and released them for the evening, Felicity's face hurt from smiling and her feet ached from her stiff new heels. She clutched Jonathan's note like a talisman as she hobbled backstage to collect her things from the dressing room. Ivy collapsed into a chair and winced as she peeled off a silver shoe and exposed several angry red blisters. "*Ow.* Haylie, you *seriously* owe me for this."

Haylie gave her a starry-eyed smile. "You'll be so glad you did it, Ives. I promise. The pageant's such a great experience."

Ivy waved her blistered foot in her friend's face. "See this? This is not a great experience. I never agreed to *bleed* for this stupid competition. I'm wearing flats from now on."

"You can't wear flats in a pageant! That's just . . . not how it works!"

"Haylie, I will go through with this ridiculous charade for you, but I will not suffer any more physical pain for it. You managed to trick me into this, but if you want me to stay in, you have to let me do it my way." Ivy dropped the silver heels into her backpack. "These are going back to the store tomorrow."

Haylie yanked off her own shoes. "Felicity, tell her she has to play by the same rules as the rest of us."

Felicity watched a fierce and determined Ivy lace up her green Converse sneakers, and she knew Haylie would never win this fight. Ivy never let anyone manipulate her or tell her what to do, and she never tried to hide who she was. Felicity admired and envied those qualities, especially because she knew she'd never have that kind of freedom. "Let her do what she wants, Hays," she said. "She's making a sacrifice just by being here."

"*Thank you,* Felicity." Ivy stood up and grabbed her bag. "You guys ready to go?"

"You can go ahead," Felicity said. "I need to ask my

mom if she wants me to pick up the twins. I'll see you guys tomorrow."

Haylie shot her a glare and headed toward the parking lot, Ivy close behind her. Felicity hoped they'd make it to their cars without throwing any punches.

She made her way back to the stage, where she expected to find her mom giving instructions to the pageant volunteers. But instead she found her chatting with Gabby, who was inspecting a box of metallic gold envelopes. It was the first time Felicity had seen Gabby since she'd learned about the exposé, and a pulse of fury ran through her. *It'll all be over in less than a week,* she reminded herself. *Once you expose the salon to the mayor, she won't be able to touch you.*

"See, the judges have already written the girls' interview questions, and they've numbered them one through twelve," Ginger was explaining. "The girls drew numbers tonight to determine their order, so that ensures that the questions are assigned randomly." She looked up and noticed Felicity. "Oh, hi, baby. I was wondering if you were still here. Gabby's interviewing me for the *Crimson Courier.*"

Felicity was certain Gabby had more sinister motives for lurking around the pageant rehearsal, but she just swallowed hard and said, "I see that."

"These envelopes are so great," Gabby said. "Where did you get them? I need some just like this for a project we're doing for the newspaper."

"Crafty Cathy's, right by the post office."

Gabby riffled through the envelopes. "What number are you, Felicity?"

Providing Gabby with personal information seemed like a terrible idea—the pageant was still five days away, and until then Felicity knew she wasn't safe. But her mom was giving her a look that begged her not to antagonize Gabby. "I'm number four," she said.

Gabby flipped the page of her notebook and made one final note before giving Ginger a big smile. "I think we're done here, Mrs. St. John. Thanks so much for talking to me. I'll be back to cover the pageant on Saturday."

"Perfect," Ginger said. "Baby, I'm going to pick up the twins, and then I think we need to work on your pivot turns. They weren't quite as sharp as I'd like them to be."

But Felicity wasn't listening to her mother. Scrawled across the page of Gabby's notebook, which was now casually angled in her direction, were the words

I have another job for you. Get ready.

Now that Felicity had ammunition, she knew she could hold her own in a fight against Gabby. If necessary, she could probably even find a way to expose the salon to the mayor before the pageant. Every time she walked into school, she steeled herself as if she were walking into the trenches, her nerves strung taut as a tightrope.

But for three days, nothing happened.

Gabby clearly knew that Felicity feared uncertainty, and she used that to her advantage. As she waited for her enemy's summons, Felicity existed in a constant state of fight-or-flight. Everything sent her into a startled panic: her brother knocking over his milk at dinner, a classmate using a staple gun in the art studio, excited cheerleaders shrieking in the hall. Every day, she lived for the moment when she could get into bed with her iPod, let her guard down for a few hours, and let Sharks in Heaven sing her to sleep.

Felicity still hadn't heard from Gabby by the time she visited Rouge-o-Rama on Thursday. To Rose, this appointment was the same as any other, and she chattered away about how excited she was about the pageant. But Felicity knew this might be her last time at the salon, and a deep sense of nostalgia and sadness began to eat away at her steely resolve. For her whole life, this room had been her sanctuary, the one place where she didn't have to pretend to be something she wasn't. Rose's flawless work had secured her popularity and kept her from being ridiculed at school. It had ensured that she wasn't a disappointment to her mother. In a way, Felicity had Rose to thank for everything she'd become. Could she really repay her stylist by betraying her and bringing her whole world crashing down?

But Rose would be fine. She was an intelligent, capable adult who could easily start over somewhere else. People moved all the time. Everyone needed stylists, and outside of Scarletville, Rose wouldn't have to keep her skills with dye a secret. Felicity told herself that by keeping herself safe, she might actually be doing the Vaughns a favor.

Her appointment sped by in a haze of distraction, and before Felicity knew it, her hair was dry and perfumed. Rose walked her to the door and gave her a big hug and a kiss on each cheek. "I'd say good luck, but I know you don't need it," she said. "You'll be just beautiful up there. I'm so proud of you."

The warmth in Rose's eyes ignited Felicity's guilt, and she suddenly felt as if a small animal were trying to chew its way out of her gut. "Thanks," she choked. "And thanks for . . . you know, everything." She held up a lock of coppery hair.

"Of course," Rose said. "But there's so much more to you than that."

She ushered Felicity into the down elevator with a smile and closed the salon door. Despite Felicity's best efforts, a few renegade tears slipped down her cheeks as she rode the juddering elevator to the second floor.

She arrived at City Hall half an hour before her sound check slot, so she headed for one of the stone benches that flanked the front door. She cued up "Cookie-Cutter Girl" on her iPod as she walked, eager to feel those strong opening chords crash through her body and chase away some of her guilt and sadness. And that was why it took her a minute to notice Gabby, who was basking in the sun on the next bench over.

Felicity cursed under her breath. For a minute, it seemed like Gabby might be asleep, and she wondered if she could sneak away unnoticed. But then her enemy sat up, stretched like a cat, and smiled. "Felicity," she said lazily. "What a nice surprise. Come on, let's go inside and have a little chat."

As she followed Gabby into City Hall, Felicity reached into her pocket and wrapped her fingers around Jonathan's note for comfort—she'd been carrying it with her as a lucky charm since Monday. *You can do this*, she told herself. *You have just as much power as Gabby does*. But her heart obviously didn't get the message, because it refused to slow down.

Gabby led her up a flight of stairs and down a long, echoing hallway, then ushered her into a room near the end. When she turned on the single bare bulb hanging from the ceiling, Felicity saw that they were in the Scarletville Community Players' props closet. The shelves were piled high with random items that appeared to be completely unsorted: a stack of shields, a lace parasol, a basket full of Mardi Gras beads, a plastic ham. Three taxidermy deer heads gazed down at her from a high shelf with their creepy glass eyes. The closet was tiny, forcing Felicity and Gabby to stand uncomfortably close together, and the overly warm air was filled with dust. Felicity sneezed several times in rapid succession.

Gabby dug through her bag, then presented Felicity with a gold envelope marked with the number four and a folded sheet of white paper. "This is your new interview question for the pageant, and this is the answer you're going to give," Gabby said. "Make sure you memorize it by Saturday."

Felicity stared at the envelope. "My . . . what? But . . . my mom already has the questions. What am I supposed to do with this?"

Gabby rolled her eyes. "Seriously, it's like I have to spell everything out for you. You're going to go into your mom's office and swap them, genius."

"You want me to tamper with pageant materials? I could get disqualified!"

"Only if you get caught. And you won't get caught, will you?"

Felicity unfolded the white paper. It read:

> As a redhead, I certainly understand the founder of Scarletville's original mission. That being said, I think it's incredibly important to have people with other hair colors in Scarletville. It's small-minded and irresponsible to have a community that's entirely made up of one sort of person. That kind of environment fosters intolerance and stereotyping. And there's actually still a lot of that here in Scarletville, even though we're not all the same. The way redheads are automatically placed at the top of the social hierarchy whether or not they deserve it is incredibly unfair. Many blondes and brunettes would probably excel in leadership roles in our community, but people just assume they're not worthy and don't even give them a chance. I mean, look at the girls in the pageant this year. There are at least twenty blondes and brunettes in our class, but none of them are up here today. The pageant committee is clearly biased toward redheads,

*and that's just one example of the prejudiced behavior of
our community's leaders. It's not right or fair. I think
we all need to examine the way we treat people with
other hair colors and make an effort to change.*

Felicity gave Gabby an incredulous look. "You seriously think I'm going to stand up in front of the entire
town and accuse my own mom *and my mom's boss* of being prejudiced?"

Gabby shrugged. "Well, that's your call. But you
know what the alternative is."

The wave of fury that crashed through Felicity was
so strong it nearly knocked her over, and words burst
from her mouth before she could control herself. "What
is *wrong* with you? Do you seriously not see what you're
doing to me? This is not some fun little case study,
Gabby—this is my *life*. This is my *family*. I am not your
freaking experiment!"

Gabby's face registered genuine surprise. "Who told
you there was an experiment?"

"I heard you've been blowing off all your work in
journalism to write up some secret case study for a stupid internship application. Can't you see how messed
up it is to destroy someone's life for research? I'm a *person*, Gabby, and I never even did anything to you!"

"Keep your voice down," Gabby hissed. "Do you
want everyone to know we're in here? And for your
information, you are *not* the case study. You don't know
anything about what I'm doing."

"You are such a liar. I bet you love playing these

sadistic little mind games. I bet you enjoy every second of—"

"*I'm* the case study," Gabby snapped. "Not you, you self-centered baby."

Felicity stared at her. "How are *you* the case study? That doesn't even make sense. I'm the one being tortured and blackmailed!"

"I don't have to discuss this with you." Gabby turned to grab the doorknob, but Felicity was faster and managed to block her way. She stared her enemy right in the eyes, and for the first time, she saw something other than sarcasm and contempt.

Gabby was uncertain. And Felicity suddenly understood something: Gabby needed her. For whatever reason, she needed her to say the words on this paper on Saturday. And that meant Felicity had more control than she'd thought.

"I won't swap the questions unless you explain to me what you're doing," she said.

Gabby snorted, but Felicity could tell her bravado was faltering. "You're totally bluffing. You'll do whatever I want you to do, because you know I'll expose you if you don't."

Felicity shook her head. "You don't know me at all. You have no idea what I'll do."

They stared each other down for what felt like an eternity. It was so hot and musty in the closet that it was hard to breathe, and Felicity feared she might faint. But she stood her ground, the doorknob gripped tightly in her sweaty hand.

And finally, Gabby looked away first.

"I'm writing an exposé about Scarletville High for an internship at the *Chicago Tribune*," she said quietly. "It's supposed to showcase my investigative journalism skills. It's about how people react when a brunette gets the kind of publicity and attention that's usually reserved for popular redheads like you. All the stuff I've had you do made me visible in ways I could never have been on my own. And then I listened to the gossip, and I learned what people considered 'acceptable' for someone of my 'status.'"

"What about this?" Felicity held up the interview question. "This isn't making you visible. This has nothing to do with you. Now you're just trying to humiliate me."

"Why can't you get it through your thick head that this isn't about you? That has *everything* to do with me. It says I have a right to be given a *chance* in this ridiculous town. Someone needs to say it out loud, and nobody ever does. You know as well as I do that nobody in Scarletville gets treated with respect unless they have red hair. If you didn't know that, you wouldn't be so terrified of someone finding out what you really are."

Felicity shoved the paper back at Gabby. "If you want someone to say this out loud, why don't you say it yourself? Leave me out of your stupid crusade!"

"Nobody *cares* if I say it, Felicity! It's always 'Oh, look at the bitter brunette, she's just pissed she's not popular.' People automatically listen to you. You can do whatever the hell you want, and there are never any consequences. God, you have *no idea* what it feels like to grow up in a place where nobody takes you seriously."

"If you hate it here so much, why don't you just leave?" Felicity shouted, forgetting to keep her voice down. "Go to boarding school or something. Nobody's forcing you to live here! Nobody *wants* you to live here!"

"You think my mom has the money to send me to boarding school? I have three little sisters, and my dad's been unemployed for two years! If we could afford boarding school, trust me, I'd be out of here in a hot second. But at this point, the internship at the *Tribune* is my fastest ticket out of this hellhole. So if I have to take you down to get it, Felicity, I will take you down. You're just another shallow redheaded clone, and there are plenty more to take your place when you fall."

Felicity was afraid she would start clawing at Gabby's eyes if she spent one more second with her in that oppressively stuffy closet. So she pushed her way out and stumbled down the hall to the stairs, gulping deep breaths of dust-free air. She dashed into the bathroom and was horrified by her red-faced, wild-eyed, sweaty reflection in the mirror. She looked like a hunted animal. No one should be allowed to debase her like this. She was finished being ordered around, being forced to scrabble and scrape and make a fool of herself. She was done lying to her loyal friends and hurting the people she loved. Enough was enough.

On Saturday, up on that stage, she would finally take back all the power Gabby had stolen from her. She wouldn't wait until after the pageant to approach the mayor and tell him where Rouge-o-Rama was located. Instead of saying the words Gabby had scripted for her, she would march up to that microphone during the interview portion and expose the salon in front of the entire town. Gabby would be finished, and Scarletville would never know Felicity had been living a lie.

It was time for her sound check, but Felicity couldn't let her mom see her like this. She splashed cold water on her face and patted herself dry with paper towels. After a whirlwind few minutes with powder, mascara, and lip gloss, she looked more like the pageant girl Ginger expected her to be. She heard her mom's voice in her head: *It's the face you present to the world that matters, not how you feel inside.*

She forced a smile and went down to the auditorium.

Lorelei was just finishing her sound check, belting out the final lines of a sappy power ballad Felicity didn't recognize. Ginger hurried over and kissed Felicity's damp cheek. "We'll be ready for you in a minute," she said, failing to notice that her daughter was on the verge of exploding into a million pieces.

While Felicity laced up her tap shoes, a sullen, pumpkin-haired boy checked the floor mikes, then plodded back up to the sound booth at a glacial pace. "Ready for your music?" he finally called.

There was nothing in the world that Felicity wanted to hear less than "Red Is the Color of My Heart," but there was no getting around it. She took a deep breath. "I'm ready."

The cheesy trumpet riff began, and Felicity gritted

her teeth to keep from screaming. *If I hear this song one more time, I am going to lose it,* she thought. She danced through the routine, trying to keep a smile on her face, but she could tell there was no life or joy in her performance. Although she executed the choreography perfectly, her mom's face was lined with worry when the song ended. "Baby, you know you need to dance with much more energy than that," she said.

Felicity nearly snapped at her mom just like she'd snapped at Gabby, but she caught herself in time and counted to five inside her head. When she felt calm enough to speak, she said, "I know, I'm just tired. I'll do better at the dress rehearsal tomorrow."

"We need to get the sound levels right today. If you're tapping harder tomorrow, it's going to sound all wrong. I need you to be consistent and dance this routine the same way every time, Felicity. Matty, cue up the music again, please."

Felicity nearly burst into tears of frustration, but she struck her opening pose without complaint. She told herself that after her performance in forty-eight hours, she would never have to hear this song again. But Ella-Mae Finch's saccharine voice frayed her nerves, and forty-eight hours seemed like eons.

As soon as she was finished and Ginger announced her approval, Felicity grabbed her bag and fled the auditorium in her tap shoes, her purple flats forgotten by the edge of the stage. Her feet echoed sharply as she ran down the corridor of City Hall, out the front door, and across the lawn to the parking lot. Slumped in the front seat of her car, Felicity tore through her bag until she found her iPod. When she jammed in her earbuds and pressed play on "Cookie-Cutter Girl," the strength of the opening chords sent the memory of Ella-Mae's voice running for cover. The music felt like aloe on a blistering sunburn, and the relief of it finally made Felicity's tears spill over.

Despite her mom's claims that everything she did was for Felicity's own good, Ginger was no better than Gabby. She, too, had forced Felicity into a life of secrets and lies that Felicity hadn't chosen for herself. Ginger had carefully molded her daughter to serve her endgame—to climb the social ladder and better the family. And now the only way out was through. Winning this horrendous pageant was Felicity's only chance to turn her life around.

The worst part of it was that there was only one person who could actually relate to what she was experiencing. One more smart, ambitious girl who was trapped in a life she didn't want and who was desperate for a way out. One more girl who had spent years keeping secrets to protect her family. One more girl who didn't have the money to follow her dreams and would do whatever it took to get it, even if it meant tearing other innocent people down.

And that person was Gabby.

The song ended, and Felicity started it over a second time, then a third. She closed her eyes and breathed deeply, soaking in the music, the one thing that made her feel like she wasn't completely alone. And as she finally began to calm down, she realized she was idly moving her feet to the beat, tapping out her talent routine on the floor of the car. "Cookie-Cutter Girl" was faster than the Ella-Mae Finch song, but the rhythms of her feet fit surprisingly well with the Sharks in Heaven music.

Felicity's eyes snapped open, and her tears stopped as abruptly as they had begun. She was out of the car in a flash. She started the song a fourth time, then tapped through her routine right there on the asphalt, ignoring the government employees who stopped to watch her on the way to their cars. The Sharks in Heaven song was a little shorter than "Red Is the Color of My Heart," and the verses and choruses weren't arranged in the same way. But she knew she could alter the choreography until it fit. She could make it work.

Standing in the City Hall parking lot, her face still streaked with tears and mascara, Felicity made a decision. She knew she couldn't win this pageant and get her hands on the prize money unless she was proud of what she showed the judges. She was no cookie-cutter girl, easily manipulated and controlled. She remembered how Ivy had thrown her painful silver heels into her bag and announced that from now on, she was doing the pageant her way. If her friend could do it, so could she.

Ginger had managed to force her into this pageant. But now that Felicity was in, her performance would happen on her own terms. There would be no acting, no sucking up to the judges, no horrible music.

Just her.

16

That night, as soon as Felicity was sure her mom and brothers were asleep, she grabbed her iPod and her dance shoes, crept down to the basement, and went to work. Three hours and twenty-seven repetitions of "Cookie-Cutter Girl" later, she was exhausted and sweaty, but the routine felt pageant-ready. She tiptoed back up to her room, burned a CD of her new music, and labeled it RED IS THE COLOR OF MY HEART so her subversion wouldn't be discovered until it was too late.

It was three o'clock in the morning, but there was still work to do. Felicity dug Gabby's interview answer out of her bag and started altering it to include information about where the mayor could locate Rouge-o-Rama and its proprietor. She pictured the stricken look on Gabby's face when she realized she had finally lost,

243

and it gave Felicity a perverse kind of pleasure. At long last, she'd be back in control of her own life.

Just after four o'clock, she fell asleep with the lights on and dreamed of competing wearing a pageant gown made of brown human hair.

When she arrived at school the next morning, clutching her triple mocha as if it were a life raft, Felicity found her locker wrapped in red paper, strung with balloons, and painted with the words GOOD LUCK, FELICITY! There was a pile of gifts stacked on the floor: individual roses and carnations, an entire bouquet of pink lilies, two boxes of chocolates, and a stuffed penguin. It was disturbingly reminiscent of a makeshift shrine at the site of a fatal highway accident. Everyone who passed her locker wanted to hug or high-five her, and several people she barely knew asked to take pictures with her. Felicity was so tired that the whole experience seemed like a bizarre dream.

She was storing the offerings in her locker when Haylie dashed by on the way to her first class, an enormous stuffed tiger tucked under one arm and a rose behind her ear. Her cheeks were flushed with excitement. "Isn't today *amazing*?" she squealed.

"Amazing is a good word for it." Felicity poked at the tiger, which was wearing a rhinestone-studded collar. "Where did all this stuff even come from?"

"Admirers," Haylie said. "We have *admirers*, Felicity!"

Ivy joined them and snatched Felicity's coffee, which

was sitting untouched on the floor. She took several huge gulps, then announced, "Today is *ridiculous*."

"That's another good word for it." Felicity pried the coffee cup from Ivy's fingers. "C'mon, let go. I really need that today."

A group of swim team guys passed by and let out a string of catcalls. "There's our beauty queen!" they shouted. "Knock 'em dead, Locklear!"

"I'll knock your *face* dead," she called back. They hooted louder as they disappeared around the corner.

Haylie heaved an exasperated sigh. "Come on, Ivy, can't you at least try to enjoy the attention?"

Ivy grimaced. "I'm going to physics. See you at lunch, if I even survive until then."

The rest of the day was no different. The flock of identical giggling sophomores swarmed Felicity's lunch table and assaulted her and her friends with questions about their dresses. Another crowd surrounded Madison and Lorelei on the other side of the cafeteria, and a third grouped around Jacob Sinclair next to the vending machine. When Felicity saw Jacob accept a wad of cash from a tall senior, she remembered what Jonathan had said about his pageant-gambling website. Her stomach twisted as she wondered how many of those people were betting on her.

By the time Felicity arrived at City Hall for the pageant dress rehearsal, it was a relief to be away from her adoring fans. She collapsed in an auditorium seat beside Ivy, who had scrawled PLEASE LEAVE ME ALONE across her white T-shirt with a marker. On the other side of her, Haylie snuggled the plush tiger in her lap and compared notes with Cassie about the gifts they'd gotten. Felicity closed her eyes and tried to snatch a few moments of much-needed rest.

All too soon, her mom strode out onto the stage, dressed in a yellow sleeveless blouse and bright green capri pants that made her look like an ad for a lemon-lime sports drink. She beamed at the girls with a high-wattage smile that was almost painful to look at. "Good afternoon, ladies! I'm sure you've all had a very exciting day at school, and I hope you've been reveling in all the attention. You deserve to be treated like royalty, so enjoy every second of it! We're going to run the pageant in real time today, which means you'll do your full talent routines and all of your costume changes. The dressing room will be filled with pageant volunteers, so please take advantage of their help. And remember — heads high, shoulders back, tummies tucked, and *big, bright smiles*!"

Felicity cruised through her personal introduction, her swimsuit portion, her talent routine, and her mock interview question on autopilot. Before she knew it, her mom was giving them a final pep talk and releasing them for the night. Everyone headed for the door in twos and threes, bemoaning how they'd tripped on their trains, sung wrong notes, or looked like whales in their swimsuits. Their work for the day was done.

Felicity's was just beginning.

She followed Haylie and Ivy down the hall, half listening to Haylie talk about her pre-pageant diet and meditation ritual, but when they reached the front door, she stopped short and pretended to rummage through her bag. "Crap," she said. "I think I left my car keys in my mom's office."

"Want us to wait for you?" Ivy offered.

"No, it's fine, just go."

"Okay. I hope you find them." Haylie hugged her tightly. "Oh my God, I can't *wait* for tomorrow. I'm so, *so* glad we're all doing this together."

"Me too," Felicity said before Ivy could cut in with a snarky remark.

"Think positive thoughts before you go to sleep, and don't forget to eat breakfast!" Haylie called as she pushed the front door open.

Felicity went around to the side door of the auditorium, opened it a crack, and peeked inside. She couldn't see her mom from this angle, but she could hear her having a wrap-up meeting with Brenda and Celeste, both of whom had been on the pageant committee for a decade. Felicity wondered whether she had time to slip into her mom's office and swap the interview questions now, before the meeting ended. But that seemed too risky—she should probably hold off until her mom left to pick up the twins in a few minutes. She propped the door open a bit, sat down, and settled in to wait.

After fifteen minutes, the meeting still wasn't over, and she heard her mom say, "Shoot, I'm going to be so late to pick up the boys. Let me call Felicity and ask her to go get them, and then we can talk about the florist."

Felicity's phone started vibrating in her bag, and she jerked back from the door in a panic. Thank God she'd remembered to turn off her ringer before rehearsal. She dashed up the hallway and around the corner and managed to catch the call on the last ring. "Hello?"

"Hi, baby. Where are you? Why are you out of breath?"

"I'm in the parking lot," Felicity lied. "I'm not out of breath, I was just . . . laughing. What's going on?"

"I have to be here later than I thought, so I need you to pick up the boys at day care, okay? If you could get them into their pjs, that'd be really helpful. I'll be home as soon as I can."

"Sure, okay," Felicity said. "No problem."

"You're a lifesaver. See you later."

Felicity hung up the phone, her head spinning. Waiting to swap the envelopes was no longer an option. It was now or never.

She jogged toward her mom's office on the other side of the building. Nearly all the other offices she passed were dark and unoccupied—most of the staff left early on Fridays. *Please be unlocked, please be unlocked*, Felicity begged silently as her mom's door came into view. Through the window of the office, she spotted the box of gold envelopes on the desk—she could easily make the exchange and be out in thirty seconds. After one final glance up and down the hall to make sure she was alone, she turned the doorknob.

It was locked.

She cursed under her breath. Maybe someone at the

security desk could open the door for her. She was hesitant to involve another person in her criminal activities, but she didn't have much of a choice. Every second she waited was one second closer to being caught.

When she reached the desk near the front door, Felicity saw that her favorite security guard was on duty, and her heart lifted. Arthur had always had a soft spot for her. Today he was napping in front of his bank of monitors, his long Santa Claus beard spread out on his chest, and he startled awake when Felicity touched his shoulder. "Felicity!" he boomed. "How you doing, honey? It's so good to see you!"

"You too," Felicity said. "Listen, could you do me a huge favor? I think I left my car keys in my mom's office, and she's in a meeting. Would you mind opening the door for me?"

"Anything for my girl." Arthur hoisted himself out of his chair with a grunt and started down the hall at approximately the speed of a Galápagos land tortoise.

It took nearly five minutes to reach her mom's office. Felicity plodded alongside her old friend, answering his questions about the pageant and trying not to betray her panic. Even when they reached her mom's door, the ordeal was far from over—Arthur had a key ring the size of a grapefruit, and he had no idea which key was the right one. After sixteen tries, the lock finally clicked open, and Felicity nearly did a cartwheel.

"Thank you so much," she said.

Arthur flipped on the office lights. "Now, let's see what we can find."

Felicity's relief flickered out like a birthday candle in a strong wind. The gold envelopes on the desk beckoned to her. All she needed was ten seconds alone with them. But Arthur was feeling around on the tops of the filing cabinets and didn't seem likely to leave. If she got him to turn his back, maybe she could make the swap with him in the room. Felicity gripped the replacement envelope in her bag, waiting for her moment of opportunity. "I was sitting over there by the window," she said.

Arthur took the bait. As soon as he lumbered over to search the window ledge, Felicity lunged toward the box on the desk and whipped Gabby's envelope out of her bag. For a moment, her brain couldn't even process what she saw. One entire edge of the precious replacement envelope was covered with a gooey stain. With mounting panic, Felicity tore open the front pocket of her bag and saw that her strawberry kiwi lip gloss was missing its top. There was sparkly pink slime everywhere.

"Crap," she muttered, stuffing the envelope back into the bag.

"What's the matter, honey?"

"My stupid lip gloss opened up all over my bag." Felicity's mind raced. Now she would need to start the computer, retype the fake interview question, find a new envelope, and make the switch before her mom finished her meeting. And that meant she needed to be alone *right now*.

While Arthur still had his back turned, Felicity

closed her sticky fist around her car keys and slipped them behind a picture on her mom's desk. "Oh, here they are," she exclaimed, forcing a laugh. "God, I'm always leaving these everywhere. I need to put a tracking device on them or something."

"Keys are so mischievous, aren't they? Sneaky little buggers." Arthur trudged toward the door. "Ready to go?"

"Sure. After you." On her way out, Felicity pushed the button on the doorknob that kept the lock from engaging, then pulled the door shut behind her. "You're my knight in shining armor, Arthur," she said. "Thanks so much for the help."

"It was my pleasure. You show them who's boss tomorrow, okay?" The old security guard patted her cheek and gave her a paternal smile before plodding back toward his post.

As soon as he turned the corner, Felicity slipped back into the office, closed the door, and turned on her mom's prehistoric computer. While it booted up, she flipped through the box of gold envelopes until she found number four. If she was going to do this convincingly, she had to know how the original question was formatted. *This is it*, she thought. *This is the moment I become a criminal*. She took a deep breath and ripped the envelope open.

Inside was a sheet of white paper with her question typed in the center: "What food do you think you are most like, and why?"

Seriously? This was supposed to be her all-important

interview question, worth thirty percent of her score? She wondered if the other competitors spent time making lists of foods, animals, and colors they resembled, just in case. What answer could she possibly have given?

"I'm like a bag of barbecue potato chips—mild on the surface, but hotter and spicier the deeper down you get."

"I'm like a coconut—hard to crack, but rewarding if you make the effort."

"I'm like a cherry—red, sweet, and hard-hearted."

The computer finally whirred to life. Felicity opened a word-processing program and gingerly extracted her gloss-smeared replacement question from its envelope: "Scarletville was founded as a sanctuary for redheads. How do you think having non-redheads living in our town enriches or detracts from our community?" It was infinitely better than the other question, and for a moment, she was actually grateful to Gabby. She retyped the question and hit print, then nearly jumped through the ceiling when the printer started making horrible grinding noises.

"Come on, come on, come on," she begged in a whisper, stroking the machine as if it were a cat. "It's just two lines. You can do it."

As soon as the paper dropped into the tray, Felicity heard an even more horrifying sound—her mother's laughter in the hall. And then a key clicked in the lock.

There was nowhere to run.

In a desperate attempt to save herself, Felicity scooped up the papers and torn envelopes, hit the computer's power button, and dove under the desk. There was no time to grab the new question from the printer. Her heart began performing an Irish step dance, and she curled into a tight ball as the lights flipped on.

And then she heard Celeste's voice. "Oh, hang on, Ginger. Do you mind coming to my office for a sec? I brought that dress I was telling you about, and I want to know if you think it's too slutty for tomorrow."

"Cece, I've known you thirty years, and I've never seen you look slutty, including at Lisa Randall's 'Dress Like a Stripper' birthday party senior year." Felicity jumped as her mom dropped a stack of papers on the desk directly above her head.

Celeste giggled. "That was the first time I ever saw pasties. I was *mortified*. Come on, will you just look at it? It'll take two seconds."

"All right, fine." The footsteps moved back toward the door.

"Hey, do you really think Matty can handle running sound? That kid is — " Celeste's voice cut off as the door slammed.

Felicity couldn't believe her luck. She scrambled out from under the desk, snatched the paper from the printer tray, and ransacked the office for extra gold envelopes. After three horrible minutes, she finally located one in the filing cabinet next to the Miss Scarlet crown. She stuffed Gabby's question inside, scrawled a number four across it with a Sharpie, and slipped it into the box. Then, with the ripped, oily papers balled in her fist, she bolted out of the office and up the stairs.

As she crouched on the landing, panting, she heard her mom emerge from Celeste's office and open her own door. "I could swear this was locked," she mused aloud. "I must be going crazy." Felicity fled before Ginger had time to think too hard about it.

She raced across the second floor, pounded down the stairs on the other side of the building, and burst out into the spring twilight. As she cut across the lawn toward the parking lot, Felicity could barely keep from skipping. Sure, she'd had a few very close calls, but the questions were swapped, and now she could execute her plan. She did a little jig next to Yoko before collapsing into the driver's seat. She was only fifteen minutes late to pick up the twins. If her mom got home before her, Felicity could easily attribute her delay to the boys losing their shoes. *I am a criminal mastermind,* she thought as she plunked down her lip-gloss-smeared bag and turned on the car.

It was only when the Sharks in Heaven album started blasting through the speakers that she realized she'd forgotten to swap the music for her tap routine.

17

Felicity woke to the strange experience of hearing her own name on the radio.

The DJs at KRED were in a festive mood. "As we all know, Scarletville takes these competitions *very* seriously," said one DJ. "We're expecting a tremendous turnout at City Hall—all seven hundred Miss Scarlet tickets sold out twenty-three minutes after they went on sale."

"Several of these girls competed in the Miss Ruby Red pageant five years ago, including winner Madison Banks and first runner-up Felicity St. John," added the other DJ. "I can't wait to see them go head to head again this afternoon. We also have some promising newcomers to the scene. Who will take the crown? Join us at two o'clock as we broadcast live from City Hall."

Two o'clock—that was only five hours away. Felicity's stomach tied itself into a series of complicated knots. Five hours from now, she'd be waiting in the wings, ready to act the part of a pageant girl for the very last time. Six hours from now, she would take Gabby down in front of the entire town, and the blackmail would finally end. Seven hours from now, if all went well, she'd be a titleholder armed with the money she needed for art school.

Or everything could fall apart.

Her door burst open, and her brothers came barreling in. "Lissy, you're on the radio!" Tyler announced.

Felicity rolled over and shut off her clock radio as Andy climbed onto the bed and bounced up and down on her feet. "Are you going to win?" he demanded.

"I hope so. Do you want me to win?"

"I guess, but not as much as Mom. She *really* wants you to win."

Felicity smiled grimly. "Yes, I know."

As if she had been summoned, Ginger bustled into the bedroom, carrying a breakfast tray adorned with a tiny vase of flowers. She kissed Felicity on the forehead and deposited the tray in her lap. "Breakfast in bed for my beauty queen!"

Felicity looked with dismay at the scrambled eggs, buttered toast, fruit salad, and orange juice. The gesture was sweet, but she wasn't sure she could force any of the food down.

"Thanks, Mom. You're the best," she said with a

wan smile. She took a small bite of toast. It tasted like dust in her mouth.

"Make sure you eat all the eggs. You need extra energy today."

Felicity reached for her napkin and found a sky-blue envelope tucked underneath. "What's this?" she asked.

"It came in the mail for you. Call me when you're done showering, and I'll do your hair and makeup before I go over to City Hall, okay?"

Ginger herded the twins out of the room as Felicity tore open the envelope. Inside was a handmade construction paper card decorated with a child's drawing of twelve girls in evening gowns. In the middle stood the winner, a glitter glue crown on her head and a bunch of flowers in her hand. Underneath, in careful block print, she was labeled FELICITY.

Inside, the card read:

Dear Felicity,
    Good luck in the Miss Scarlet pajent! I can't wait to see youre beautiful dress. I am youre biggest fan. I am sure you will be the pretiest one. I really really really really hope you win!

                            Your friend,
                            Katie Vaughn

Felicity's stomach lurched and twisted dangerously, and she pushed her breakfast tray aside. She wanted nothing more than to have Gabby thrown out of Scarletville, and she was just starting to come to terms with exposing Rose. But she had completely forgotten about Gabby's little sisters. Katie was in Andy and Tyler's class—Felicity saw her all the time when she picked up the twins from day care. She was small for her age, with cartoonishly large eyes, long brown pigtails, and an adorable gap between her front teeth. Picturing her little face made Felicity feel even sicker, and she tucked the card out of sight under her duvet. She tried to banish all the empathy from her mind and replace it with steely resolve.

The blackmail had to stop. There was only one way to make it stop. Gabby had left her no choice.

Felicity abandoned her untouched breakfast and took a long, hot shower, then sat quietly as her mom curled her hair and peppered her with competition pointers. When Ginger was happy with her work, she pulled out the hair spray and enveloped her daughter in a sticky cloud. Felicity coughed, tasting the bitter chemical tang at the back of her throat.

"Perfect," her mom announced. "That should hold just fine, but spray it again before you go onstage. Now, let me see your nails."

When Felicity was thoroughly painted and primped, her mom stepped back, clasped her hands, and regarded her daughter with misty eyes. "Oh, Felicity, you look *so* beautiful. I'm so proud of you I can barely stand it. You have no idea how wonderful this is for me, watching you up there, dancing to my music. You're just like a mirror of what I used to be." Ginger hugged Felicity fiercely, careful not to muss her hair. "You know I can't show favoritism once we get to City Hall, but remember that I'm sending you all the love in my heart and rooting for you with every cell in my body."

The toast churned in Felicity's stomach as she thought about how furious Ginger would be when she saw the new tap routine. Her mom had spent seventeen years forcing her into a mold she didn't fit, but Felicity knew that every moment had been out of love. It wasn't just about the prize money—Ginger believed in Miss Scarlet with her entire heart and soul and truly thought this was the best possible path for her daughter. The guiltaconda slithered back around Felicity's chest and began to squeeze, and she was suddenly afraid she might cry. "I could never have gotten here without you," she said.

"I know you'll pay me back by winning." Ginger pulled back and touched Felicity's cheek. "I always knew you were a winner, right from the second you were born, and today you get to prove it to everyone. Just do everything exactly like we practiced, and I know that crown will be yours. Do you need anything else before I go?"

Felicity shook her head. "I'll be fine. But thanks, Mom. For everything."

Ginger embraced her one last time, and Felicity hugged her back, hoping that somewhere deep down, her mom would understand that she couldn't go through with the pageant exactly as planned. She wanted to win, but she needed to do it her own way and for her own reasons. Even though her mom loved her and wanted the best for her, she had no idea who Felicity really was.

Today, it was time to show her.

It was time to show everyone.

City Hall was in a state of jubilant chaos. When Felicity opened the front door, a cheer rang through the packed lobby, and she had to swim through a sea of patting, squeezing hands to reach the auditorium. She gave the crowd a quick wave, as she knew her mom would want her to, and a fireworks display of camera flashes went off in her face. Momentarily blinded, she stumbled through the auditorium doors. "This is insanity," she muttered as she heard another cheer go up outside.

The room was empty except for two volunteers tapping down cables on the stage. Felicity made her way to the sound booth, praying it would be unoccupied so she could swap her music before anyone noticed her. Unfortunately, the scrawny, sullen sound operator was already there, bent over a graphic novel.

"Hi," Felicity said. "Matty, right?"

The boy looked up slowly, as if it took incredible effort to raise his head three inches. His squash-colored hair fell over his eyes, and he made no effort to brush it away. "Uh-huh. 'Sup."

Felicity put on an authoritative voice. "I'm Felicity St. John. The music for my talent sounded a little weird yesterday, so I burned a new CD, and I need you to swap them."

She worried for a moment that he'd argue with her, but Matty was far too catatonic to care what she did. He leaned sluggishly to the side like a melting snowman, providing her access to the box of CDs on the table. Felicity slipped into the booth and swapped the discs, stuffing the old one into her bag. "There," she said. "Thanks."

"Uh-huh." Matty righted himself and returned to his book.

"Hey, listen," Felicity said. "When you play this, someone might come running up here to tell you it's the wrong music, but it's not. Don't let anyone turn it off, no matter what, even the people in charge. Okay?"

Matty shrugged one shoulder and mumbled something that might have been "Whatever." Felicity wasn't sure her comment had registered, but there was nothing else she could do. She headed backstage.

The dressing room reeked of hair spray and hot curling irons and was packed with pageant volunteers, mothers, and contestants in various states of undress. The sickly-green linoleum floor, fluorescent lights, and rolling costume racks were hardly glamorous, but they were familiar to Felicity from past pageants, and the sight of them made her relax a little. Ginger was nowhere to be found, so Felicity checked in with Brenda, then found an empty spot at the mirrors next to Haylie. Her friend was sitting perfectly still in one of the orange plastic chairs, eyes closed and earbuds in, oblivious to the chaos around her as she did breathing exercises.

As she did before every competition, Felicity lined up her beauty supplies in tidy rows on the table: magnifying mirror, hair spray, curling iron, round brush, bobby pins, tissues, makeup, antistatic spray, Topstick fashion tape, lint brush, sewing kit, stain stick, and a Sharpie for blacking out unexpected scuffs on her tap shoes. Seeing everything laid out neatly made her feel safer, like she had some small measure of control over the day.

Ivy found her as she was digging through a costume rack for her personal introduction outfit. "It's completely *insane* out there," her friend said, eyes wide. "Is it like this every year?"

"Pretty much." Felicity found her outfit and extracted it. "Are you nervous?"

"I wasn't before, but I am now. I'm kind of afraid people are going to mob the stage and start speaking in tongues or something."

"Is Darren coming?"

"Are you kidding? I'd never subject him to a pageant."

"Hey, Ives?" Felicity said. "Thanks for going through with this. I know how much you hate being here."

Ivy shrugged. "It's okay—it's not that big a deal. I know how important it is to you and Haylie. And it might be fun for the audience to see something a little different up there for once."

Cassie bounded over to retrieve her costume. She looked as if she'd had a play date with a jet engine and then dipped her head in shellac. "Wow, Cass," Felicity said. "Your hair is . . . really something."

"Isn't it?" Cassie spun around to show off the back, which resembled a mound of cotton batting that had been gnawed by rats. "My stylist said messy was all the rage this year."

"Is her stylist a category-five hurricane?" Ivy muttered under her breath, and Felicity tried to cover her giggles with a coughing fit.

They were headed back toward the mirrors when Felicity noticed Ariel, the pageant's token strawbie, sitting across the room and roughing up the bottoms of her new heels with sandpaper. Her long straight hair fell around her shoulders like a curtain as she leaned forward over the shoes, and Felicity was surprised by how beautiful it looked. All the other girls were mingling and chatting, but everyone looked right through Ariel as if she were invisible. When she thought back, Felicity realized she hadn't seen anyone speak to Ariel during the rehearsals, either. She certainly hadn't made any effort to do so herself, despite the fact that underneath a coat of dye, they were exactly the same.

She was no better than the rest of Scarletville. No matter what Felicity's new music said, she *would* be a cookie-cutter girl until she stopped acting like one.

"Go ahead," Felicity told Ivy. "I'll be right there." And before she could think too much about it, she marched over and sat down next to her fellow strawbie.

"Hey," she said.

Ariel looked up, surprised, and glanced over her shoulder. When she finally determined that the greeting was intended for her, she gave Felicity a tiny, puzzled smile. "Hi?"

Felicity realized too late that she had nothing to say, and a long, awkward silence stretched between them. Finally, she blurted out, "So . . . how're you feeling about this whole . . . thing?"

"I'm so excited, but I'm really, really nervous. You have any tips? You were so great in Miss Ruby Red—I still remember that dance you did, with the feathers on your costume? You totally should have won over Madison."

Felicity smiled. "Thanks. Don't worry, you're going to be fine out there. It's all about confidence. Even if you have no idea what you're doing, just act like you do, and everyone will believe it." *That's what I do every day of my life.* "What's your talent? I didn't get to see yesterday."

"Scottish Highland dancing. I'm doing a sword dance."

"A *sword* dance? Like, with real swords?"

"Yup." Ariel reached into her duffel bag and pulled out two long blades, and Felicity recoiled. "It's okay, they're not sharp. And I don't swing them around like a ninja or anything. I just put them on the floor and jump over them a lot."

Across the room, Haylie finished her meditation and flickered back to life, and she beamed and waved when she spotted Felicity. "I should go get ready," Felicity told Ariel. "But break a leg today."

"Thanks." Ariel flashed her first genuine smile, and it lit up her whole face. "Kick Madison's butt this time, okay?"

Felicity returned to her table, and Haylie jumped up to hug her. "I am so ready for this," she squealed. "I feel like I'm totally in the zone, you know?"

Before Felicity could respond, Madison brushed by. "Hey, Felicity, I meant to tell you yesterday that your dance costume is *super* cute. I used to have a jacket just like that, with a big sparkly heart on it. I think I was in . . . second grade?" She gave a simpering smile and flounced away, her curls bobbing in an excellent imitation of Georgia Kellerman's.

"Don't let her get to you," Haylie said. "Your tap costume *is* cute."

Felicity sighed; her stupid costume was the only thing she hadn't been able to fix at the last minute. "No, she's right. That heart is hideous."

"There's nothing you can do about it now, so just try to forget about it," Ivy said. "You only have to wear it for three minutes."

"Hey, can I use this?" Haylie asked, reaching for Felicity's lint brush. She bumped the black Sharpie, which fell off the table and rolled across the linoleum. As Felicity bent to pick it up, she froze, suddenly struck by a flash of inspiration.

There *was* something she could do about the jacket.

"Felicity?" Haylie asked. "Can I—"

"Yeah, go ahead," Felicity said. "I'll be back in a few minutes."

She snatched her tap costume off the rack and took it into one of the three individual bathrooms off the dressing area. She could hear someone retching in the next stall—a common occurrence on pageant days—and tried her hardest not to listen. Sitting cross-legged on the tile floor with her jacket spread over her knees, she uncapped her Sharpie and very carefully started blacking out jewel after jewel.

Ten minutes later, the center of the heart was adorned with a large black skull and crossbones.

"Take that," Felicity whispered, not entirely sure if she was speaking to Ella-Mae Finch, the pageant judges, Gabby, or her mother.

Fifteen minutes before the pageant began, Felicity was fastening her lucky shamrock necklace when her mom bustled in, clad in a gold cocktail dress. "The dressing room is now closed to visitors," she announced. "Family members and friends, please wish your girls luck and take your seats in the auditorium. Enjoy the pageant, everyone!"

After a flurry of emotional good-byes, Ginger gathered all the contestants in a circle. "This is the moment we've been waiting for, girls," she said. "You're all ready for this, so hold your heads high, be proud, and respect yourselves and each other. I want to see humble winners and gracious losers out there." She didn't bother to say, "All of you are winners," as most pageant directors would. She clearly didn't believe that for a second.

"All right, everyone, hands in the middle," she directed, and the girls squished together, piling up their manicured hands. "'Go, Miss Scarlet' on three. Ready? One, two, three!"

The girls shouted, *"Go, Miss Scarlet!"* no one louder than Ginger. "Five minutes till lineup, ten minutes till showtime!" she called as everyone flew back to their mirrors for last-minute touch-ups. Felicity's stomach gave another lurch when Ginger blew her a kiss from the doorway, her smile full of warmth and pride. For a mad moment, she considered chasing her mom into the hallway and spilling out all her secrets. *I'm not the sweet, obedient daughter you think I am. I don't even like pageants. I can't stand your music, so I'm using my own. I tampered with the interview questions. Oh, and I'm about to fight my blackmailer in front of the whole town, even though you explicitly told me not to.*

But confessing wouldn't change anything—it would only make her mom hysterical. These were burdens she had to carry alone. But in just a few hours, it would all be over. Her hand automatically sought her right hip, where Jonathan's note had been nestled all week, before she remembered she had no pockets in her skirt. She felt strangely unmoored without the little square of paper.

Haylie reached out to take Felicity's and Ivy's hands. "I love you guys," she said, her voice weighty with

267

emotion. "No matter what happens out there, I'm just so glad we're all here together."

"Love you too," Felicity said. She squeezed Haylie's hand. "Break a leg out there. You too, Ives."

"You probably shouldn't say that," Ivy said, looking around at everyone's spiky heels. "I wouldn't be surprised if someone actually did." True to her word, she was wearing flats.

Before she headed upstairs, Felicity took a last long look at her reflection. Her royal-blue blouse and black pencil skirt were crisp and wrinkle-free. Her makeup looked perfect, and her hair was as red as it had ever been. She gave a practice smile, and the girl who beamed back at her from the mirror looked relaxed, confident, eager to command the stage. She thought of Gabby sitting in the press section, prepared to expose her at any moment, but her reflection betrayed no anxiety. Her pageant-girl mask was flawless.

"Time to show everyone what you're made of," she whispered to herself.

The girls filed up the stairs and into the wings, an army of high heels punching the hardwood floor. When they were all lined up, Haylie in the lead and Madison in the rear, Brenda spoke into her headset. "I have all twelve girls stage right, ready to go. Stage left, do you have Ginger, Georgia, and the emcee?" There was a pause, and then Brenda said, "Great. Let's get started. Send Ginger out."

Light flooded the stage, and Felicity watched her mom step up to the lectern, grinning and waving with both hands as the entire auditorium erupted in cheers. "Good afternoon, Scarletville!" she called. "I'm Ginger St. John, pageant director and the head of the Scarletville Pageant Committee! Welcome to the seventy-fifth-anniversary Miss Scarlet Pageant! The twelve spectacular girls you're about to see are upholding a time-honored tradition today. They have some very big shoes to fill, but I have no doubt they'll rise to the challenge."

She introduced each of the five judges, and wave after wave of applause and cheering crashed through the auditorium. It sounded like there were thousands of people in the house. Felicity could feel the adrenaline starting to pump through her body, and she shook out her hands to release some nervous energy. In front of her, Ariel was breathing in shallow little gasps.

Ginger handed the microphone to the emcee, Donna Marie Sullivan, who had been crowned Miss Scarlet ten years ago. She stood at least six foot three in her heels and shimmered like a mermaid in her iridescent turquoise gown. Donna Marie explained how the pageant was scored—thirty percent for the interview portion, forty for the talent portion, and ten percent each for the personal introduction, swimwear, and evening wear portions. Then she introduced Georgia, who bounced onstage in a little black dress and belted out "Our Sacred Scarlet Home." The crowd roared its approval, and then Felicity saw Brenda tap Haylie on the shoulder and nod toward the stage.

It was time.

A fast pop song blasted through the speakers, and Donna Marie shouted, "Ladies and gentlemen, I give you this year's Miss Scarlet contestants!"

Radiant smiles in place, shoulders back, and chins held high, the girls looped around the stage, waving at the packed house and trying not to squint under the bright stage lights. The walk lasted only about ninety seconds, but Felicity heard voice after voice screaming her name. By the time she was back in the wings, her heart was pounding in her ears. She had forgotten how scary and thrilling it was to be onstage in front of so many people.

When it was time for her personal introduction, she strode toward the microphone, trying to radiate confidence and enthusiasm. She smiled at the judges first, then scanned the cheering crowd, taking stock. There was her mom, sitting next to the judges' table and grinning so broadly Felicity feared her face might shatter. There was the mayor, his tiny mustache twitching with excitement. There was Gabby in the press section, her pen flying over her notepad. There were Andy and Tyler, sitting with her neighbor Victor a few rows back and waving madly. There in the back was a bored-looking Brent, his arm wrapped around the skinny shoulders of Gretchen Williams. There was Ms. Kellogg with a group of teachers.

And there, sitting just in front of her, was Jonathan.

Jonathan, who had no Scarletville spirit. Who couldn't care less about pageants.

Who was smiling at her now as if they were the only two people in the room.

Felicity's stomach did a little twirl, and it had nothing to do with being nervous.

She forced her eyes back to the judges and gripped the microphone. With a bright smile, she said, "Hi, everyone! I'm Felicity St. John. I'm seventeen years old, and I was born right here in beautiful Scarletville. I was first runner-up in the Miss Ruby Red Pageant when I was twelve. This year, I was the cocurator of the student art show and served on the prom committee, for which I designed all the decorations. I also helped organize and run the winter recital at Red Shoes Dance Studio, where I've been a student since I was three. I'm so excited to be here, following in my mom's footsteps as I compete for the title of Miss Scarlet." The crowd cheered, and Felicity made sure to smile at each judge individually before she turned and walked into the wings.

She headed downstairs to the dressing room, walking slowly so she'd have a moment alone to think. Why was Jonathan here? Had he come to see *her*? Tickets had gone on sale long before the two of them were friends, so maybe he was here for another reason entirely. But the way he'd smiled at her just now made her doubt he was here for someone else. The memory of it made her feel tingly all the way to her fingertips. His presence also anchored her somehow — having him here in person was so much better than carrying his

271

note in her pocket. Everyone else was looking at her sparkly facade, but she knew Jonathan was looking at the real Felicity behind the mask.

She found her swimsuit—black with white polka dots, just like her prom dress—and joined Haylie at their table. "How'd your intro go?" Haylie asked as she tied her turquoise bikini top.

"Good, I think." Felicity unbuttoned her blouse and stepped out of her skirt, then draped a robe over her shoulders before swapping her underwear for her bikini. "How was yours?"

Ivy rushed into the dressing room and grabbed her swimsuit off the rack. "A whole bunch of swim team girls are here," she said, obviously distraught. "They're wearing these stupid T-shirts that spell out 'Go, Ivy, go!' It's so embarrassing."

"Only you would be upset that people came to cheer for you." Felicity started applying Topstick to her butt.

Ivy gave her a horrified look. "Are you *taping* your suit to your ass?"

"Yeah, everyone does. There are some things the entire town doesn't need to see."

"There's nothing worse than a wedgie onstage," Haylie stated with great authority.

Ivy shuddered. "I sincerely hope I never have to experience that firsthand." She pulled on her full-coverage tank suit, which was emblazoned across the chest with the Scarletville High School Rubies logo. As Haylie rolled her eyes, Ivy accessorized her outfit with flip-flops, a rubber bathing cap, and goggles.

Brenda called six minutes to lineup, and Felicity went over to inspect herself in the full-length mirror. She stretched and shimmied for a minute, making sure her tape held and everything stayed securely in place. When she glanced around the room, she found that nearly half the girls were wearing shades of turquoise. Cassie's suit was covered in ruffles, as if she were going underwater salsa dancing, and Madison was struggling into something that looked more appropriate for the bedroom than the pool. No one else had a pattern on her suit, and Felicity smiled, pleased that her polka dots would stand out.

It wasn't until she was standing in line in the wings that she realized she was about to parade out onstage, nearly naked, in front of Jonathan. Somehow, the hundreds of other people in the audience didn't bother her—the swimsuit competition had never seemed scarier than walking around at the public pool. But even when Felicity was fully dressed, the way Jonathan looked at her was sometimes so penetrating that she felt unclothed. Her palms started to sweat, and she wiped them on her bare thighs as she watched Ariel pose and turn.

Ariel headed off into the wings, and Donna Marie called Felicity's name. Felicity took a deep breath, smiled, and ordered her feet to move forward.

She strode out onto the stage, one hand cocked on her hip, and kept her eyes on the judges for her first set of poses and pivots. And then she moved toward the other side of the stage, where Jonathan was sitting. He sat on the very edge of his seat, staring intently with his lips slightly parted, and the moment Felicity locked eyes with him, a delicious heat suffused her. She forbade herself to blush—even the slightest pink tinge would be obvious on the exposed, milk-white canvas of her skin. Even when she forced herself to break eye contact and turn around, she could still feel his gaze hot on her back. She spun once more, gave him a final dazzling smile, and walked offstage, breathless.

"You looked great out there," Haylie whispered as she got in line for the full-group walk. "Way to flirt with the audience!" Felicity felt the blush she'd been holding back rush to her cheeks, and she was grateful no one could see it in the dark.

During the full-group walk, Felicity caught her mom's eye and saw that Ginger was teary with joy—so far, everything was going just as she had hoped. Felicity felt sick as she pictured what her mom's expression would look like when "Cookie-Cutter Girl" started blasting through the auditorium. But the judges would probably love her edgy new tap routine, and if she scored well, Ginger would have to forgive her subversion. Maybe she'd even respect Felicity for taking charge.

The thought buoyed her, and Felicity felt strong as she changed into her tap costume. She looked forward to being out there on the stage, showing off who she really was for the very first time. After she did some quick warm-ups in the hall, she found Ivy, and together they went upstairs to watch Haylie's talent routine.

Felicity and Ivy both hugged her for luck, and then Haylie ran out onstage in her red toe shoes, gave the crowd an enthusiastic wave, and struck her opening pose. When her music began, Haylie was transformed. Felicity had watched her friend dance countless times, and she had never doubted that Haylie was talented. But today's performance went far beyond anything Felicity had ever seen. Haylie seemed to feel the music down to her core, and emotion radiated from her tiny body all the way to the back row. When she jumped, hair flying and legs stretched to their full extension, she embodied reckless abandon and precise control all at once.

When the routine ended, the audience leapt to its feet. Haylie took a gracious bow and ran offstage. "Was it good?" she asked, her face glowing. "It felt really good."

"Are you kidding? It was *amazing*!" Felicity said. "I've never seen you dance like that."

"You've got this in the bag, Hays," Ivy agreed.

A volunteer rushed out onstage to reset the microphone, and then Cassie hurried by them, the lights glinting off her windswept cloud of hair. "What's she doing for her talent?" Felicity whispered.

"I'd like to share with you a poem I wrote," Cassie said, as if in response. "It's called 'Diva Power.'"

Ivy's eyes widened. "Oh my God, I can't *wait* to hear this."

Cassie cleared her throat and began her recitation.

"Yeah, I'm a diva,
don't try to pretend like I'm not.

275

You might not like my sassy attitude,
but you definitely think I'm hot.

"Yeah, I know I look good,
my makeup takes me an hour.
But that doesn't mean I'm not tough and badass;
I am *totally* about girl power."

Felicity turned to give Ivy an incredulous look and saw that her friend was doubled over, both hands clapped over her mouth as she giggled uncontrollably. The sight of her nearly undid Felicity as well, but she bit her tongue hard and tried to keep herself in check. Cassie continued reciting, a strange swagger creeping into her voice.

"Yeah, I've got mad skills, too.
You'll see what I mean.
When you see me strut my stuff,
with jealousy you will turn green.

"Yeah, I'm the greatest one here.
I won't go off on a tangent,
but I'm gonna crush my competition
and win this pa-pa-pageant."

The audience was deathly silent for a minute, unsure whether Cassie was finished. Finally, she said, "Thank you," which triggered tentative applause. Cassie strode offstage, looking pleased with herself. Much to Felicity's relief, she headed straight to the dressing room without stopping to chat.

Ariel appeared in the doorway, decked out in a plaid skirt and argyle knee socks, and waited in the wings for the volunteer to remove the microphone. She was clutching her swords so tightly her knuckles were white. When Felicity walked over and put a reassuring hand on her shoulder, she jumped as if she'd been zapped with a Taser.

"You're going to do great," Felicity whispered.

"Go, Ariel," Brenda told her. "You're on deck, Felicity."

The sword dance flew by in a flash, and before Felicity knew it, Brenda was saying, "Any time you're ready, honey." Then Haylie was squeezing her hand, and Ivy was massaging her shoulders as if she were a boxer. Felicity stood at the edge of the wings with her eyes closed, breathing deeply and centering herself. *You can do this*, she thought. *You are going to rock those judges' worlds.*

Her eyes flew open when Brenda gasped behind her. "Felicity, *what* did you do to your beautiful costume?"

It was time to go.

Before Brenda could grab her, Felicity ran out onto the stage. She smiled at the judges, then struck her first pose.

The opening chords of "Cookie-Cutter Girl" crashed through the speakers. And as Felicity danced to the song she loved, the rest of the world fell away, and all that mattered was the music pulsing through her body and the staccato rhythms of her feet on the floor. She flew over the stage, knowing every step was right, and she finally felt as if she were exactly where she was supposed to be. She didn't even have to try to smile.

When the Sharks in Heaven song ended, the swell of applause pulled her back down to earth. There was no full-crowd standing ovation, but Felicity was pleased to see that many people were on their feet. Jonathan was one of them, a goofy grin plastered on his face. She smiled back in a way that she hoped said, *That was for you.* "Go, Lissy!" her brothers shrieked over and over, and she looked right at them as she took her bow. She glanced at the judges and tried to gauge their reactions, but their faces were unreadable as they scribbled in their notepads.

Finally, when she couldn't avoid it any longer, she forced herself to look at her mom.

She had expected to see anger and confusion, but she wasn't prepared for the look of pure devastation she saw. Ginger sat perfectly still as the crowd clapped and cheered around her, both hands pressed to her chest as if her heart were in danger of falling out. Her eyes were huge and uncomprehending, like a dog who had just been kicked by its loving owner.

It's just a song, Felicity wanted to tell her. *Don't take it personally—I rejected Ella-Mae Finch, not you. And didn't you see how much better I danced when I was actually proud of what I was doing? Can't you tell how much everyone liked it?*

But she couldn't say any of that. Her three minutes were up, and it was time to get off the stage. Felicity turned and walked away, wondering how it was possible to feel defiant, proud, relieved, and heartbroken all at the same time.

Haylie embraced her the moment she was in the wings. "You were fabulous," she whispered. "I couldn't believe how fast your feet were going. How'd you get your mom to agree to that awesome new music? She was so set on that stupid jazz song."

"She didn't know. I went in the booth and swapped the CDs this morning. I just couldn't go through with the other song. It was just so . . . not me." Haylie's eyes widened, and all the excitement drained from her face. "Hays, what's the matter? Are you okay?"

"You didn't get it approved?" Even at a whisper, Haylie's voice was laden with anxiety.

"No. I know my mom's probably going to throw a fit about it later, but it's just a song, so I'm hoping she'll get over it when—"

"Felicity, didn't you read the pageant rule book? You're not allowed to change anything about your routine after the last rehearsal unless you get it approved by the pageant committee."

Felicity's blood turned to ice. Her mom's dire expression suddenly made sense. It wasn't just a song; it was a punishable offense. The pageant rule book was Ginger's bible, and she knew exactly how much trouble her daughter was in.

279

"What are they going to do to me? Will they dock points?"

"Maybe, but . . . Felicity, they could vote to disqualify you."

As if from a very great distance, Felicity heard Ivy start playing "You're a Grand Old Flag" on the kazoo. And that was the last thing she heard before she fled.

18

Felicity sat on the bathroom floor, her back against the locked door and her tearstained face buried in her hands. Her mascara was rubbing off all over the place, but it didn't matter now. It was hard to believe she'd been in here less than two hours ago, blacking out the jewels on her jacket and feeling optimistic.

If she really was disqualified, she had just traded a lifetime of pursuing her dreams for three minutes of defiant individuality. Maybe there was a reason she had spent her whole life letting other people tell her what to do, how to look, and who to be. She clearly couldn't be trusted to make good decisions for herself.

Haylie had been knocking on the door unrelentingly for the past five minutes. "Come on, Felicity, let us in," she called for the thousandth time. "I know you're

281

upset, but you can't cry now. You'll have to totally redo your eye makeup."

"Too late," Felicity called back. Her voice sounded wet and choked, as if she had a goldfish in her throat.

"Then let me in so I can help you. We've got twenty minutes. But you have to stop crying now, or you'll look all red and puffy."

Felicity grabbed a wad of toilet paper and blew her nose. She wanted to spend the rest of the day locked in this bathroom, where she couldn't make any more stupid mistakes. But Gabby was in the audience, watching her every move and waiting for her to slip up. If Felicity didn't stand up on that stage and take her enemy down today, she might never get another chance. Maybe the mayor could even convince the pageant judges to go easy on her in exchange for the juicy information about the salon. Maybe it wasn't too late to redeem herself.

She stood up and unlocked the door.

Haylie and Ivy pushed inside carrying Felicity's makeup bag, shoes, and gown. "Wash your face," Haylie ordered, shoving a towel and a tube of face wash into her hands.

Felicity took them—there was no resisting tough-love Haylie. "Sorry I didn't get to see your talent," she told Ivy. "I totally freaked out up there."

"It's fine. You really didn't miss much. But I'm happy to play you a medley of patriotic tunes on the kazoo while walking on my hands any time, if you feel deprived."

"I should have been there to support you, though.

282

I'm screwing everything up." A fresh flood of tears threatened to spill over, and Haylie pointed sternly at the sink.

"If you don't wash your face, I'm going to have to do it for you," she said.

Felicity obediently scrubbed off her makeup, then sat slumped on the closed toilet lid as Haylie applied a new layer of foundation. "This is hardly even worth it now," she complained. "You guys should just go get yourselves ready. At least you're still in the running."

"It'll take me two minutes to get dressed," Haylie said. "Keep your eyes closed. Besides, it *is* worth it. They might not disqualify you. And if all they do is dock points, you have to pull yourself together and rock the interview section. Which is fine, 'cause you're great at this part. You never get tongue-tied or say stupid stuff."

"God, what do you think Cassie will say?" mused Ivy. "Do you think she'll go off on a tangent? 'Cause then she'll never win this pa-pa-pageant." Felicity smiled despite herself.

Haylie expertly blended Felicity's eye shadow with quick, gentle strokes. "It would be worth it even if you *were* disqualified. We're all in this together, remember? We've got your back, even when you mess up. No, don't you dare cry again."

Felicity sniffled, then laughed. "Okay. Thanks."

By the time she was fully made up and dressed, it was impossible to tell she had ever been crying. "There," Haylie said, pleased with her handiwork. She gripped Felicity firmly by the shoulders. "Now, you're going to go out there and finish this thing with your head held high, like nothing ever happened, okay? The judges want to see confidence and composure, and that's what you're going to show them. Right?"

Felicity nodded, feeling a little stronger. "Right."

"And you look bitchin'," Ivy chimed in. "You have the best dress out of everyone. No offense, Haylie."

Felicity laughed. "Did you seriously just say 'bitchin''?"

"Seven minutes!" shouted Brenda from the other side of the bathroom door.

"We have to go get ready." Haylie grabbed Ivy and dragged her out of the bathroom.

"That's right," Ivy called over her shoulder. *"Bitchin'."*

Felicity glided through the evening-wear portion in a daze. She beamed at the judges as she floated around the stage in her perfect gown, but Gabby was the only thing on her mind. She might have lost the Miss Scarlet prize money, but in five minutes she would have an even better reward: her secret would be safe.

When the girls formed a semicircle around the microphone for the interview portion, Felicity's heart began to pound so hard she feared it might climb up her throat and fly out of her mouth. Haylie went first, chic and glittering in her backless gown. She was eloquent and composed as she answered a question about the role of social networking in society. Cassie's question dealt with whether the pageant's swimsuit competition was becoming archaic, and she stumbled through a disjointed response, obviously unclear on the meaning of the pivotal adjective. Ariel gave a heartfelt speech about how her older sister was the most influential person in her life.

And then it was Felicity's turn.

She stepped up to the microphone. Donna Marie opened envelope number four and smiled at her, blissfully unaware that the question she held was a fake. "Felicity, Scarletville was founded as a sanctuary for redheads. How do you think having non-redheads living in our town enriches or detracts from our community?"

Felicity met Gabby's expectant eyes, and suddenly, she wasn't afraid. *This ends now,* she thought. But just as she was about to speak, she heard a little voice yell, "Go, Felicity!"

On the far left side of the auditorium, Felicity spotted tiny Katie Vaughn, who was being violently shushed by everyone around her. She was wearing a brilliant red party dress and bouncing up and down in her seat. Gabby's two middle sisters sat on her right, and Rose was on her left. All four pairs of chocolate-brown eyes shone with admiration as they looked up at Felicity. The Vaughns were rooting for her, and here she was, about to destroy them.

Felicity felt as if she'd been punched in the stomach, and her breath caught in her throat. She closed her eyes and struggled to regain the impassive determination she'd felt just a moment before. She concentrated on how much she hated Gabby, how horrible it had felt to be manipulated, and she opened her mouth and tried again to speak.

But it was no use. She couldn't go through with it.

Gabby had no qualms about ruining an innocent life to better her own chances. But Felicity wasn't like her, and she couldn't stoop to that level. No matter how furious she was, it just wasn't in her to take someone else down so that she could keep standing.

She opened her eyes and looked at Jonathan, who respected her for being herself. She looked at Ms. Kellogg, who had told her there were places in the world where strawberry-blond wasn't less than red. And she realized there was another way to end this.

She gripped the microphone tightly.

"I think it's incredibly important to have people with other hair colors in Scarletville," she said, speaking the words Gabby had written. "It's small-minded and irresponsible to have a community that's entirely made up of one type of person. That kind of environment promotes intolerance and stereotyping."

Gabby's lips curled into a smile—everything was going according to her plan.

And then Felicity deviated from the script.

"People in this town are terrified no one will respect them if they don't have red hair, that no one will even see them. And I know that firsthand, because I've had those same fears my whole life."

Gabby's smile faltered, and Felicity stared right into her adversary's eyes as she said the words she had been holding back for seventeen years.

"I'm a strawbie," she said. "My hair is dyed, and it has been since I was two years old. My mom knew I wouldn't have the opportunities I deserved unless I altered the way I looked. Every single day, I've lived in fear that someone would find out what I really was. And when someone did discover my secret, I let her blackmail me. I lied to my best friends for her. I lied to my boyfriend, and I lost him because of it. I did everything she told me to do because I was so afraid she'd expose me and I'd lose everything I had. But I hurt people I loved to protect my secret, and it wasn't worth it. It's just hair." She grabbed a handful of perfect coppery curls and held them up for everyone to see. "This is not who I am, and I'm done hiding behind it."

Felicity turned back to Donna Marie, whose mouth was hanging open. "That's all I have to say," she finished. And then she turned around and got back in line.

For a moment, the auditorium was so quiet Felicity could hear her own heartbeat. And then everyone started whispering at once, including the girls on the stage. All five judges stared wide-eyed at Felicity, their notepads forgotten in their limp hands. Ginger was doubled over in her chair, hyperventilating, while another former Miss Scarlet rubbed her back. Brent was slack-jawed, thoroughly horrified by the thought of all the intimate things he'd unwittingly done with a strawbie. Even under all her makeup, Haylie's face looked ashen, and she stared at Felicity as if she had never seen her before.

But Jonathan and Ms. Kellogg were still smiling at

her, and Gabby's eyes were wide with dismay as she watched her powerful hold on Felicity slip away. Ariel gave Felicity's shoulder a quick, reassuring squeeze. And when Felicity turned and searched Ivy's face for signs of disgust, she found nothing but genuine surprise.

"Way to go out with a bang," her friend whispered. "Now, excuse me, I have to think of something really shocking to say. I can't let you outdo me like that."

Ivy strode toward the whispering crowd, her green Converse sneakers peeking out from under the hem of her gown, and adjusted the microphone as if nothing were out of the ordinary. She looked at Donna Marie expectantly. The emcee stared back, uncomprehending, and fanned herself with the stack of interview envelopes.

"Hi," Ivy finally said. "Do you have a question for me, or are we done here? Because I've got a pint of Coffee Heath Bar Crunch and last week's episode of *Granny Smackdown* waiting for me at home."

Somehow, the interview portion of the pageant finally came to an end. "Now we'll take a break while the judges tally the scores," Donna Marie said, obvious relief on her face. "When we return, we'll crown our new Miss Scarlet!"

Ivy attached herself to Felicity's side like a barnacle the moment they were offstage. "If people want to mess with you, they'll have to mess with me first," she said in answer to Felicity's questioning look.

Felicity was so grateful she almost cried. "Where's Haylie?" she asked.

"She's probably already downstairs. That girl moves like a—"

Ivy broke off when Felicity went flying into her, propelled by an accidentally-on-purpose shoulder shove from Madison. "Oh, sorry, *strawbie*," Madison sneered. "I didn't notice you there. You people really *are* harder to see." She brushed past and flounced down the stairs.

Felicity stared after her. "Way to defend me, Ives."

"Not even worth it," Ivy said. "She's a stupid cow."

When they reached the dressing room, Felicity paused. Her adrenaline was wearing off, and she didn't think she could put on a brave face for one more second. "Ives, I can't go in there right now. I just—I need a minute, okay?" She eyed the small, empty hallway that ran along the side of the dressing room.

Ivy straightened up to her unimpressive full height. "I'll cover you if you want to hang out over there for a while."

"Great." She hugged Ivy tightly. "Thanks for not freaking out."

"About what? Your hair? Do you seriously think I care what color your *hair* is? Hey, listen, if you want to shave your head, I'll totally do it with you. I've been looking for an excuse anyway. It makes you so aerodynamic."

"Thanks, but no thanks. Tell Haylie I'm out here, okay?"

Felicity took off her heels and spent a few minutes

pacing up and down the cold, empty hallway in her bare feet, thinking about what she had just done. Her whole life teetered precariously like a building after an earthquake, not quite sure whether to collapse. She no longer had any idea who her friends were, how she should expect to be treated, where she fell on the social ladder. She had never had to think about things like that before. Nobody did when they were at the top.

But even amid all that uncertainty, there was a part of her that felt gloriously free. The thing she had always feared most had happened, and she was still standing. For the first time in her entire life, she had nothing to hide.

When she heard footsteps behind her, Felicity whirled around, hoping it was Haylie. But it was only Brenda, her mouth pressed tight into a thin line of displeasure. "The judges want to see you in conference room C," she said. "It's just down the hall from your mom's office. Do you think you can find it on your own?"

Felicity hadn't expected the judges to call her in. Were they going to let her plead her case? It seemed unlikely after the stunt she had just pulled. But maybe they had appreciated her boldness and honesty. Maybe she had earned their respect.

Or maybe they knew she had swapped the interview questions, in which case she was in even bigger trouble than she'd thought. Was it possible to go to jail for tampering with pageant materials?

Brenda was still staring at her, and Felicity nodded. "I can find it."

When she tapped lightly on the conference room door, a stern female voice called, "Come in." All five judges were seated on one side of the conference table, as if Felicity were there for a job interview. None of them smiled. Ginger sat at the head of the table with a defeated expression on her face and several used tissues balled in her fist. Felicity took a step toward her, but her mom shot her such a hostile look that she retreated, chastened. Nobody offered her a seat. She stood with her hands clasped penitently in front of her and waited for her sentence.

The head judge, a severe-looking woman with white hair, stared her down over a pair of half glasses. "Felicity St. John," she said, "you've certainly made this competition interesting."

"Yes, ma'am." Felicity wasn't sure if she was being complimented or insulted.

"As you're probably aware, your talent routine was in violation of section 103b of the pageant code, which states that a contestant may not alter her routine in any way after the final dress rehearsal without formally petitioning the pageant committee. Are you familiar with this rule, Miss St. John?"

Felicity nodded. "I wasn't at the time I switched the music, ma'am, but I am now."

"May I take that to mean that you did not, in fact, *read* the pageant rules prior to the competition?"

Felicity had flipped through the rule book briefly when she'd received her Miss Scarlet packet in the mail, then tossed it in the recycling bin. She had assumed her mom would keep her from doing anything that wasn't allowed. "I read some of it, ma'am. But I must have missed that part."

"Apparently." The judge made a note on her legal pad. "Are you aware, Miss St. John, that failure to abide by the pageant code is grounds for disqualification?"

"I am aware of that. Yes." Felicity realized her hands were trembling, and she clasped them together more tightly.

"The judges will take a vote to determine whether you will remain in the running for the title of Miss Scarlet. Ordinarily, the pageant director would conduct said vote, but obviously that won't be possible today. Mrs. St. John, please step into the hall with Felicity, and we'll let you know when we've made a decision."

"We'll wait in my office," Ginger said. Felicity was horrified to hear how broken her mother's voice sounded. She followed her down the hall, grateful that the judges hadn't brought up the forged question. That, at least, was a small mercy.

"How could you do this to me?" her mother snapped the moment the office door closed behind them. "I spent *seventeen years* preparing you for today! I gave you everything, *every* opportunity, because I was sure you were a good investment! But I guess I was wrong, Felicity, since you decided to repay me by getting yourself disqualified and *then telling the entire town I'm a liar!*"

"Mom, I—"

"All I ever asked from you was that you take this competition seriously and win that prize for us, and I told you *exactly* how to do it. All you had to do was follow my instructions. You couldn't even do *that* for me, after all I've given up for you!"

Felicity felt as if all the air had been sucked from the room. "I know how much you've done for me," she pleaded. "And I appreciate all of it, I swear. I've tried so hard to be everything you wanted me to be, but I just . . . I'm not that girl, Mom. I don't belong in pageants, and I never have. I'm not even a real redhead."

"I made you into a redhead, and you threw it all away!" Ginger screamed. "I lied for you and sacrificed for you so you could have the life I thought you deserved! But because of what you did out there today, Felicity, everyone will think you're *nothing* from now on. Not to mention you've put my job and my reputation on the line. Are you satisfied? Is this what you wanted?"

"I was being blackmailed!" Felicity yelled back. "I didn't do this for the *fun* of it! I know you didn't want me to fight Gabby, but I couldn't just lie down and let her take everything away from me!" Tears sprang to her eyes, and she angrily swiped them away with the back of her hand. "This sucks for me, too, Mom, trust me! Everyone probably hates me now. But even that will be better than living every single second terrified someone is going to expose me. My entire life was a lie! You have no idea what that's like!"

Ginger took a quick step forward, her face crimson with fury, and Felicity thought for a moment that her mom was going to hit her. But Ginger just leaned close to her ear and hissed, "I know *exactly* what it's like, Felicity, but unlike *some people,* I can handle it!"

It took Felicity a minute to figure out what her mom was implying.

And then she finally put the pieces together.

Her mouth dropped open.

"Are you saying—" she stammered. "But . . . *you?* You're a str—"

"Don't say it out loud," her mom snapped.

"But I—"

"How do you think it feels to protect a secret for *forty-two years,* Felicity, only to have it thrown out in the open by the person you love the most?"

Ginger and Felicity both whipped around as the head judge opened the office door. "We're ready for you now," she said.

Numb with shock, Felicity followed her mother back into the conference room. She stood before the row of judges, trying not to show that her whole world had just been turned inside out.

"Felicity St. John, the judges have voted to disqualify you from the Miss Scarlet Pageant," the head judge announced. "In an effort not to humiliate you, this decision will not be made public. You will stand on the stage with the other girls for the coronation. Nobody ever has to know."

Ginger put her head down on the table and cried as if the world were ending.

Felicity sat on the cold marble floor outside the dressing room, too shocked even for tears. Ever since she was a child, she had thought she was alone in the world, that nobody really knew what her life was like. But there had always been someone who empathized; Ginger had merely opted not to reveal herself. Felicity wondered what it would have been like to grow up knowing that her mom understood her on a deep level. Now it was too late, and she would never know.

Ginger's words echoed through her mind over and over: *everyone will think you're nothing from now on.* Now that the euphoria of outwitting Gabby had worn off, Felicity wondered if she really had destroyed her entire world by outing herself. Spending the next year at Scarletville High as a strawbie would be a living hell. And now, without the prize money, art school would always be just a dream. Her life stretched before her, gray and flat and featureless.

Ivy stuck her head through the doorway. "Brenda wants us to line up soon. Why are you on the floor?"

Felicity wanted to blurt out everything, but her mom's secret wasn't hers to tell. "I got disqualified," she said instead. "It's all over."

Ivy shrugged and sat down next to her. "So you won't be a beauty queen. I think you'll live. Honestly,

I'm relieved you're out of the running. One fewer person between me and that sparkly, sparkly tiara."

Felicity gave her friend a feeble smile, but it only lasted a moment. "It's not about the title. I don't care about that. But I really needed the prize money."

"For what?"

"For art school."

"You want to go to art school? Felicity, that's *awesome*!"

"It would have been. But now I guess I'm going to Scarletville Community College. If they'll even take me."

"Hang on, what about financial aid?" Ivy asked. "Lots of people go to schools they can't afford."

"My mom doesn't believe in that stuff. Apparently, 'St. Johns don't accept charity.'"

"Financial aid is not *charity*. And you're about to turn eighteen. You don't need her permission. You can apply for whatever you want. Plus, I'm sure there are merit-based art scholarships. You should ask Ms. Kellogg. And maybe your mom would even help you out with the money a little."

"She won't," Felicity said. "She hates me for what I said up there."

"She doesn't *hate* you. I'm sure she's pissed now, but she'll get over it eventually. All you did was stand up for yourself."

"You should have heard the things she said to me, Ives. It was really horrible. Can I sleep at your house tonight? I don't even want to see her."

"Of course. That's fine."

The dressing room door opened, and Haylie poked her head out. "It's almost time, Ivy," she said.

Felicity moved to get up. "Hays, I was wondering where you were. Do you want—"

But Haylie didn't even look at her. She just closed the door in Felicity's face.

Felicity gaped at Ivy. "What just happened?"

"I think she's having a hard time with this whole thing. She feels like you lied to her." Ivy picked at her nail, suddenly unable to meet Felicity's eyes.

"I only lied because of the blackmail. I explained that. And I thought she was over the whole prom nomination thing, anyway. We were totally fine an hour ago."

"Not about the prom thing. About your hair."

Felicity felt as if she'd been stabbed with an icicle. "What happened to 'We're all in this together and I'll have your back no matter what'?"

"That's exactly what I said to her, but she's so emotional, I don't think I got through to her at all. And she's nervous about the coronation on top of everything else. She'll probably snap out of it as soon as the pageant's over."

"We've been best friends since preschool! She seriously won't talk to me because my hair is four shades lighter than she thought it was?"

"Two minutes! Everyone upstairs now!" hollered Brenda.

Ivy stood up and offered Felicity her hand. "We should go," she said. "We'll talk about it later, okay? Ten more minutes and this will all be over."

297

Felicity considered just staying there in the hallway until the pageant ended. What was the point of putting herself on display for hundreds of judgmental eyes, just so everyone could watch her lose? But then she thought of her brothers and the Vaughns and Ms. Kellogg and Jonathan. They were still out there rooting for her, and they would want her to hold her head high and finish what she'd started. She couldn't let them down.

Felicity let Ivy pull her to her feet and lead her up the stairs to the stage.

She tried to get Haylie's attention again, but her friend stood motionless at the front of the line and pretended not to hear when Felicity whispered her name. Donna Marie, who was back at the podium in a different dress, asked the audience to give a big round of applause to all the Miss Scarlet contestants. The girls starting filing onto the stage, and Felicity followed them out into the glare of the lights.

"Aren't they gorgeous?" Donna Marie squealed. "Look at those dresses, just like tropical flowers. Well, ladies and gentlemen—girls—the most exciting moment of the pageant is upon us! Right here in this envelope, I hold the name of this year's Miss Scarlet! It's time to crown her now."

The audience went wild as Georgia appeared from stage left, holding the Miss Scarlet crown on a red velvet pillow. The rhinestones twinkled furiously under the stage lights. The twelve girls on the stage clasped hands as Donna Marie tore open the envelope containing the winner's name. As Felicity entwined her fingers with

298

Ivy's and Ariel's, she thanked the universe for placing her between the only two competitors who wouldn't recoil from her touch. Both girls squeezed her hands, and she felt just a tiny bit stronger as she squeezed back.

"This year's first runner-up, who will take Miss Scarlet's place if she is unable to perform her duties, is . . . Madison Banks!"

In all the pageants she had attended, Felicity had never seen a less happy first runner-up. Madison, whose gold-sequined gown was painfully bright under the lights, scowled as she stepped to the front of the stage to acknowledge her applause. When a pageant volunteer presented her with a huge bouquet of red roses, Madison looked as if she might eat her. "The fact that she didn't win just made my life," whispered Ivy, who wasn't even bothering to clap. Felicity nodded. She glanced over at Haylie and gave her a supportive smile, but her friend wouldn't meet her eyes. She was visibly trembling and gripping Cassie's hand with bone-crushing force.

"And now, Scarletville, the moment you've all been waiting for," announced Donna Marie. "This year's highest-scoring contestant, in a rare unanimous decision by the judges, is . . . Haylie Adams!"

The entire shrieking crowd was on its feet in an instant, and Felicity cheered, too. For the first time since becoming an official strawbie, she experienced a moment of genuine happiness, even as she watched her mom storm up the aisle and out of the auditorium. The press photographers rushed the stage like children mobbing an ice cream truck and vied for the best shots of Haylie, who was screaming, laughing, and crying all at once. Her chandelier earrings caught the light of countless camera flashes as she jumped up and down, unable to contain her joy. Donna Marie had to hold her down so Georgia could pin the crown to her hair.

A pageant volunteer draped a Miss Scarlet sash over Haylie's shoulder, and another heaped her arms with red flowers. As Haylie raised her hand in the beauty queen wave she'd been practicing since first grade, confetti cannons erupted on both sides of the stage and showered everyone with glittery paper streamers.

"She deserves it," Ivy shouted over the noise. "She was seriously amazing."

Felicity nodded. "I'm glad she won."

"Let's go say congratulations."

Haylie's parents fought their way onto the stage and swept their daughter into their arms as she repeatedly screamed, "I won, I won, I can't believe I won!" Ivy and Felicity waited for Haylie's mom to release her. When Haylie finally noticed them, she launched herself directly at Ivy, nearly smothering her with the enormous bouquet. After a long moment, she let go and turned to Felicity.

And as Haylie looked at her, Felicity saw something slam shut behind her best friend's eyes.

She reached for Haylie anyway, but her friend was stiff and awkward in her arms and pulled away after only a few seconds. Felicity wanted to shake her and say, *Haylie, I'm still me. I'm exactly the same person I was an hour ago.* But instead, she just said, "Congratulations, Hays. I'm so proud of you. You really deserve this."

"Thank you." Haylie smiled, but it was a polite, distant smile. Then she pushed past Felicity and was gone.

Parents were swarming the stage now, and as Felicity watched them embrace their emotional, sparkle-clad girls, a wave of loneliness engulfed her. This wasn't how things were supposed to go. Whether she won the pageant or not, her friends and family were supposed to be there when it was over. There were supposed to be flowers and kisses and congratulations. There were supposed to be shoulders to cry on.

But here she was, alone, filled with a strange numb emptiness.

Without speaking to anyone, she made her way into the wings and down the stairs to the empty dressing room. She changed into her old jeans, then methodically packed up her pageant supplies and took one last look around. She would probably never see this room again.

Felicity didn't want to face the crowded lobby, so she slipped out the back door of City Hall and skirted the far side of the building until she reached the parking lot. After stuffing her garment bags into the trunk of her car, she collapsed into the driver's seat and rested her forehead against the steering wheel.

She had absolutely no idea what to do next.

After several long minutes, Felicity's phone beeped, and she dug it out of bag. She had one new text message.

GABBY: well played, st. john. I underestimated you.

19

Felicity spent Saturday night and most of Sunday hiding in Ivy's bedroom, watching horrible reality TV and trying not to think.

Ivy provided a steady supply of Twizzlers, popcorn, and smoothies and didn't ask any touchy-feely questions. But when the sun started setting on Sunday and Felicity still hadn't moved from her nest of blankets, Ivy switched off the television and stood menacingly in front of the screen. Felicity reached for the remote, but Ivy snatched it away.

"You have *got* to snap out of it," she announced. "If everyone doesn't stop making such a big deal about your hair, I will seriously cut it all off myself. You've been sulking over here for an entire day because you're freaking out about everyone *else* freaking out. It's *hair*,

302

Felicity! It's a bunch of stringy keratin! What is everyone's problem?"

"They should be apologizing to *me*! I shouldn't have to run after them."

Ivy sighed and flopped down next to her on the bed. "I know. The whole thing just drives me insane. I mean, who cares if you have the MC1R gene or not? Everyone loved you on Saturday morning, and aside from the fact that you're a little less clean now, you haven't changed at all. God, *everywhere* but here, people dye their hair right out in the open, and nobody cares. I cannot wait to get out of this place."

Felicity had never heard a genuine redhead rail against Scarletville before, and the wheels in her brain slowly started spinning again. "What do you mean? Where do you want to go?"

"Stanford. Everyone has weird hair in California. Maybe I'll go platinum."

"Was that Haylie you were yelling at on the phone earlier?" Felicity asked. "What has she been saying about me? Is she coming around at all?"

"She keeps being like, 'Felicity lied to us, how can we ever trust her again?' It's absolutely ridiculous. Maybe when we see her at school tomorrow—"

Felicity's mouth dropped open. "I'm not going to school tomorrow!"

"Yes, you are. You have to. You made this big, bold public statement, which was totally awesome and bad-ass, by the way, and you made everyone think you were proud of who you were—which you should be. But if

303

you hide now, everyone's going to know you're actually ashamed, and that's when they'll try to take you down. They sniff out fear like dogs. If you don't hold your head up, this is not going to go away."

Felicity looked at her friend. "You're kind of wise, you know?"

"That's me. Tiny and wise. Just like a Magic Eight Ball."

Felicity's phone rang, and she lunged for it. Her heart started beating wildly when she saw her mom's name on the screen. "Hello?"

"Felicity." There was hurt and sadness in her mom's voice, but all the fury was gone. "Are you at Ivy's house?"

"Yeah."

"I'm still not happy about what you did yesterday."

"I know," Felicity said.

There was a long moment of silence, and then her mom said, "I'd still like you to come home, please. Your brothers would like to see you." She paused. "I would, too."

It wasn't an apology, but even the tiniest start was better than nothing.

So Felicity went.

Monday morning was like The Dream come to life.

When Felicity walked through the doors of Scarletville High, everyone stared at her, even the littlest freshmen. Nobody spoke to her directly, but everyone started whispering. There were giggles. There were gasps. There was no eye contact.

The difference was that in The Dream, Felicity always woke up when she screamed. This time, there was no escape.

When she reached her locker, she saw that the GOOD LUCK, FELICITY! wrapping paper was hanging off in uneven shreds. She tore the rest down and stuffed it into the trash can, along with the chocolates and the wilted flowers she had left in her locker on Friday. She kept the plush penguin for the twins.

Ivy finally showed up as she was picking off the last of the tape. She reached for Felicity's mocha and took a sip. "How'd things go with your mom last night?"

"Okay, I guess. Dinner was pretty awkward. We didn't really talk at all. But I guess it'll take time. Have you spoken to Haylie?"

"No progress yet, but I'll get through to her eventually. There's no way that girl can beat me in a fight."

Felicity whipped around when she heard a burst of giggles behind her and found the group of miniskirted, furry-booted sophomores whispering behind their hands. They skittered off like cockroaches in the light when Felicity glared at them. "God, this place *sucks* today," she said.

Ivy nodded. "Yeah, it does. But let's be honest, this place kind of sucks all the time."

It was an abysmal day. Although very few people spoke to Felicity directly, whispers trailed her wherever she went. People let doors slam in her face as if she were invisible. A group of sophomores commandeered her table in the cafeteria, and she and Ivy ended up eating under the RED IS RAD! banner. When Brent passed her in the hallway, he pretended to vomit as Gretchen Williams clung to his arm and giggled. Even Felicity's teachers looked at her warily, as if she might go crazy and attack someone at any moment. No one called on her all day.

The one exception was Ms. Kellogg, who embraced Felicity as soon as she walked into the art room. "I didn't get to see you after the pageant," she said. "You were spectacular. That tap routine was incredible! I had no idea you were good at so many things. You're going to go very far in life, Felicity."

The affection was so unexpected that Felicity almost burst into tears. "Thanks," she said. "I'm really glad you were there."

"I am, too. And what you did during the interview— that was so brave. You said exactly what this town needed to hear. You probably inspired a lot of people."

Felicity shrugged. "I didn't do it to be inspirational."

"I know. That's usually how it goes." She pulled Felicity close again. "You did good, kid," she whispered. "Don't let anyone tell you otherwise."

After that, it was a little easier to get through the rest of the day. But only a little.

By the time the last bell rang, Felicity was so worn out that all she could think about was getting home and going to bed. But she snapped awake when she opened her locker door and a small white envelope tumbled out and landed at her feet. She jumped back in alarm, as if it might attack her toes.

"What the *hell*?" she whispered. She was not in the mood for cryptic correspondence today. She scanned the hall, looking for Gabby, but her adversary was nowhere in sight.

The envelope stared up at her, daring her to touch it.

Fine, Felicity thought, snatching it up. *It's not like my life can get any worse.* She ripped the envelope open and pulled out a card with a butterfly on the front.

> *Felicity,*
> *What you did on Saturday was incredibly brave.*
> *I'm a secret strawbie, too.*
> *I don't have the guts that you have, but maybe someday I will.*
> > *Thanks.*
> > *—A friend*

Felicity stared at the card. Somehow, it had never occurred to her that she wasn't the only artie at Scarletville High. But Rouge-o-Rama was a thriving business. Of course there would be others. It could be anyone. It could be Madison. It could be Haylie.

She left the building consumed by curiosity, thinking of something other than her own hair for the first time in days.

And that was why it took her a minute to notice Jonathan waiting by her car in the back of the parking lot, the section reserved for non-redheads.

Felicity had once read that a hummingbird's heart can beat up to 1,250 times a minute. When she saw the way Jonathan was smiling at her, her own heart started trying to break that record.

"Hi," he said quietly. "I have something for you." He held out a fat brown envelope.

There were two thick, glossy booklets inside, the kind Felicity was starting to receive in the mail from colleges. One was for the Tanglewilde Summer Arts Program, and the other was for the School of the Art Institute of Chicago. Both booklets were packed with photos of galleries and beautiful sunlit art studios. The paint-spattered students and wise-looking professors looked happy, wild, free.

It was Felicity's idea of heaven.

A scrap of paper fluttered out of the envelope, and she barely managed to catch it before it blew away. In Jonathan's handwriting, it said,

This is where you belong.
P.S. You rock my world.

Felicity looked up and met his eyes. They were warm and gentle and full of unconditional acceptance. She knew he was seeing her—really *seeing* her—and that he liked what he saw, red hair or not.

She put the booklets down on the trunk of her car.

And then she kissed him.

For once, Jonathan's hands knew exactly where to land. One of them rested against the small of her back, warm through her T-shirt, and the other cradled the back of her neck, under her traitorous hair. She wrapped both arms around him, surprised at how pleasantly solid his wiry frame felt against her body.

Kissing someone new was like learning how to kiss all over again. Felicity closed her eyes and concentrated, learning how their mouths fit together. She felt as if she had just let go of a swinging trapeze and was plunging into an exhilarating, delicious free fall, totally secure in the knowledge that there was a soft net to catch her at the bottom.

When they broke apart, Felicity noticed that the parking lot was strangely silent. Anyone who hadn't been staring at her already was certainly staring now.

"Do you want to go to that gallery in Des Moines with me?" Felicity asked.

Jonathan smiled. "Now?"

"Now."

He didn't hesitate at all. "Definitely. Let's go."

The Sharks in Heaven music wrapped around them like an embrace when she started her car. Jonathan took her hand and held it tightly as they pulled out of the parking lot. For just a moment, Felicity looked back at her classmates, standing openmouthed among the shattered remains of her old life.

And then she turned her eyes to the road ahead.

ACKNOWLEDGMENTS

I am overflowing with gratitude toward the following people:

My rock-star agent, the incomparable Holly Root, who believed in this book long before it was book-shaped. Thank you for always magically knowing when I need a pep talk and for laughing with me, not at me, when I make a complete fool of myself. You are, quite simply, the best.

My brilliant editor, Wendy Loggia, who has transformed this book into something I actually want people to read. Thank you for loving Felicity as much as I do and for making me laugh with your margin notes.

My Delacorte Press publishing team, for all the hard work you've put into bringing my book to life. Extra-special thanks to my genius copy editors, Jennifer

Prior and Colleen Fellingham, and my book designer, Heather Daugherty.

My amazing critique partners and early readers: Nicole Lisa, Liz Whelan, Lauren Billings, Christina Hobbs, Julia Reischel, Renee Lasher, Adam Bowker, Evie Gaynor, Rachel Handshaw, and Marianna Caldwell. Thank you for your honesty, your humor, and your kindness and for never letting me take the easy way out. This book is so much better because of you.

Elizabeth Little, for introducing me to the world of young adult literature and for helping me navigate the treacherous waters of publishing for the first time.

The wise and hilarious ladies of Team Root, for welcoming me into the fold with open arms and making me feel like I belonged there. I am so lucky to know all of you. A special shout-out to Rae Carson, who shared her top-secret beauty pageant knowledge with me.

My debut group, the Lucky 13s, who have been the best support system a girl could ask for. Giant hugs to Brandy Colbert, Kristen Kittscher, and Lindsay Ribar—I would never have survived revisions without you.

SCBWI, for inspiring me, setting me on the path to publication, and introducing me to such spectacular people.

My incredibly supportive friends, who understand when I sometimes disappear from society for months at a time and reappear with a slightly crazed look in my eyes. Thank you for cheering me on and for forcing me to talk about things other than writing. High fives to

Lissa Harris and Jenna Scherer, without whom there would be no Crucial Douches.

My sister, Erica Cherry, for all the times you dropped everything to read my new pages and for motivating me by incessantly clamoring for more story. You (and your brains) are too awesome for words.

And finally, my mom, Susan Cherry, my toughest critic and my biggest fan. Thank you for helping me with every single draft of this book. Thank you for being *nothing* like Ginger St. John. And thank you for passing on the genes that gave me my love of words and my red hair.

ABOUT THE AUTHOR

Unlike Felicity, Alison Cherry is a natural redhead. She is a professional photographer and spent many years working as a lighting designer for theater, dance, and opera productions. She lives in Brooklyn, New York. This is her first book. Visit her at alisoncherrybooks.com or on Twitter at @alison_cherry.